ADVENTURE TIME™ COMICS

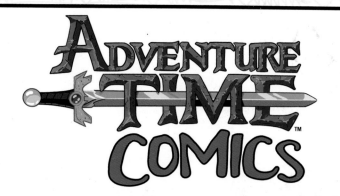

VOLUME 2

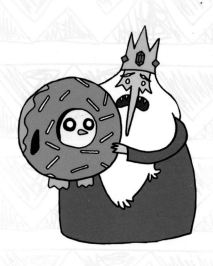

ADVENTURE TIME COMICS Volume Two, June 2017. Published by KaBOOM!, a division of Boom Entertainment, Inc. ADVENTURE TIME, CARTOON NETWORK, the logos, and all related characters and elements are trademarks of and © Cartoon Network. (S17) Originally published in single magazine form as ADVENTURE TIME COMICS No. 5-8. © Cartoon Network. (S16) All rights reserved. KaBOOM!™ and the KaBOOM! logo are trademarks of Boom Entertainment, Inc., registered in various countries and categories. All characters, events, and institutions depicted herein are fictional. Any similarity between any of the names, characters, persons, events, and/or institutions in this publication to actual names, characters, and persons, whether living or dead, events, and/or institutions is unintended and purely coincidental. KaBOOM! does not read or accept unsolicited submissions of ideas, stories, or artwork.

BOOM! Studios, 5670 Wilshire Boulevard, Suite 450, Los Angeles, CA 90036-5679. Printed in China. First Printing.

ISBN: 978-1-60886-984-8, eISBN: 978-1-61398-655-4

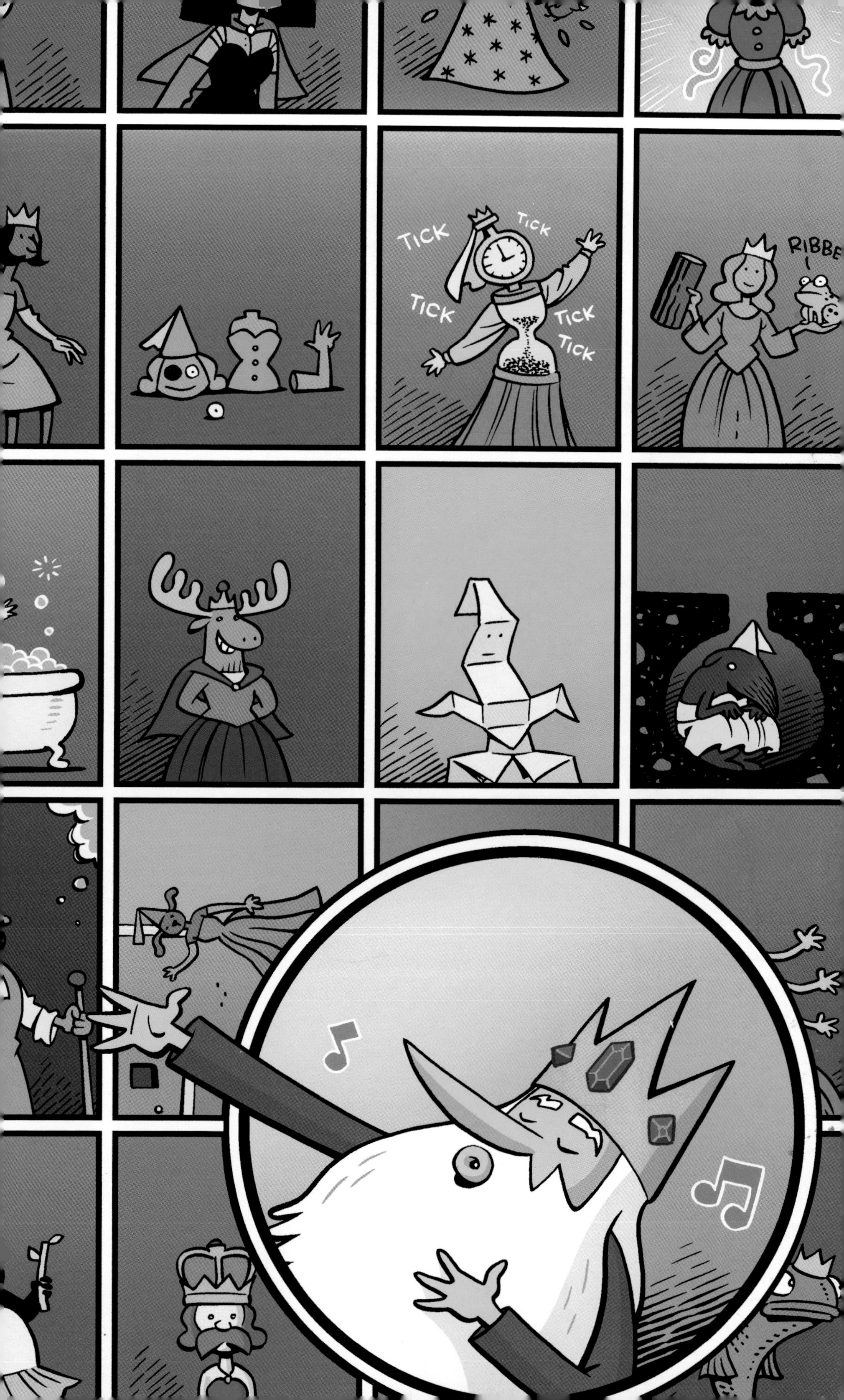
TICK
TICK
TICK
TICK
TICK
RIBBE

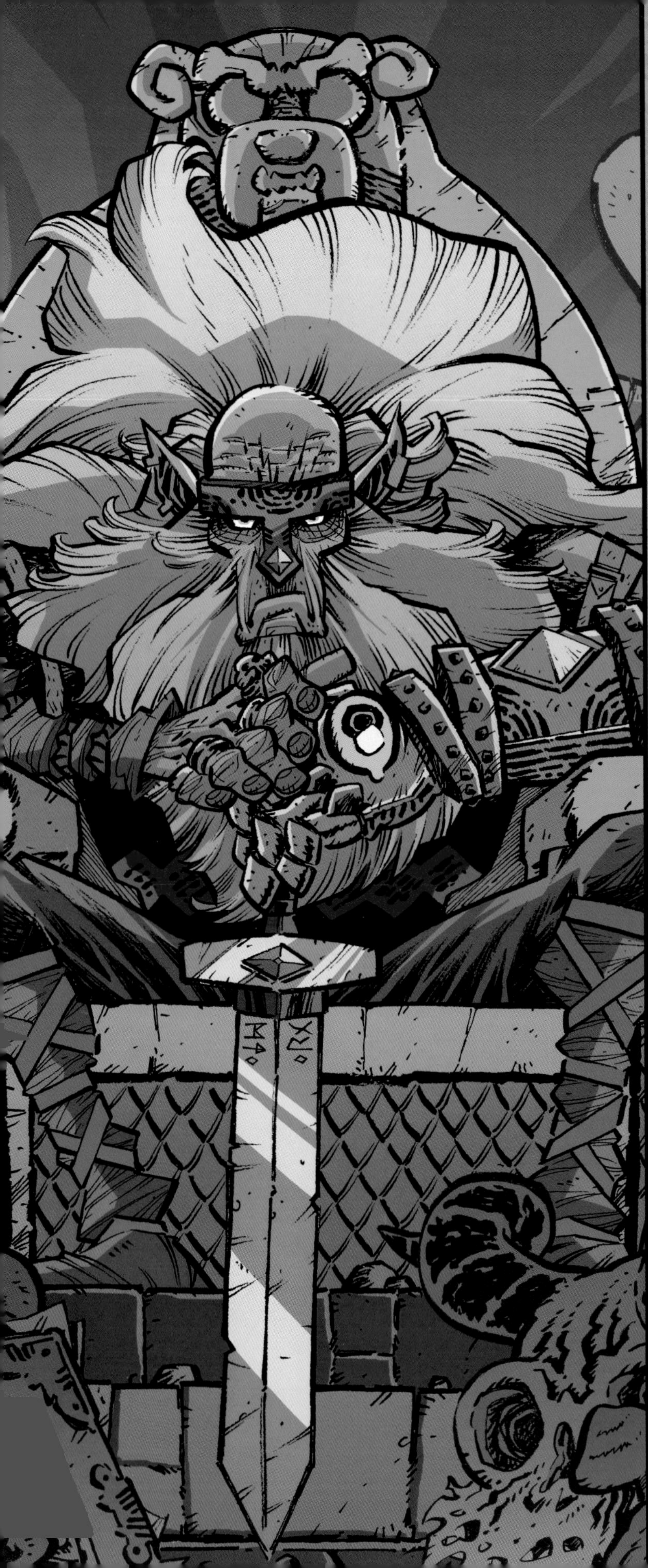

ADVENTURE TIME™
Created by **PENDLETON WARD**

"WIZARD'S QUEST"
Written & Illustrated by
DEREK FRIDOLFS
Colors by
PAMELA LOVAS
Letters by
MIKE FORIENTINO

"FRIEND OR FOE"
Written by
WHITNEY TAYLOR
Illustrated by
KYLA VANDERKLUGT

"CAKE BAKES"
Written & Illustrated by
ZACHARY STERLING
Letters by
BRITT WILSON

"BURN BRIGHT"
Written & Illustrated by
EVA ESKELINEN

"WISHING FOR DEM
SWEET WISH TACOS"
Written & Illustrated by
RYAN BROWNE

"THE PRINCESS
MEGATHALON"
Written by
SHAENON GARRITY
Illustrated by
ROGER LANGRIDGE

"THE SUBLET"
Written & Illustrated by
KELSEY WROTEN

"NO CHILL"
Written by
ANNIE MOK
Illustrated by
RACHEL DUKES

"GUNTER THE HERO"
Written & Illustrated by
KEVIN JAY STANTON

"BETTER DIET"
Written & Illustrated by
RILEY ROSSMO
Colors by
KARL FAN
Letters by
JIM CAMPBELL

"SPRING CLEANING"
Written & Illustrated by
MARINA JULIA

"SICK KICKS"
Written & Illustrated by
KIKI'SSH

"I'M LOST!"
Written & Illustrated by
FRAN KRAUSE

"SING A SONG"
Written by
MARIKO TAMAKI
Illustrated by
MEG OMAC

Cover by
ERIN HUNTING

Designer
MICHELLE ANKLEY

Associate Editor
ALEX GALER

Editors
**SHANNON WATTERS &
WHITNEY LEOPARD**

With Special Thanks to Marisa Marionakis, Janet No, Curtis Lelash, Conrad
Montgomery, Meghan Bradley, Kelly Crews, Scott Malchus, Adam Muto
and the wonderful folks at Cartoon Network.

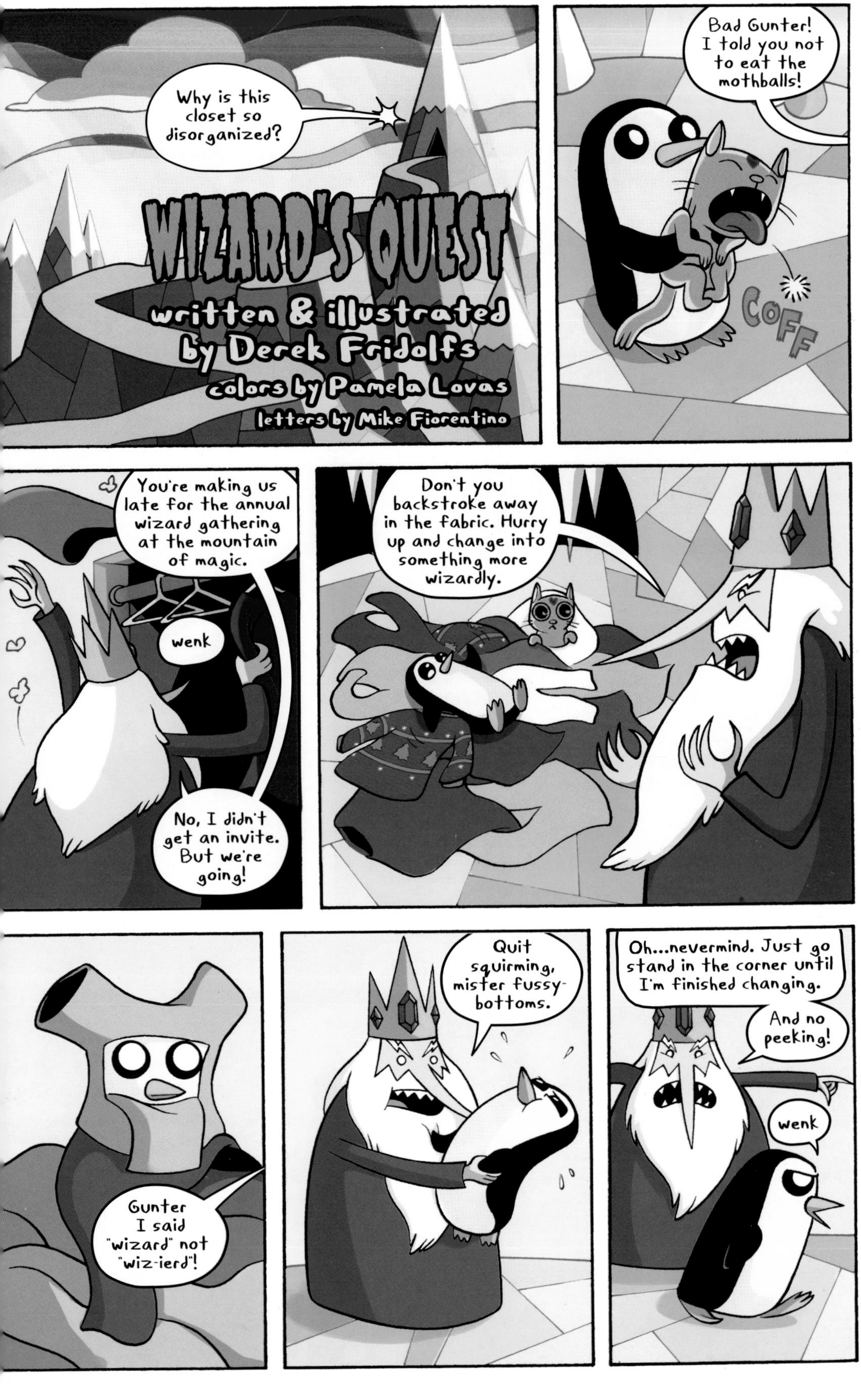
Why is this closet so disorganized?
WIZARD'S QUEST
written & illustrated by Derek Fridolfs
colors by Pamela Lovas
letters by Mike Fiorentino
Bad Gunter! I told you not to eat the mothballs!
COFF
You're making us late for the annual wizard gathering at the mountain of magic.
wenk
No, I didn't get an invite. But we're going!
Don't you backstroke away in the fabric. Hurry up and change into something more wizardly.
Gunter I said "wizard" not "wiz-ierd"!
Quit squirming, mister fussy-bottoms.
Oh...nevermind. Just go stand in the corner until I'm finished changing.
And no peeking!
wenk

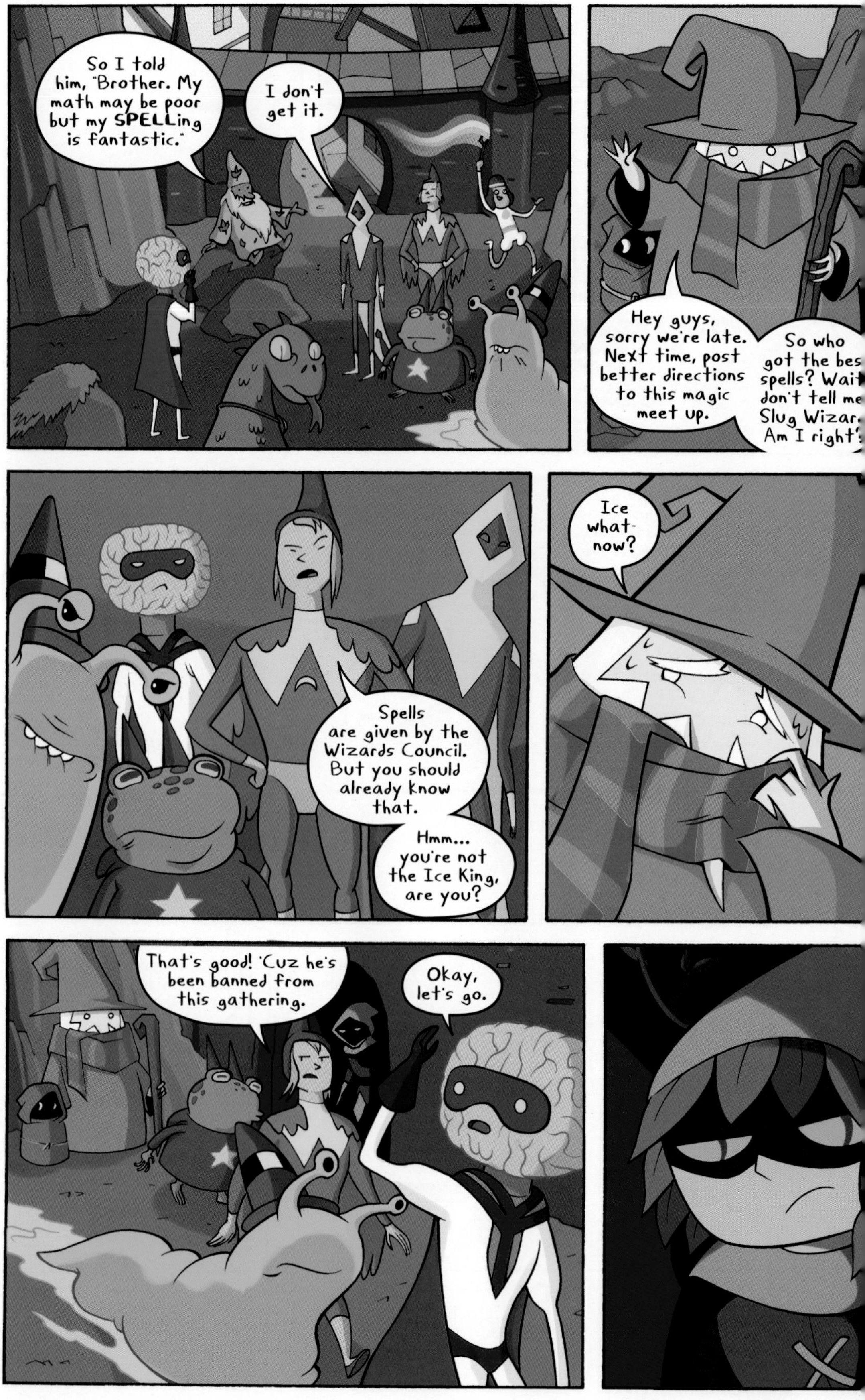
So I told him, "Brother. My math may be poor but my SPELLing is fantastic."
I don't get it.
Hey guys, sorry we're late. Next time, post better directions to this magic meet up.
So who got the bes spells? Wait don't tell me Slug Wizar Am I right?
Spells are given by the Wizards Council. But you should already know that.
Hmm... you're not the Ice King, are you?
Ice what-now?
That's good! 'Cuz he's been banned from this gathering.
Okay, let's go.

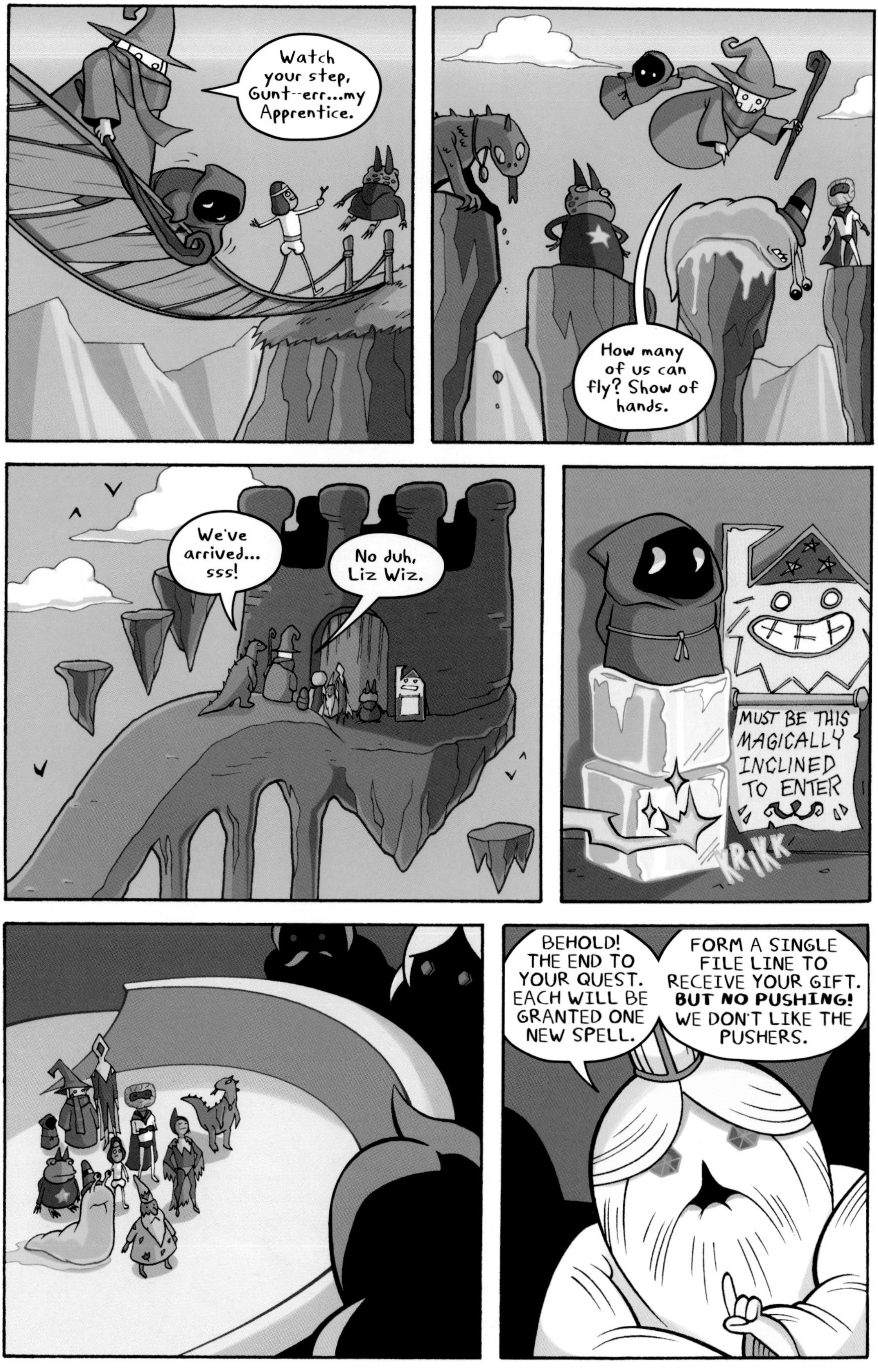
Watch your step, Gunt--err...my Apprentice.
How many of us can fly? Show of hands.
We've arrived... sss!
No duh, Liz Wiz.
MUST BE THIS MAGICALLY INCLINED TO ENTER
KRIKK
BEHOLD! THE END TO YOUR QUEST. EACH WILL BE GRANTED ONE NEW SPELL.
FORM A SINGLE FILE LINE TO RECEIVE YOUR GIFT. **BUT NO PUSHING!** WE DON'T LIKE THE PUSHERS.

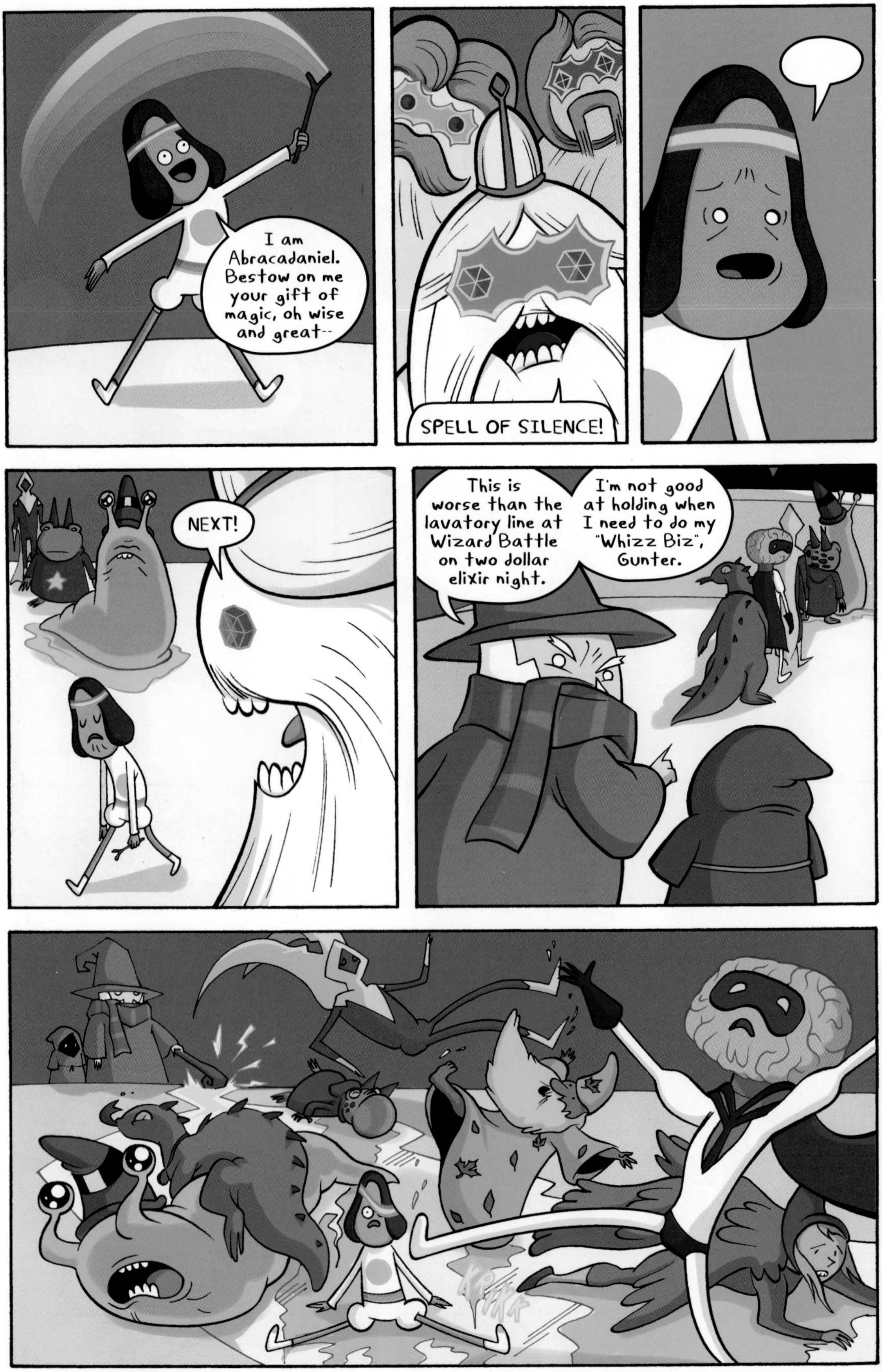
I am Abracadaniel. Bestow on me your gift of magic, oh wise and great--
SPELL OF SILENCE!
NEXT!
This is worse than the lavatory line at Wizard Battle on two dollar elixir night.
I'm not good at holding when I need to do my "Whizz Biz", Gunter.

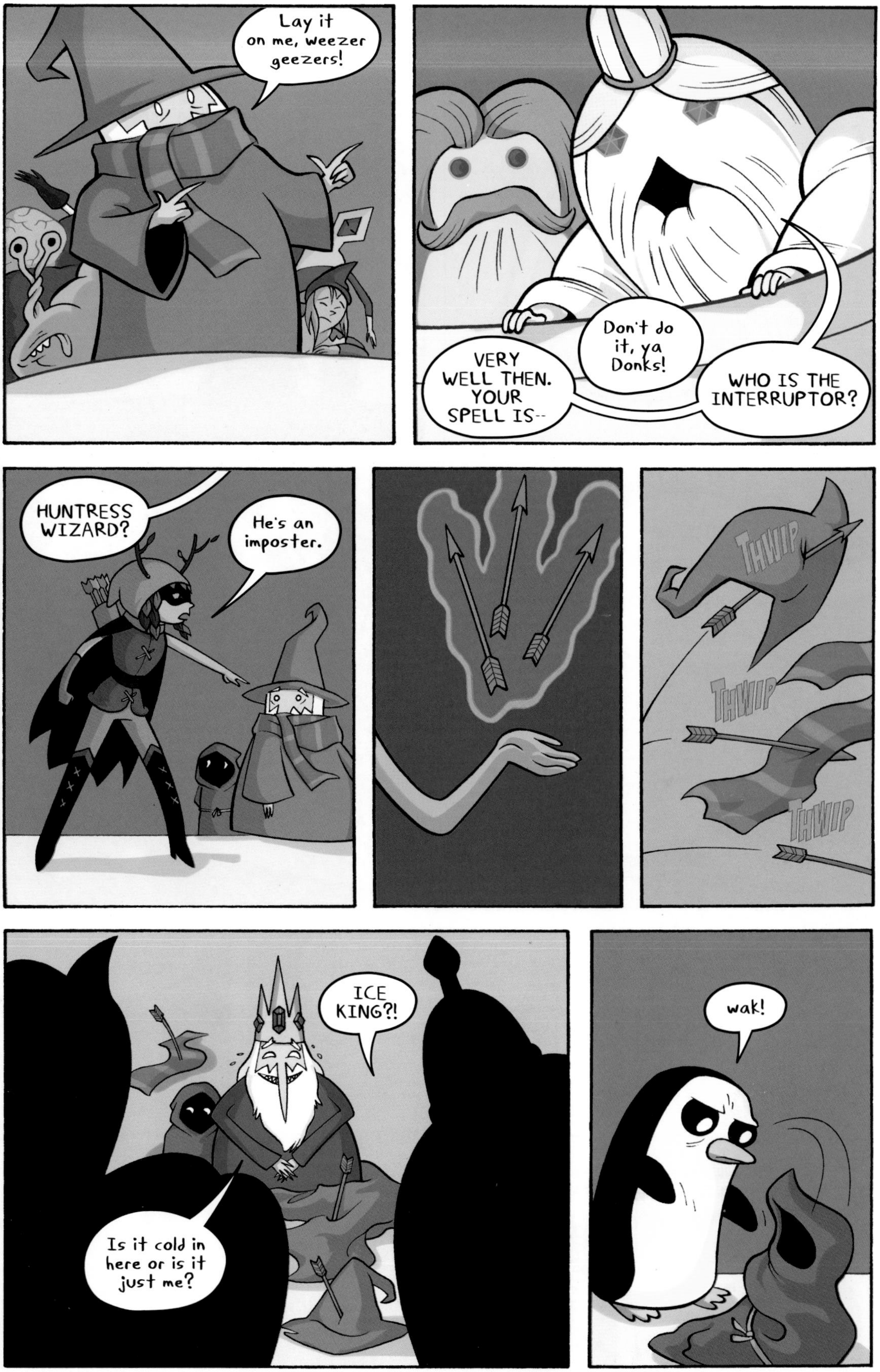
Lay it on me, weezer geezers!
VERY WELL THEN. YOUR SPELL IS--
Don't do it, ya Donks!
WHO IS THE INTERRUPTOR?
HUNTRESS WIZARD?
He's an imposter.
THWIP
THWIP
THWIP
ICE KING?!
Is it cold in here or is it just me?
wak!

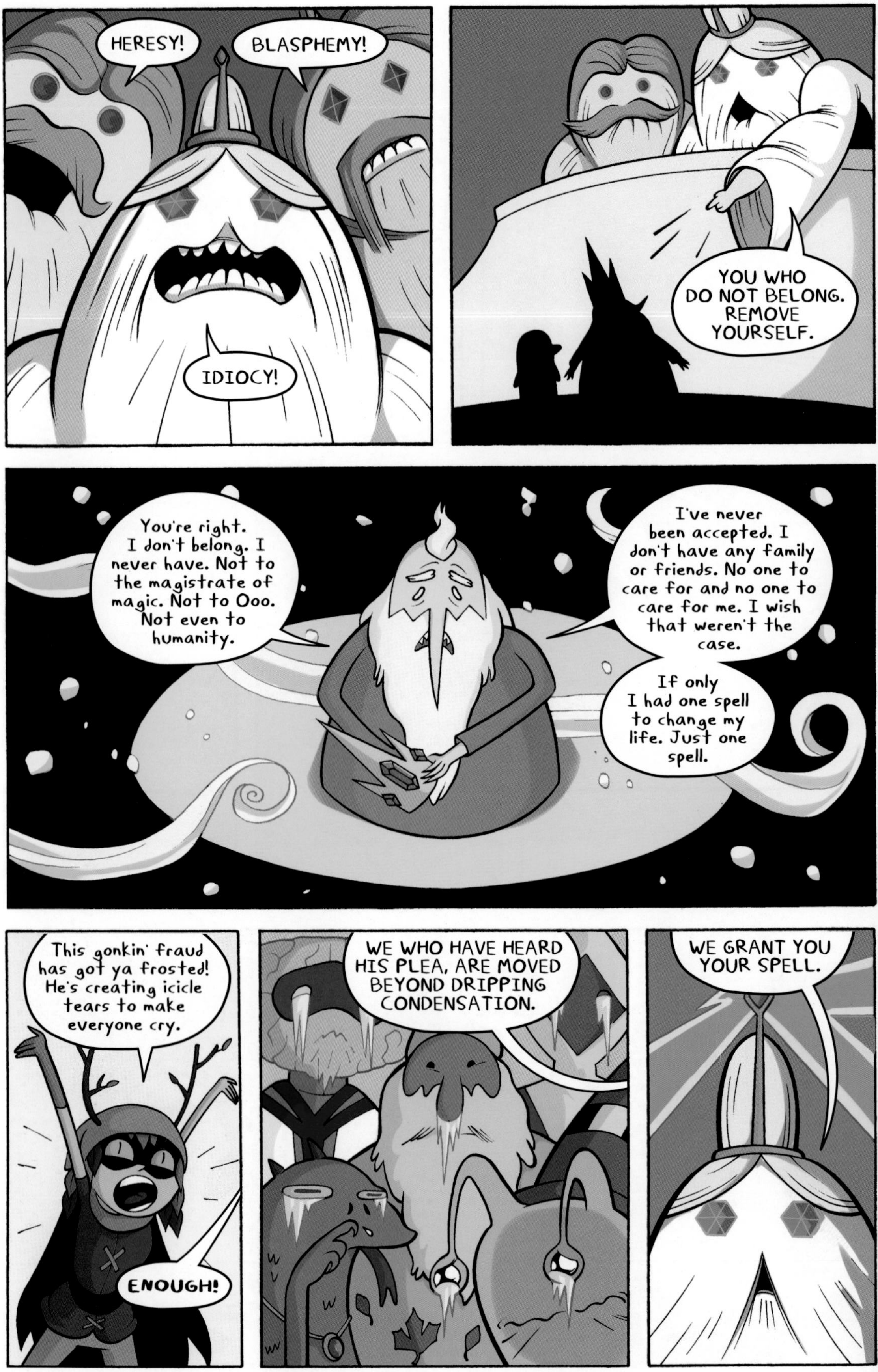
HERESY!
BLASPHEMY!
IDIOCY!
YOU WHO DO NOT BELONG. REMOVE YOURSELF.
You're right. I don't belong. I never have. Not to the magistrate of magic. Not to Ooo. Not even to humanity.
I've never been accepted. I don't have any family or friends. No one to care for and no one to care for me. I wish that weren't the case.
If only I had one spell to change my life. Just one spell.
This gonkin' fraud has got ya frosted! He's creating icicle tears to make everyone cry.
ENOUGH!
WE WHO HAVE HEARD HIS PLEA, ARE MOVED BEYOND DRIPPING CONDENSATION.
WE GRANT YOU YOUR SPELL.

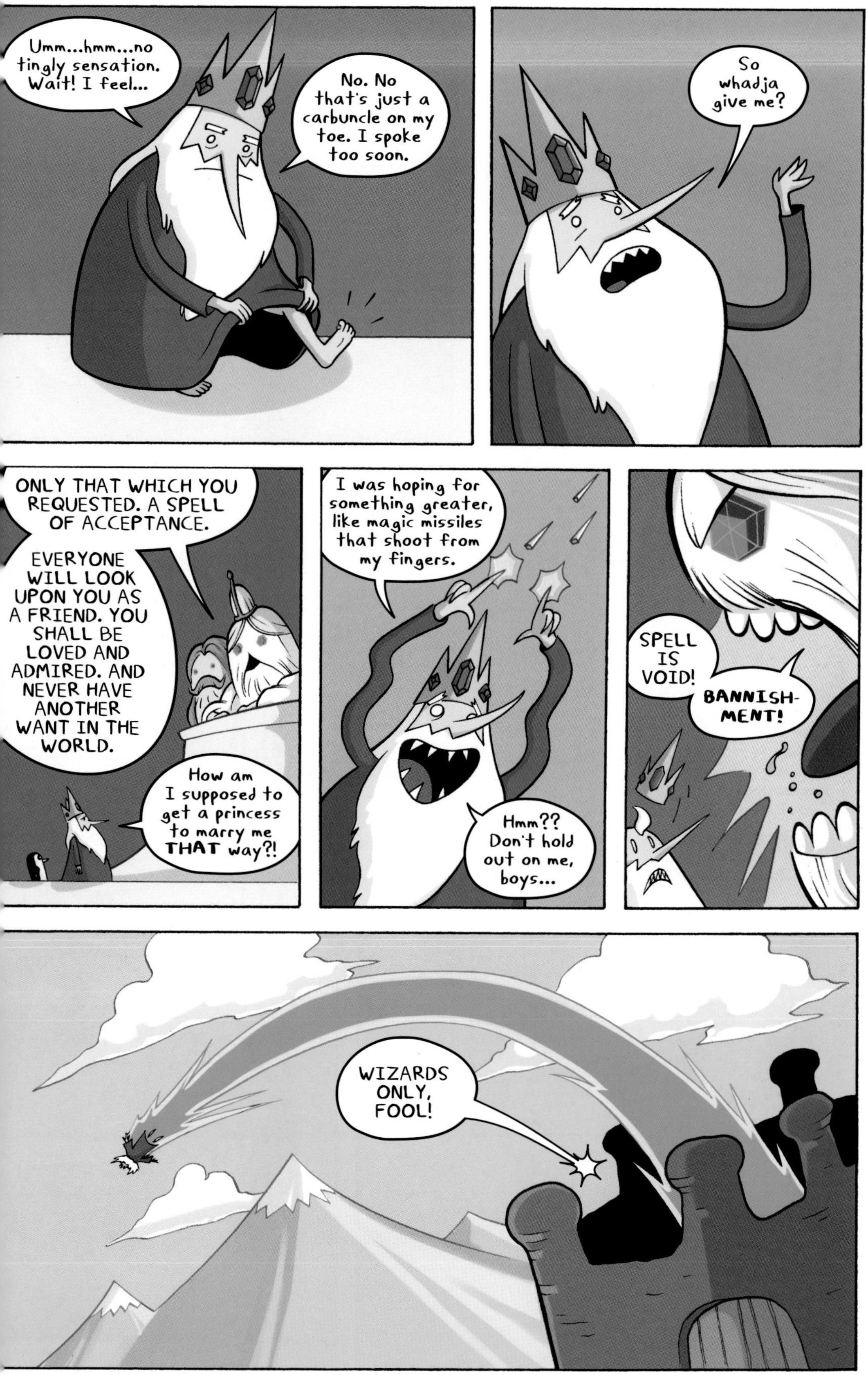

Umm...hmm...no tingly sensation. Wait! I feel...
No. No that's just a carbuncle on my toe. I spoke too soon.
So whadja give me?
ONLY THAT WHICH YOU REQUESTED. A SPELL OF ACCEPTANCE.
EVERYONE WILL LOOK UPON YOU AS A FRIEND. YOU SHALL BE LOVED AND ADMIRED. AND NEVER HAVE ANOTHER WANT IN THE WORLD.
How am I supposed to get a princess to marry me THAT way?!
I was hoping for something greater, like magic missiles that shoot from my fingers.
Hmm?? Don't hold out on me, boys...
SPELL IS VOID!
BANNISH-MENT!
WIZARDS ONLY, FOOL!

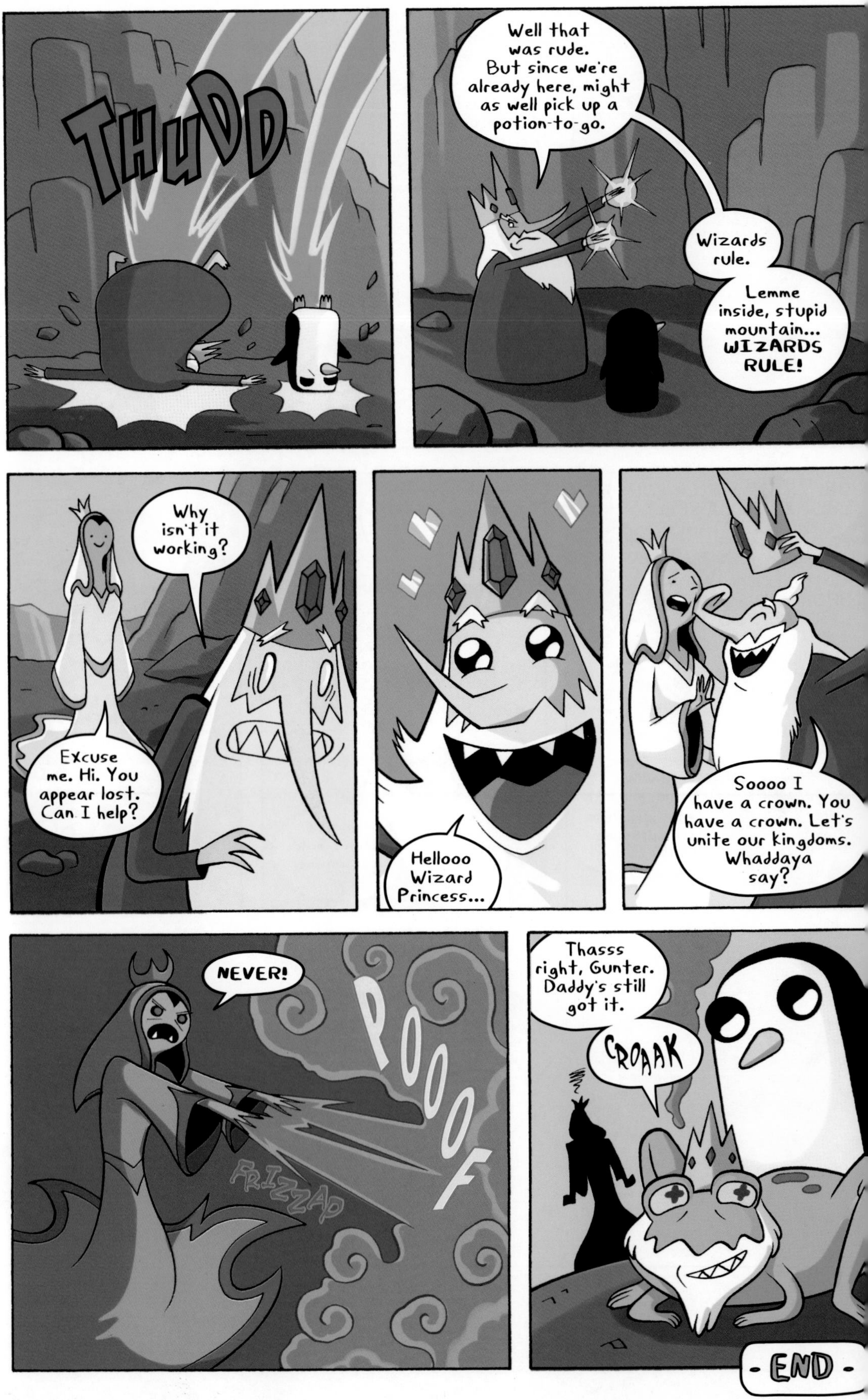
THUDD
Well that was rude. But since we're already here, might as well pick up a potion-to-go.
Wizards rule.
Lemme inside, stupid mountain... WIZARDS RULE!
Why isn't it working?
Excuse me. Hi. You appear lost. Can I help?
Hellooo Wizard Princess...
Soooo I have a crown. You have a crown. Let's unite our kingdoms. Whaddaya say?
NEVER!
POOOOF
FRIZZAP
Thasss right, Gunter. Daddy's still got it.
CROAAK
-END-

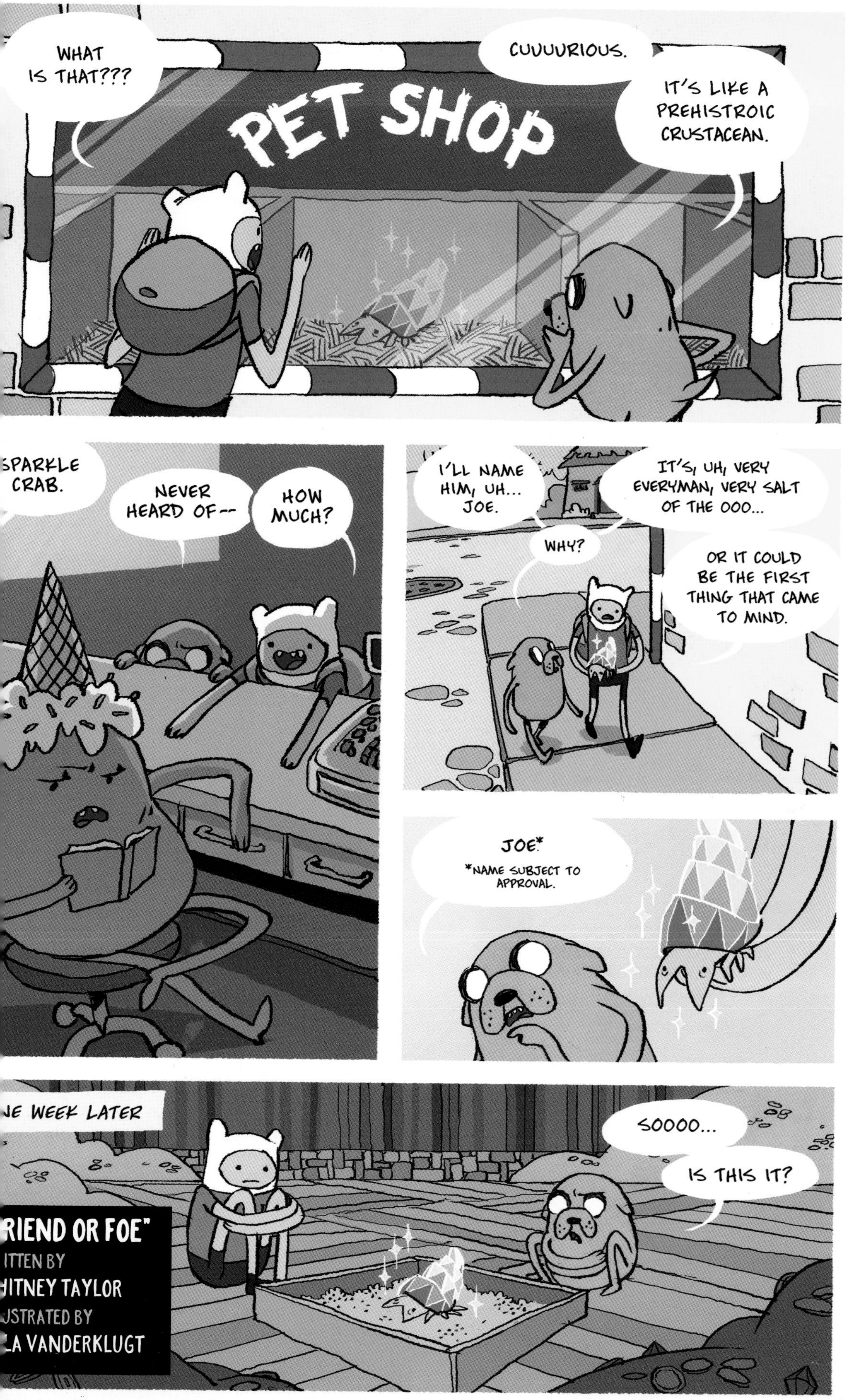
WHAT IS THAT???
PET SHOP
CUUUURIOUS.
IT'S LIKE A PREHISTROIC CRUSTACEAN.
SPARKLE CRAB.
NEVER HEARD OF--
HOW MUCH?
I'LL NAME HIM, UH... JOE.
WHY?
IT'S, UH, VERY EVERYMAN, VERY SALT OF THE OOO...
OR IT COULD BE THE FIRST THING THAT CAME TO MIND.
JOE*
*NAME SUBJECT TO APPROVAL.
NE WEEK LATER
SOOOO...
IS THIS IT?
RIEND OR FOE"
ITTEN BY
HITNEY TAYLOR
USTRATED BY
LA VANDERKLUGT

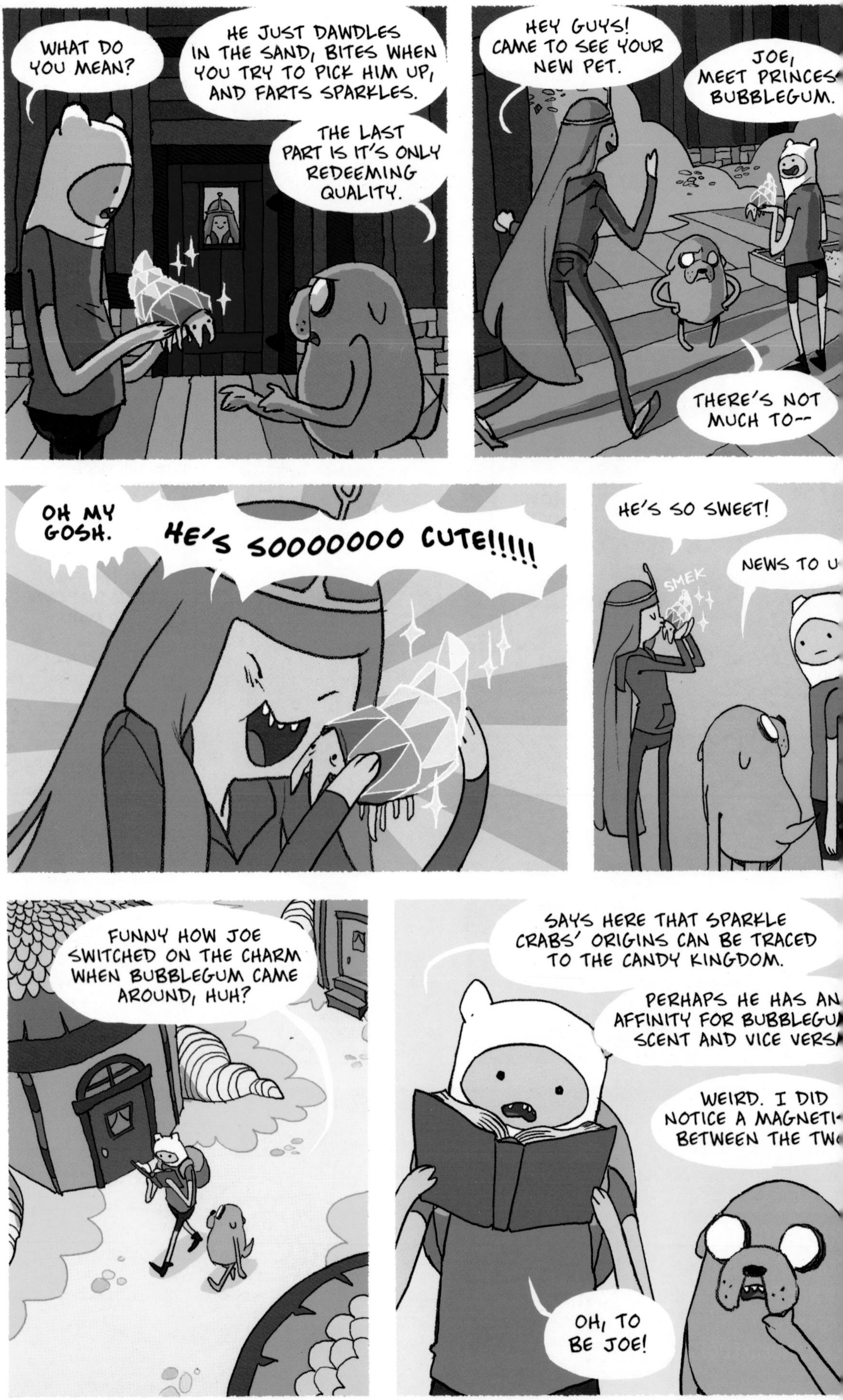
WHAT DO YOU MEAN?
HE JUST DAWDLES IN THE SAND, BITES WHEN YOU TRY TO PICK HIM UP, AND FARTS SPARKLES.
THE LAST PART IS IT'S ONLY REDEEMING QUALITY.
HEY GUYS! CAME TO SEE YOUR NEW PET.
JOE, MEET PRINCES BUBBLEGUM.
THERE'S NOT MUCH TO--
OH MY GOSH.
HE'S SOOOOOOO CUTE!!!!!
HE'S SO SWEET!
SMEK
NEWS TO U
FUNNY HOW JOE SWITCHED ON THE CHARM WHEN BUBBLEGUM CAME AROUND, HUH?
SAYS HERE THAT SPARKLE CRABS' ORIGINS CAN BE TRACED TO THE CANDY KINGDOM.
PERHAPS HE HAS AN AFFINITY FOR BUBBLEGU SCENT AND VICE VERS
WEIRD. I DID NOTICE A MAGNETI BETWEEN THE TW
OH, TO BE JOE!

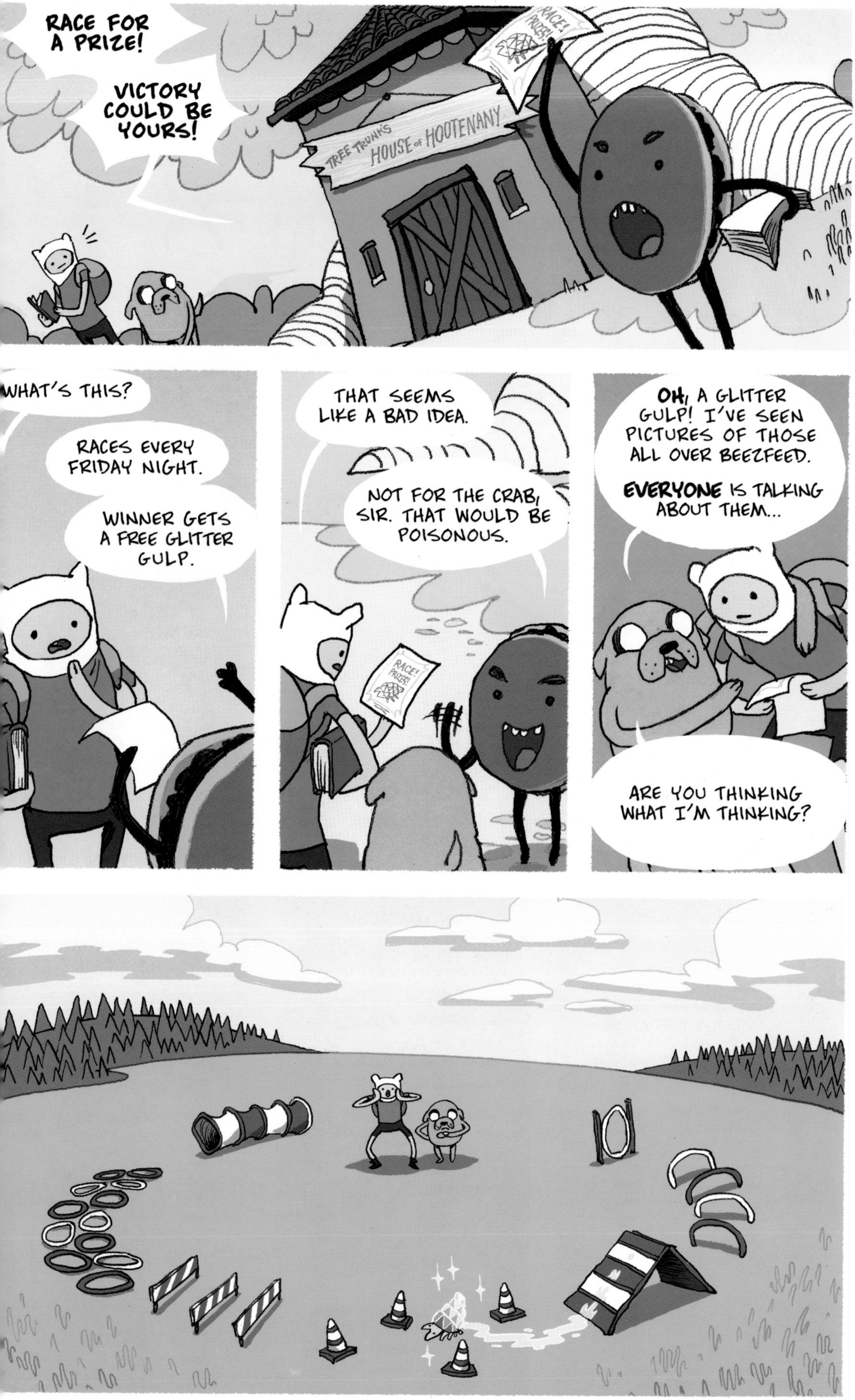
RACE FOR A PRIZE!
VICTORY COULD BE YOURS!
TREE TRUNK'S HOUSE of HOOTENANY
RACE! PRIZES!
WHAT'S THIS?
RACES EVERY FRIDAY NIGHT.
WINNER GETS A FREE GLITTER GULP.
THAT SEEMS LIKE A BAD IDEA.
NOT FOR THE CRAB, SIR. THAT WOULD BE POISONOUS.
RACE! PRIZES!
OH, A GLITTER GULP! I'VE SEEN PICTURES OF THOSE ALL OVER BEEZFEED.
EVERYONE IS TALKING ABOUT THEM...
ARE YOU THINKING WHAT I'M THINKING?

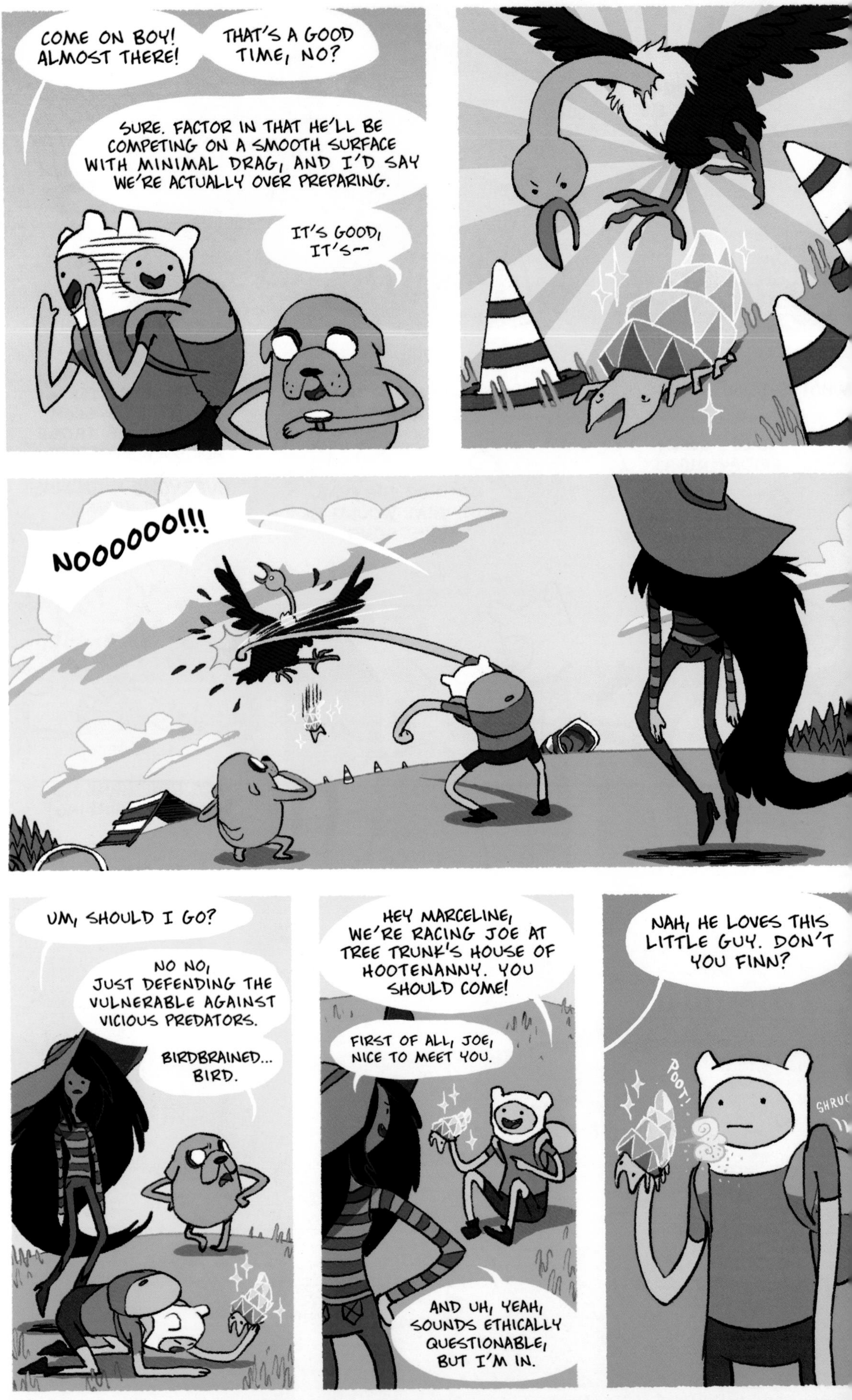
COME ON BOY! ALMOST THERE!
THAT'S A GOOD TIME, NO?
SURE. FACTOR IN THAT HE'LL BE COMPETING ON A SMOOTH SURFACE WITH MINIMAL DRAG, AND I'D SAY WE'RE ACTUALLY OVER PREPARING.
IT'S GOOD, IT'S--
NOOOOOO!!!
UM, SHOULD I GO?
NO NO, JUST DEFENDING THE VULNERABLE AGAINST VICIOUS PREDATORS.
BIRDBRAINED... BIRD.
HEY MARCELINE, WE'RE RACING JOE AT TREE TRUNK'S HOUSE OF HOOTENANNY. YOU SHOULD COME!
FIRST OF ALL, JOE, NICE TO MEET YOU.
AND UH, YEAH, SOUNDS ETHICALLY QUESTIONABLE, BUT I'M IN.
NAH, HE LOVES THIS LITTLE GUY. DON'T YOU FINN?
POOT!

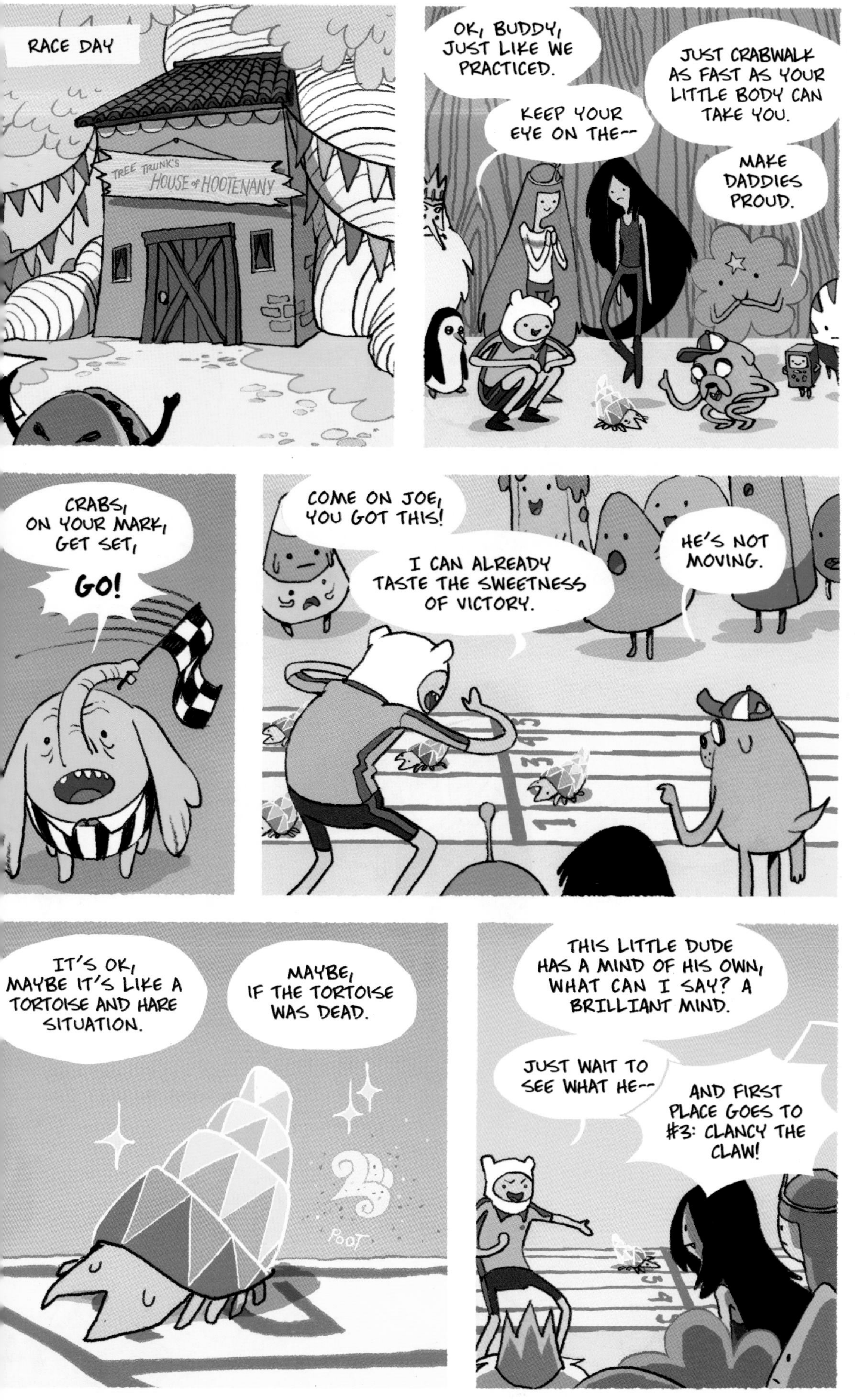
RACE DAY
TREE TRUNK'S HOUSE of HOOTENANY
OK, BUDDY, JUST LIKE WE PRACTICED.
KEEP YOUR EYE ON THE--
JUST CRABWALK AS FAST AS YOUR LITTLE BODY CAN TAKE YOU.
MAKE DADDIES PROUD.
CRABS, ON YOUR MARK, GET SET,
GO!
COME ON JOE, YOU GOT THIS!
I CAN ALREADY TASTE THE SWEETNESS OF VICTORY.
HE'S NOT MOVING.
IT'S OK, MAYBE IT'S LIKE A TORTOISE AND HARE SITUATION.
MAYBE, IF THE TORTOISE WAS DEAD.
POOT
THIS LITTLE DUDE HAS A MIND OF HIS OWN, WHAT CAN I SAY? A BRILLIANT MIND.
JUST WAIT TO SEE WHAT HE--
AND FIRST PLACE GOES TO #3: CLANCY THE CLAW!

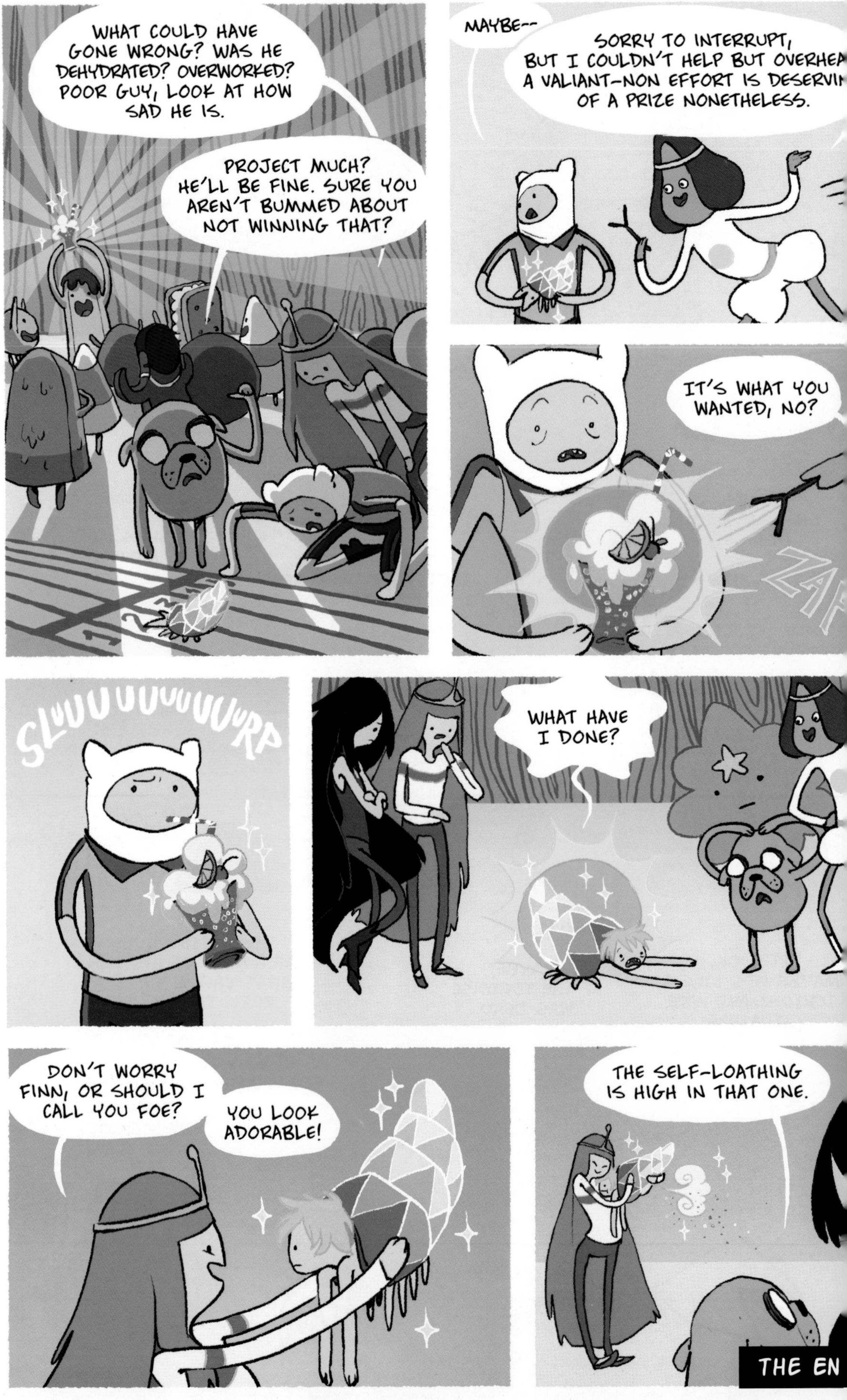

WHAT COULD HAVE GONE WRONG? WAS HE DEHYDRATED? OVERWORKED? POOR GUY, LOOK AT HOW SAD HE IS.
PROJECT MUCH? HE'LL BE FINE. SURE YOU AREN'T BUMMED ABOUT NOT WINNING THAT?
MAYBE--
SORRY TO INTERRUPT, BUT I COULDN'T HELP BUT OVERHEA
A VALIANT-NON EFFORT IS DESERVI
OF A PRIZE NONETHELESS.
IT'S WHAT YOU WANTED, NO?
ZAP
SLUUUUUUUURP
WHAT HAVE I DONE?
DON'T WORRY FINN, OR SHOULD I CALL YOU FOE?
YOU LOOK ADORABLE!
THE SELF-LOATHING IS HIGH IN THAT ONE.
THE EN

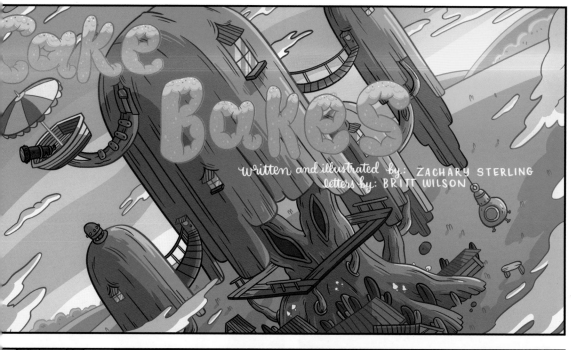

Cake Bakes

written and illustrated by: ZACHARY STERLING
letters by: BRITT WILSON

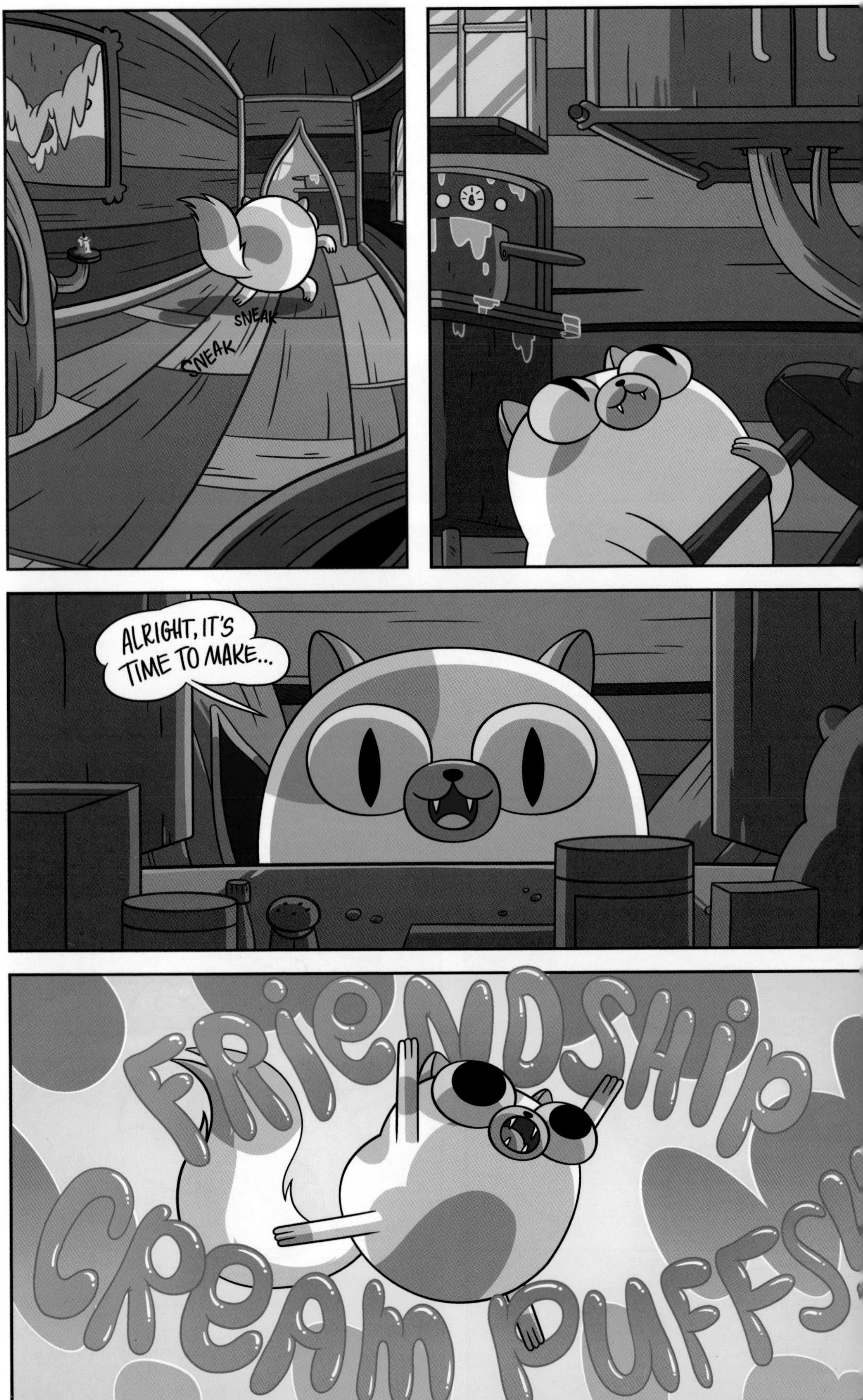
SNEAK
SNEAK
ALRIGHT, IT'S TIME TO MAKE...
FRIENDSHIP CREAM PUFFS!

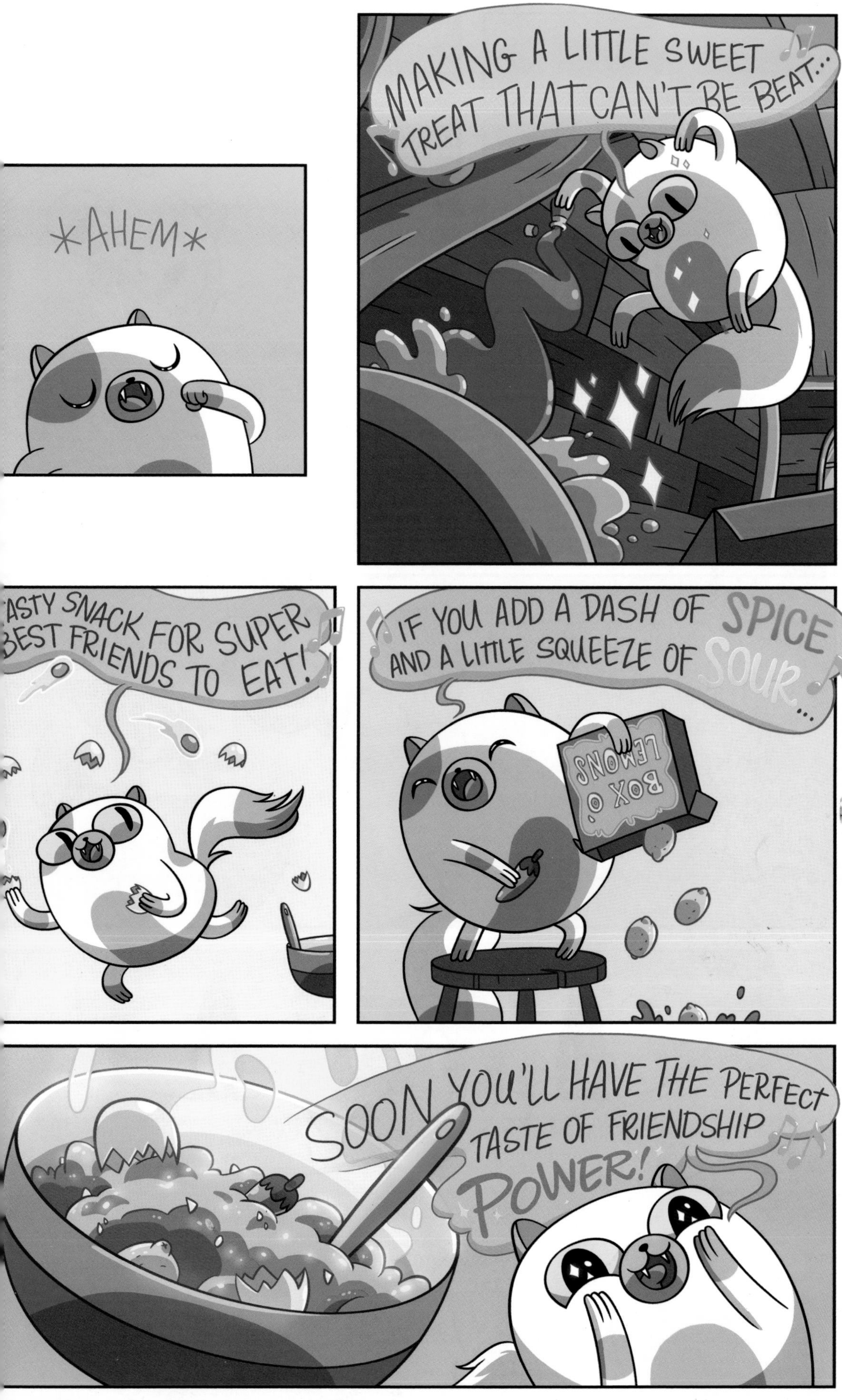
AHEM
MAKING A LITTLE SWEET TREAT THAT CAN'T BE BEAT...
ASTY SNACK FOR SUPER BEST FRIENDS TO EAT!
IF YOU ADD A DASH OF SPICE AND A LITTLE SQUEEZE OF SOUR...
BOX O' LEMONS
SOON YOU'LL HAVE THE PERFECT TASTE OF FRIENDSHIP POWER!

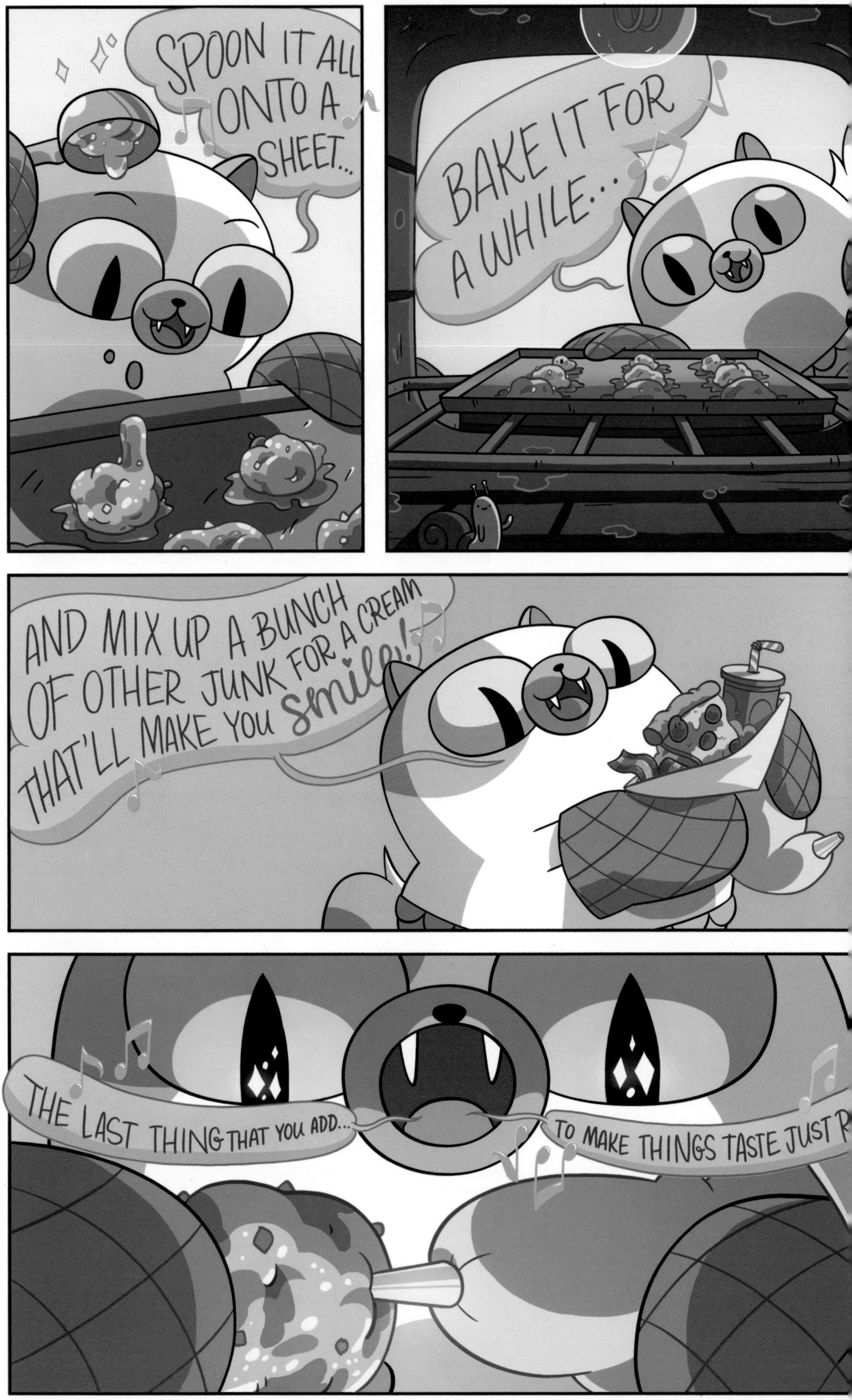
SPOON IT ALL ONTO A SHEET...
BAKE IT FOR A WHILE...
AND MIX UP A BUNCH OF OTHER JUNK FOR A CREAM THAT'LL MAKE YOU smile!
THE LAST THING THAT YOU ADD...
TO MAKE THINGS TASTE JUST

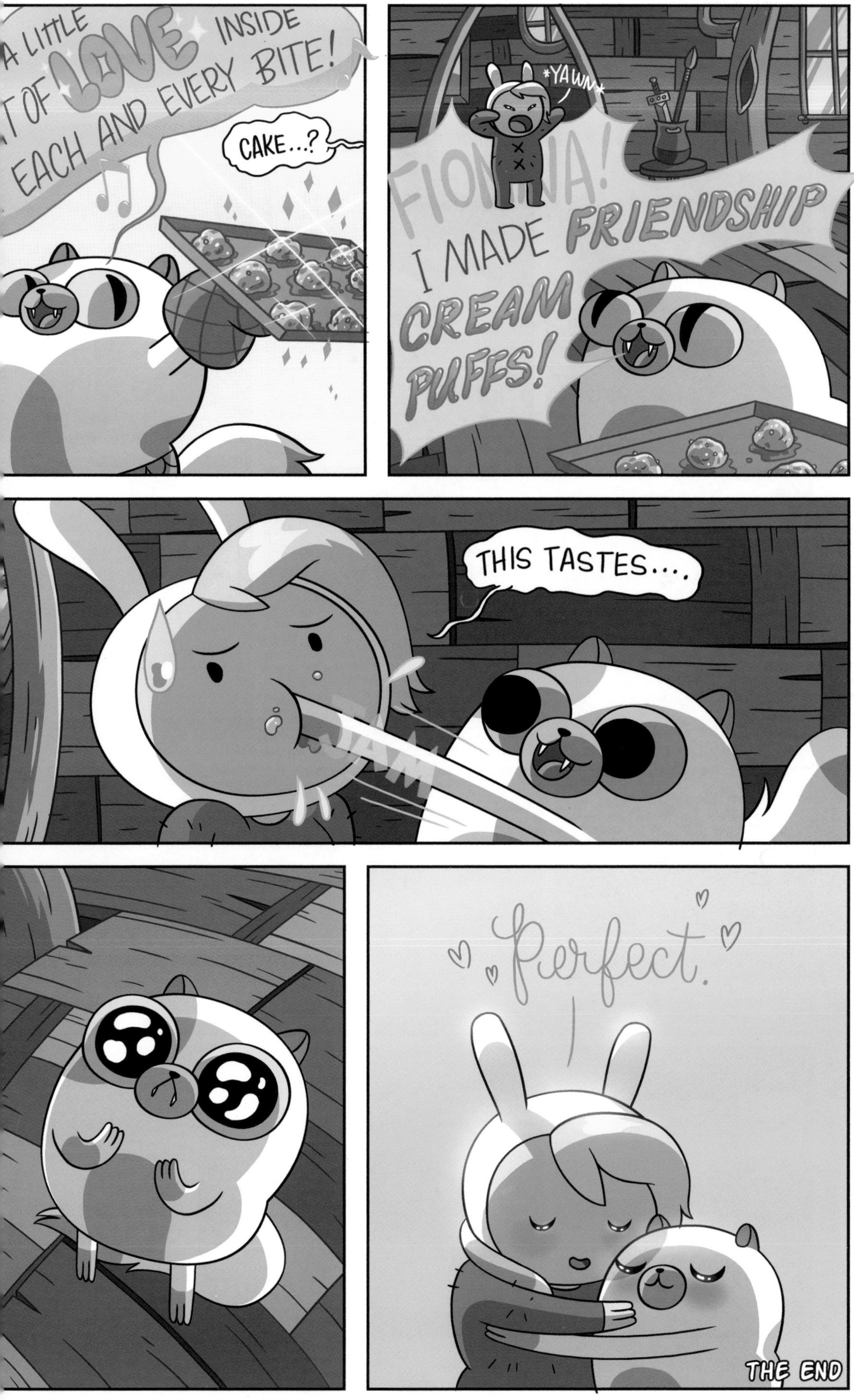
A LITTLE
...T OF LOVE INSIDE
EACH AND EVERY BITE!
CAKE...?
YAWN
FIONNA!
I MADE FRIENDSHIP
CREAM
PUFFS!
THIS TASTES....
JAM
Perfect.
THE END

FEEDBACK

STORY & ART
EVA ESKELINEN

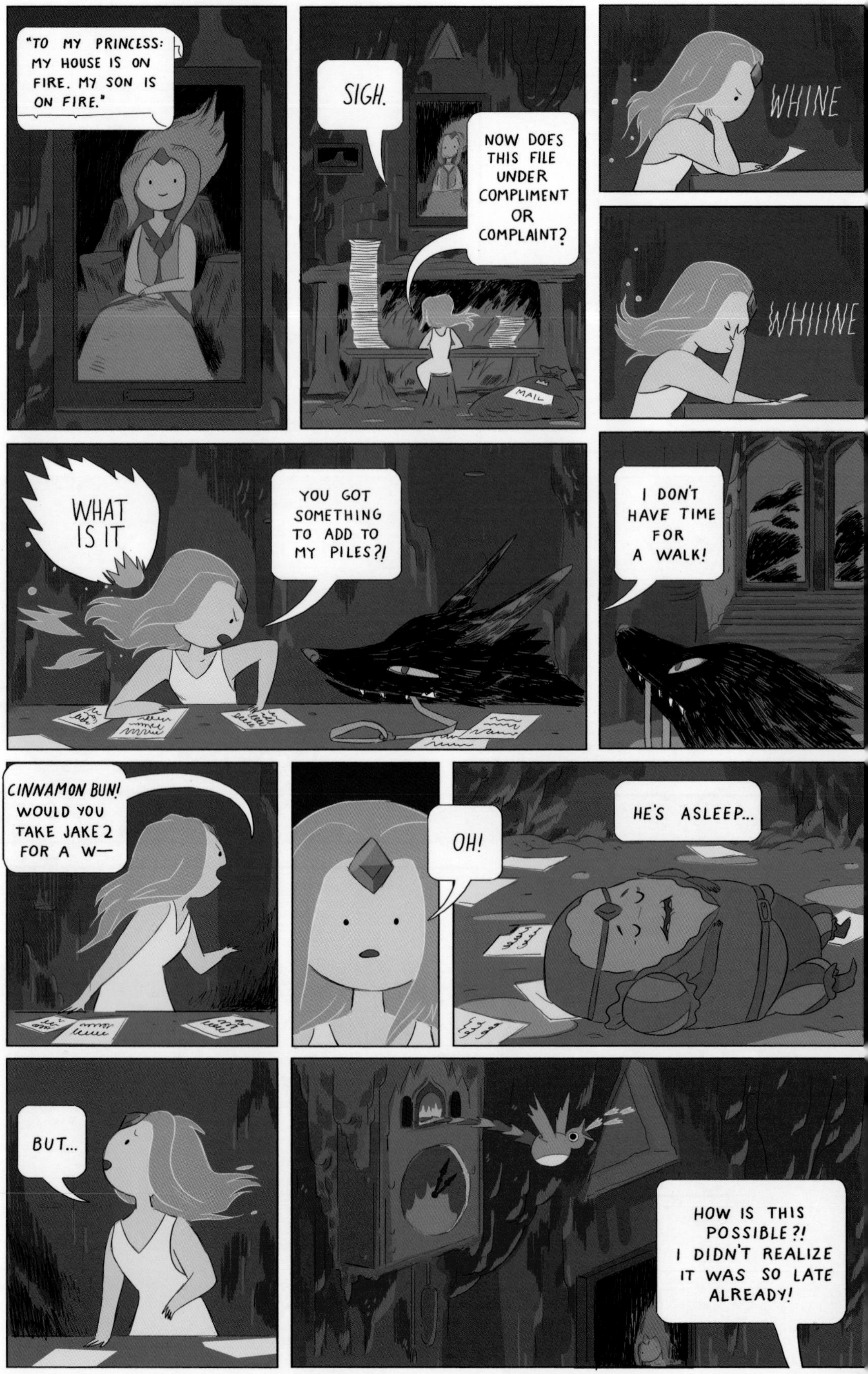

"TO MY PRINCESS: MY HOUSE IS ON FIRE. MY SON IS ON FIRE."
SIGH.
NOW DOES THIS FILE UNDER COMPLIMENT OR COMPLAINT?
WHINE
WHIIINE
MAIL
WHAT IS IT
YOU GOT SOMETHING TO ADD TO MY PILES?!
I DON'T HAVE TIME FOR A WALK!
CINNAMON BUN! WOULD YOU TAKE JAKE 2 FOR A W—
OH!
HE'S ASLEEP...
BUT...
HOW IS THIS POSSIBLE?! I DIDN'T REALIZE IT WAS SO LATE ALREADY!

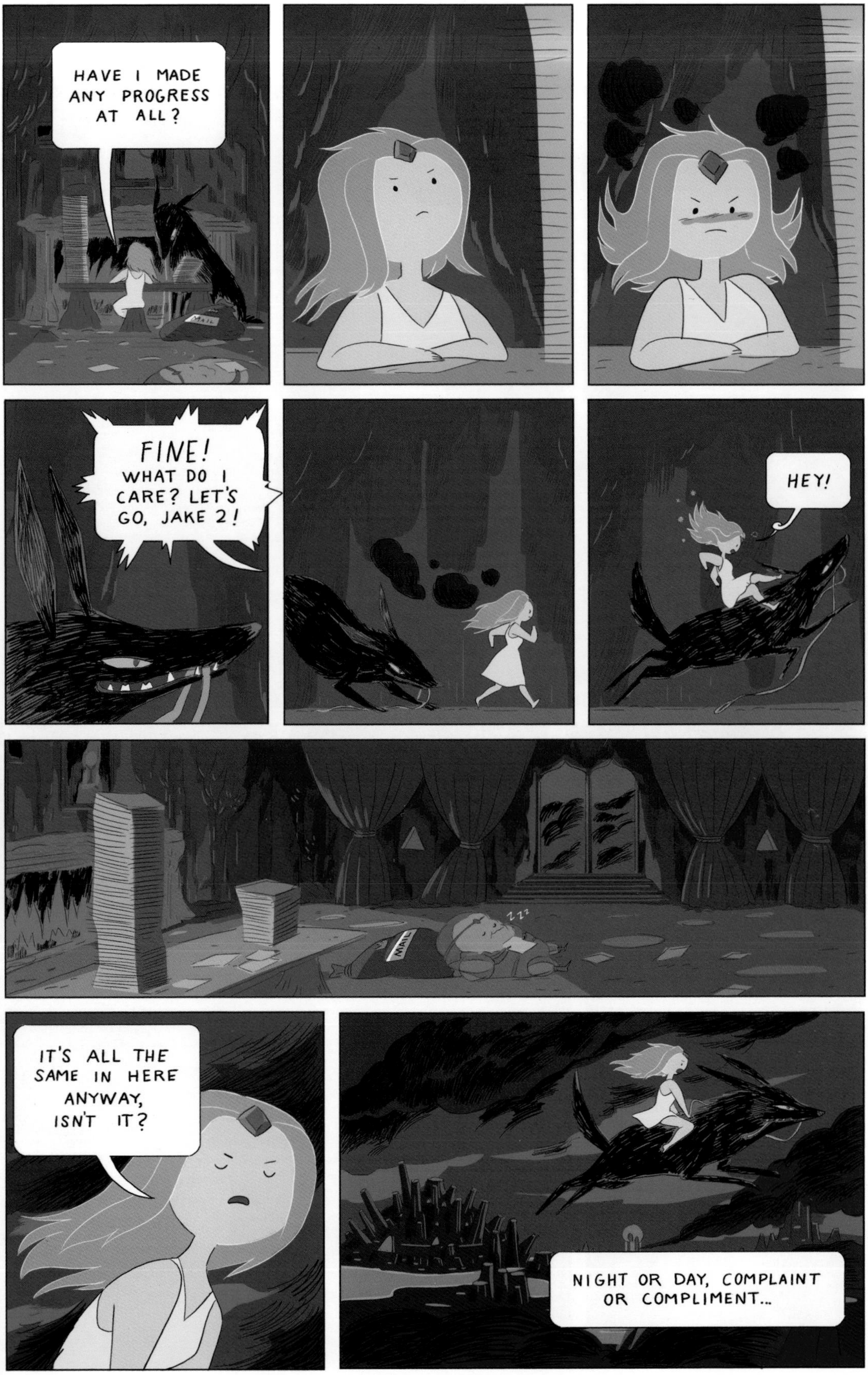
HAVE I MADE ANY PROGRESS AT ALL?
FINE! WHAT DO I CARE? LET'S GO, JAKE 2!
HEY!
MAIL
IT'S ALL THE SAME IN HERE ANYWAY, ISN'T IT?
NIGHT OR DAY, COMPLAINT OR COMPLIMENT...

JUST WHAT AM I SUPPOSED TO DO? CONTEMPLATE WHILE LOOKING AT STARS?

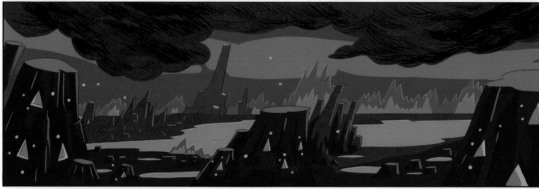

OKAY. FAIR ENOUGH.

YOU FINISH YOUR BUSINESS AND I'LL GO BACK TO MINE.

FIN.

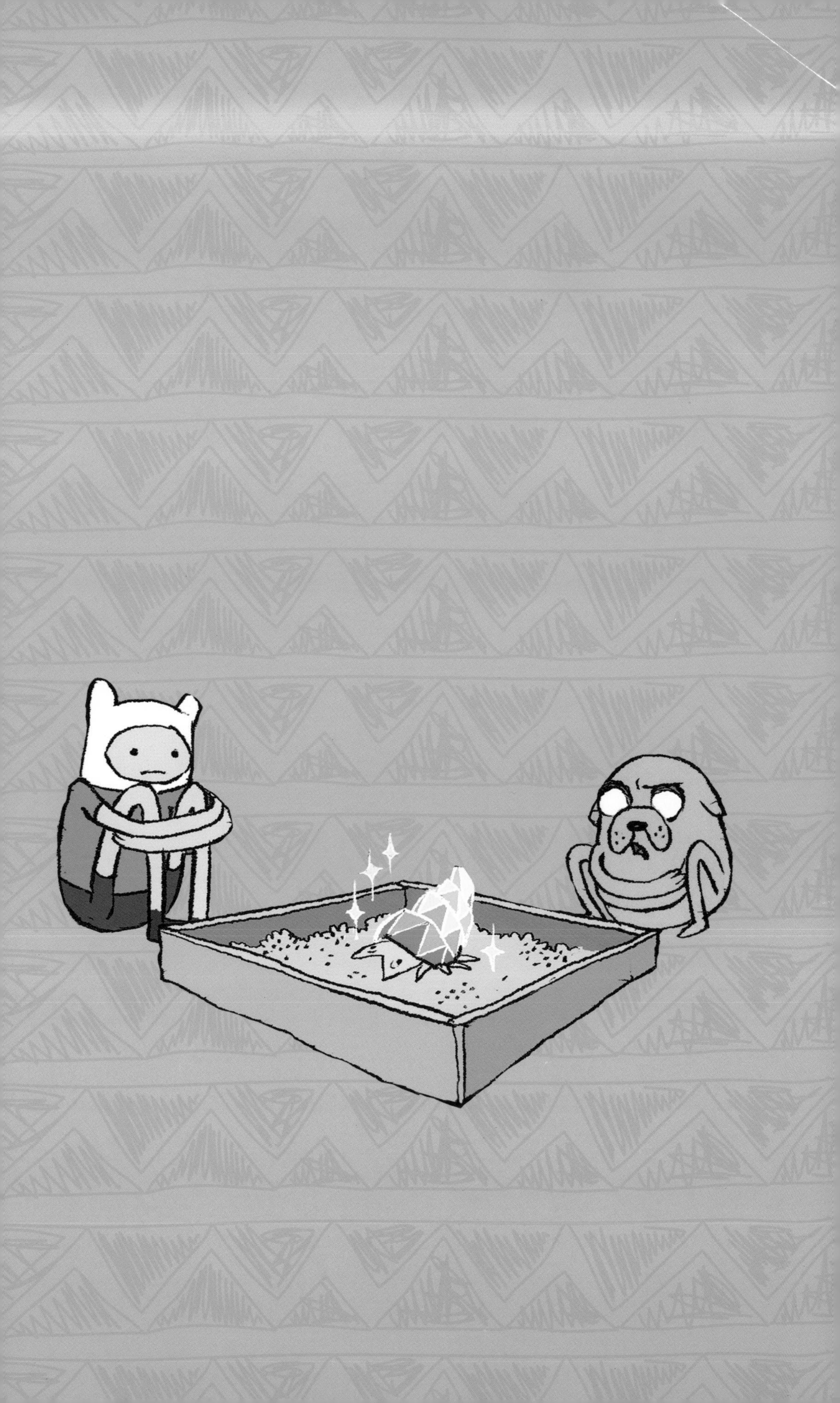

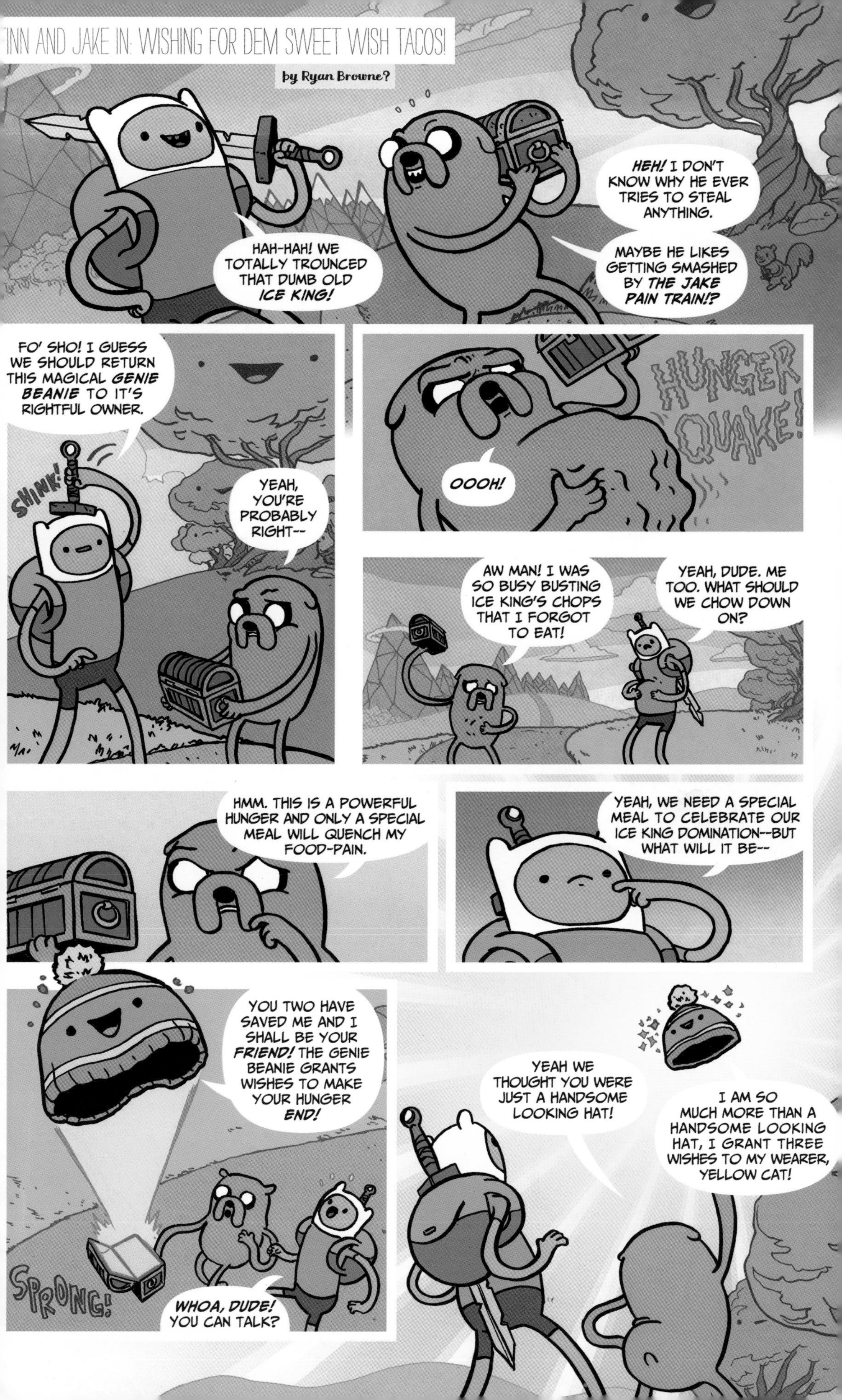

INN AND JAKE IN: WISHING FOR DEM SWEET WISH TACOS!
by Ryan Browne?
HAH-HAH! WE TOTALLY TROUNCED THAT DUMB OLD ICE KING!
HEH! I DON'T KNOW WHY HE EVER TRIES TO STEAL ANYTHING.
MAYBE HE LIKES GETTING SMASHED BY THE JAKE PAIN TRAIN!?
FO' SHO! I GUESS WE SHOULD RETURN THIS MAGICAL GENIE BEANIE TO IT'S RIGHTFUL OWNER.
SHINK!
YEAH, YOU'RE PROBABLY RIGHT--
HUNGER QUAKE!
OOOH!
AW MAN! I WAS SO BUSY BUSTING ICE KING'S CHOPS THAT I FORGOT TO EAT!
YEAH, DUDE. ME TOO. WHAT SHOULD WE CHOW DOWN ON?
HMM. THIS IS A POWERFUL HUNGER AND ONLY A SPECIAL MEAL WILL QUENCH MY FOOD-PAIN.
YEAH, WE NEED A SPECIAL MEAL TO CELEBRATE OUR ICE KING DOMINATION--BUT WHAT WILL IT BE--
YOU TWO HAVE SAVED ME AND I SHALL BE YOUR FRIEND! THE GENIE BEANIE GRANTS WISHES TO MAKE YOUR HUNGER END!
SPRONG!
WHOA, DUDE! YOU CAN TALK?
YEAH WE THOUGHT YOU WERE JUST A HANDSOME LOOKING HAT!
I AM SO MUCH MORE THAN A HANDSOME LOOKING HAT, I GRANT THREE WISHES TO MY WEARER, YELLOW CAT!

UH, ACTUALLY, I'M A DOG.

WISHES, HUH? SO THAT'S WHY THE ICE KING STOLE YOU.

ICE KING WANTED EVERY PRINCESS IN OO, BUT ALL Y'ALL BEAT HI, BLACK AND BLUE!

HAH, YEAH. WE SURE DID--OOH! SO HUNGRY!

QUICK, MAN! WEAR THAT HAT AND MAKE A DINNER WISH!

GRUMBLE!
WOBBLE!

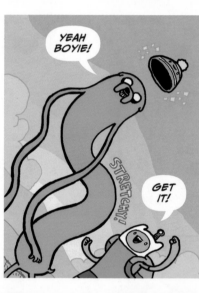

YEAH BOYIE!

STRETCHY!

GET IT!

I WISH FOR THE ULTIMATE DINNER IDEA!

MAGIC!

MAGIC TIME!

FINN AND JAKE, MAKE NO MISTAKE, HERE'S THE SOLUTION TO YOUR HUNGER QUAKE!

THIS IS AWESOME.

ULTRA-SPICY COSMIC FISH AND DEVILED SALAMI TACOS!

WISH GRANTED!

BOOOM!

DE-LICIOUS!

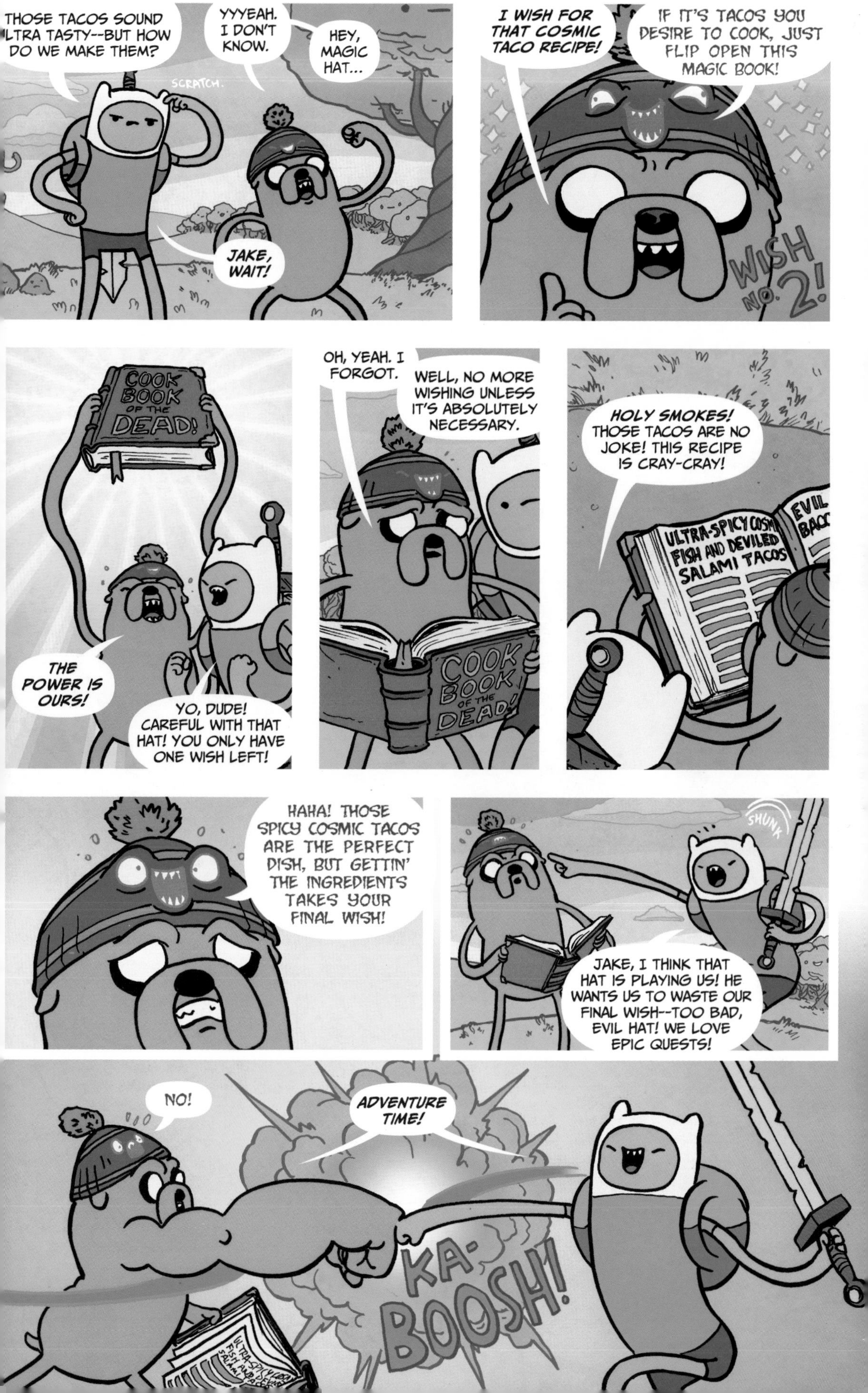

THOSE TACOS SOUND ULTRA TASTY--BUT HOW DO WE MAKE THEM?
SCRATCH.
YYYEAH. I DON'T KNOW.
HEY, MAGIC HAT...
JAKE, WAIT!
I WISH FOR THAT COSMIC TACO RECIPE!
IF IT'S TACOS YOU DESIRE TO COOK, JUST FLIP OPEN THIS MAGIC BOOK!
WISH NO. 2!
COOK BOOK OF THE DEAD!
THE POWER IS OURS!
YO, DUDE! CAREFUL WITH THAT HAT! YOU ONLY HAVE ONE WISH LEFT!
OH, YEAH. I FORGOT.
WELL, NO MORE WISHING UNLESS IT'S ABSOLUTELY NECESSARY.
COOK BOOK OF THE DEAD!
HOLY SMOKES! THOSE TACOS ARE NO JOKE! THIS RECIPE IS CRAY-CRAY!
ULTRA-SPICY COSMI FISH AND DEVILED SALAMI TACOS
HAHA! THOSE SPICY COSMIC TACOS ARE THE PERFECT DISH, BUT GETTIN' THE INGREDIENTS TAKES YOUR FINAL WISH!
SHUNK
JAKE, I THINK THAT HAT IS PLAYING US! HE WANTS US TO WASTE OUR FINAL WISH--TOO BAD, EVIL HAT! WE LOVE EPIC QUESTS!
NO!
ADVENTURE TIME!
KA-BOOSH!

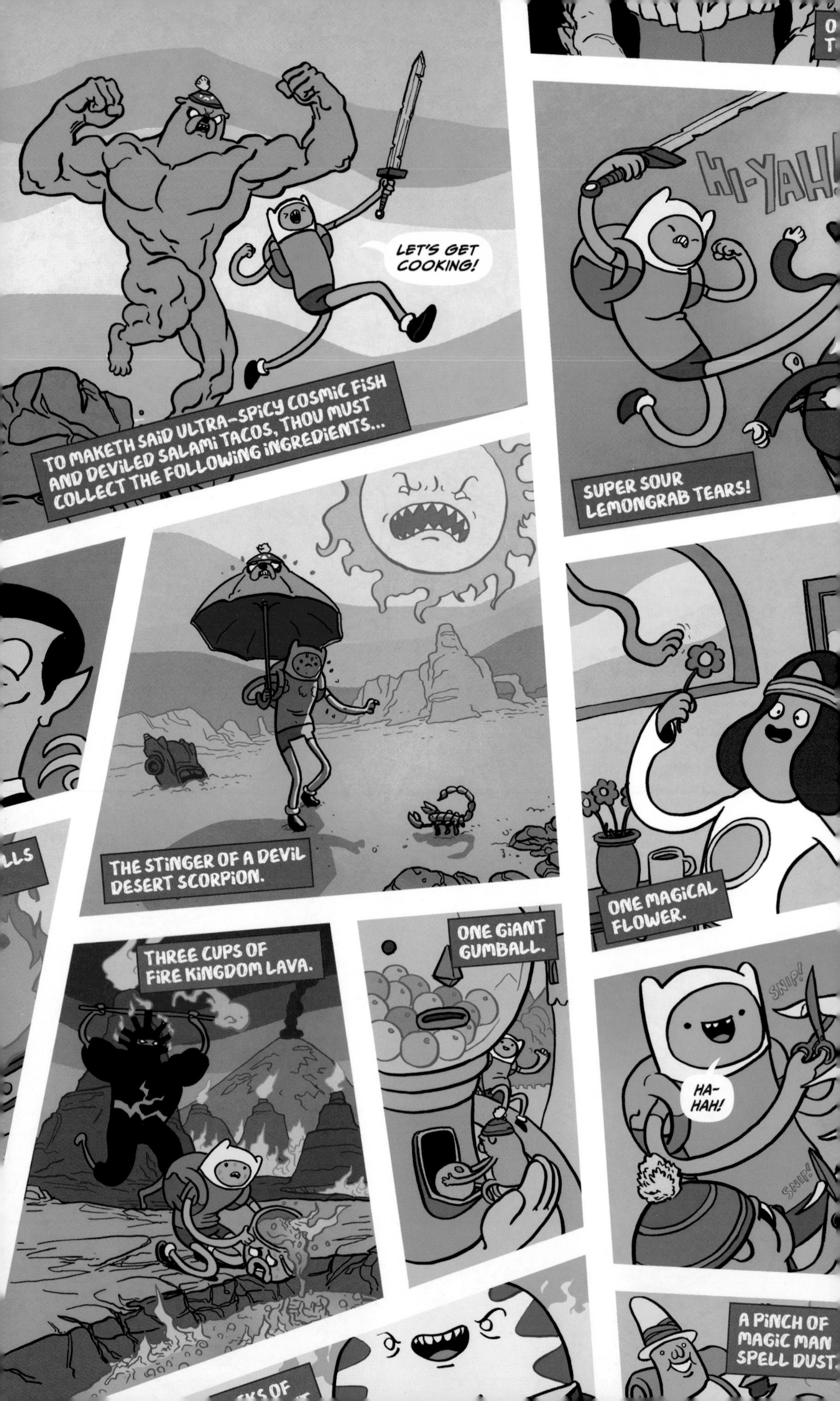

LET'S GET COOKING!
TO MAKETH SAID ULTRA-SPICY COSMIC FISH AND DEVILED SALAMI TACOS, THOU MUST COLLECT THE FOLLOWING INGREDIENTS...
HI-YAH!
SUPER SOUR LEMONGRAB TEARS!
THE STINGER OF A DEVIL DESERT SCORPION.
ONE MAGICAL FLOWER.
THREE CUPS OF FIRE KINGDOM LAVA.
ONE GIANT GUMBALL.
SNIP!
HA-HAH!
SNIP!
A PINCH OF MAGIC MAN SPELL DUST.

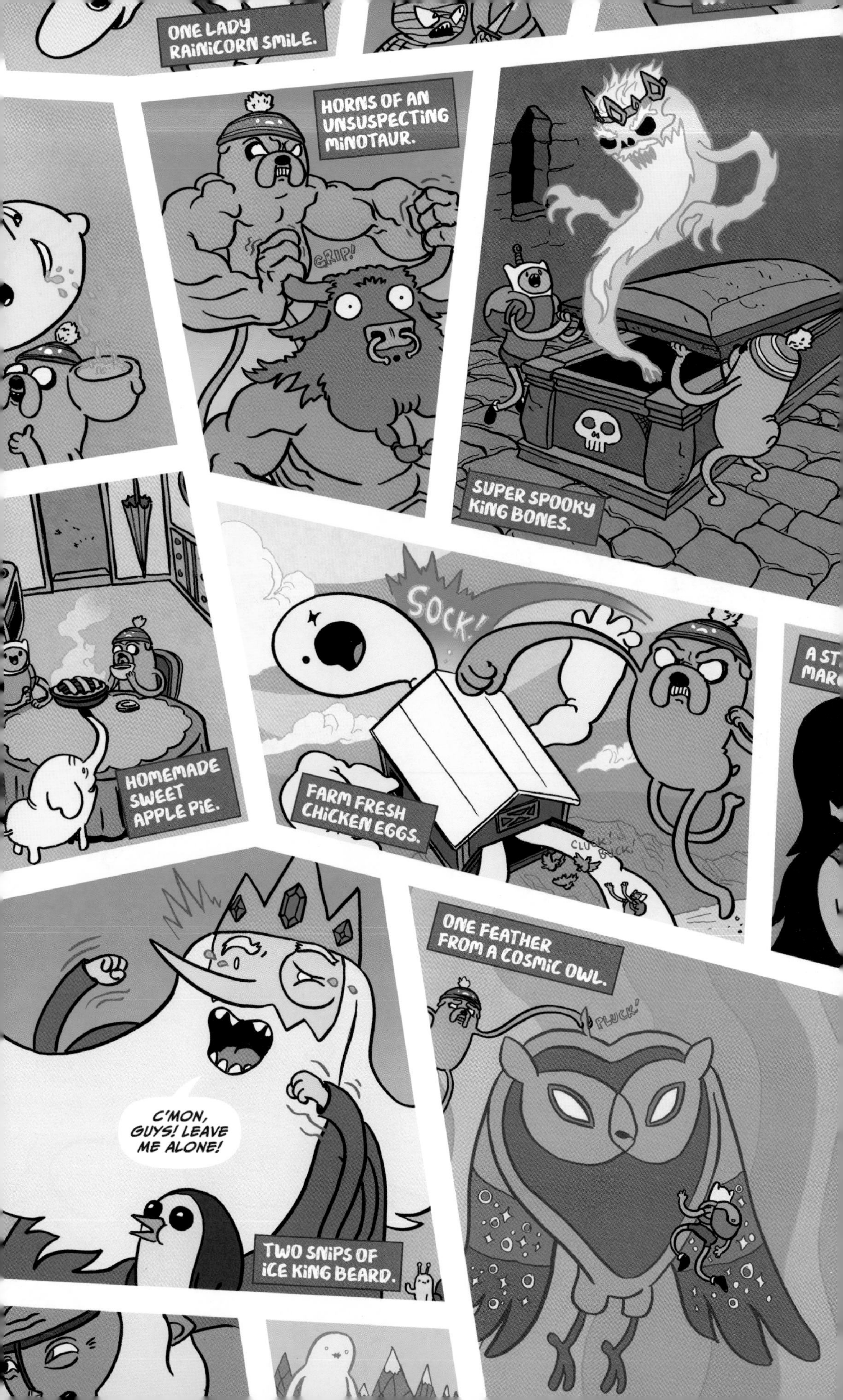
ONE LADY RAINICORN SMILE.
HORNS OF AN UNSUSPECTING MINOTAUR.
GRIP!
SUPER SPOOKY KING BONES.
HOMEMADE SWEET APPLE PIE.
SOCK!
FARM FRESH CHICKEN EGGS.
CLUCK! BUCK!
A ST
MAR
C'MON, GUYS! LEAVE ME ALONE!
TWO SNIPS OF ICE KING BEARD.
ONE FEATHER FROM A COSMIC OWL.
PLUCK!

HUFF WE--
HUFF--WE FINALLY
GOT ALL OF IT.

SSSSSOOO
HUNG-REEEEY!

I--I'M SO HUNGRY
I CAN BARELY SEE.
H-HOW ARE WE GONNA
COOK THIS...

FWUMP!

DOOF!

GIVE UP WITH
YOUR QUEST FOR
FOOD? MAKE THE
WISH AND I'LL
COOK IT GOOD!

F-FINE. I-I
WISH THESE TACO
WERE COOKED...

YES! ADVENTURERS
I DID FINALLY
BREAK, NOW EVIL
TACOS I SHALL
MAKE!

WISH No.3!

JEEPERS!

EVIL TACO
TIME!

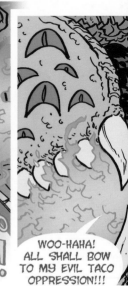

WOO-HAHA!
ALL SHALL BOW
TO MY EVIL TACO
OPPRESSION!!!

GROW!

WAIT,
WHAT--

CHOMP!
CHOMP!
CHOMP!

JAKE! YOU
SCARFED THE
WHOLE TACO!

ALRIGHT, *GENIE
BEANIE!* I WISH
FOR A HUNDRED
COSMIC TACOS
THAT JAKE
CAN'T EAT!

SWIPE!

AW,
SORRY, BRO.
MY BAD.

GIMMIE
THAT!

YOUR WISH IS
MY COMMAND, BEHO
MORE TACOS THA
YOU CAN STAND!

NO
FAI

The E

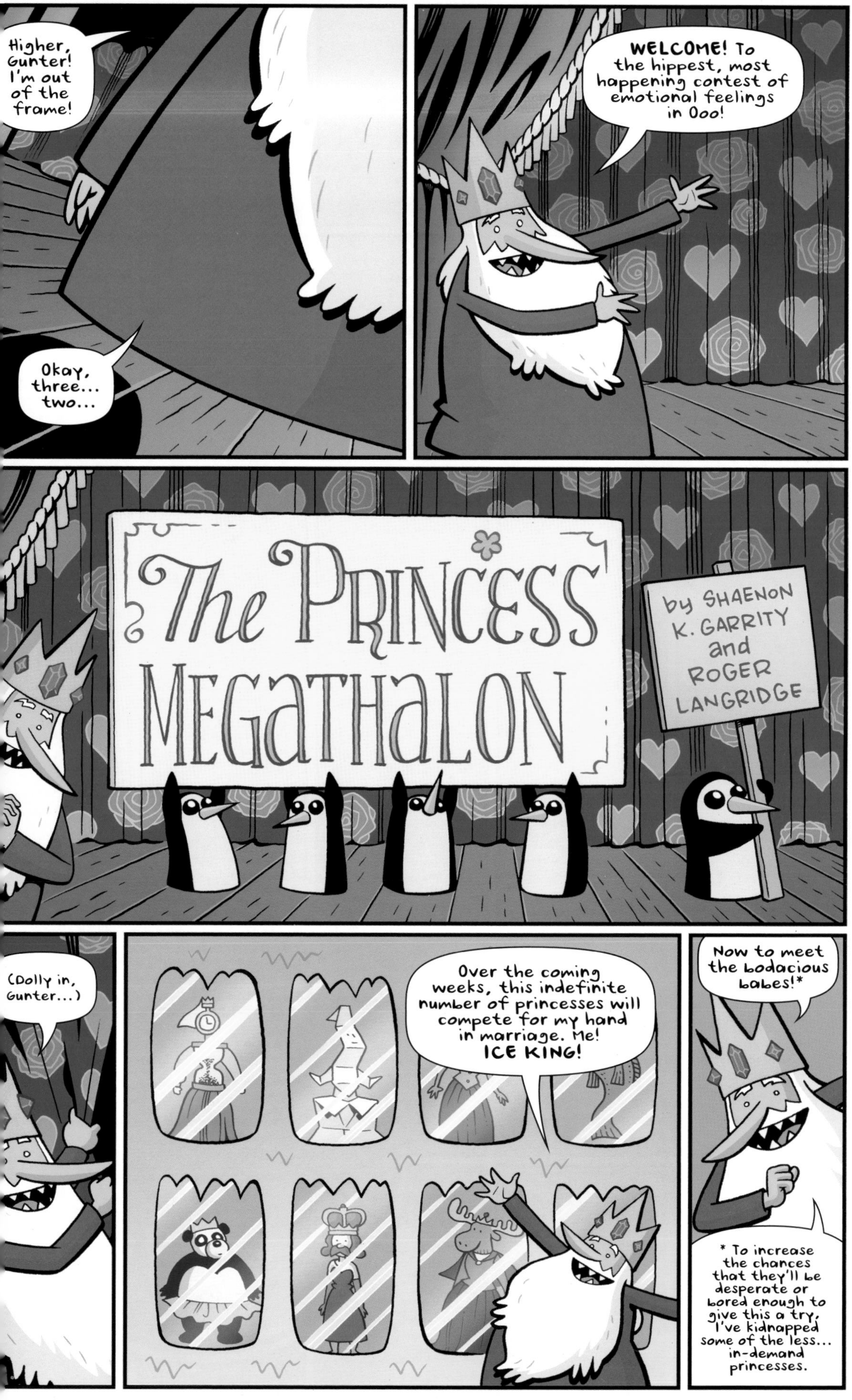
Higher, Gunter! I'm out of the frame!
Okay, three... two...
WELCOME! To the hippest, most happening contest of emotional feelings in Ooo!
The PRINCESS MEGATHALON
by SHAENON K. GARRITY and ROGER LANGRIDGE
(Dolly in, Gunter...)
Over the coming weeks, this indefinite number of princesses will compete for my hand in marriage. Me! ICE KING!
Now to meet the bodacious babes!*
* To increase the chances that they'll be desperate or bored enough to give this a try, I've kidnapped some of the less... in-demand princesses.

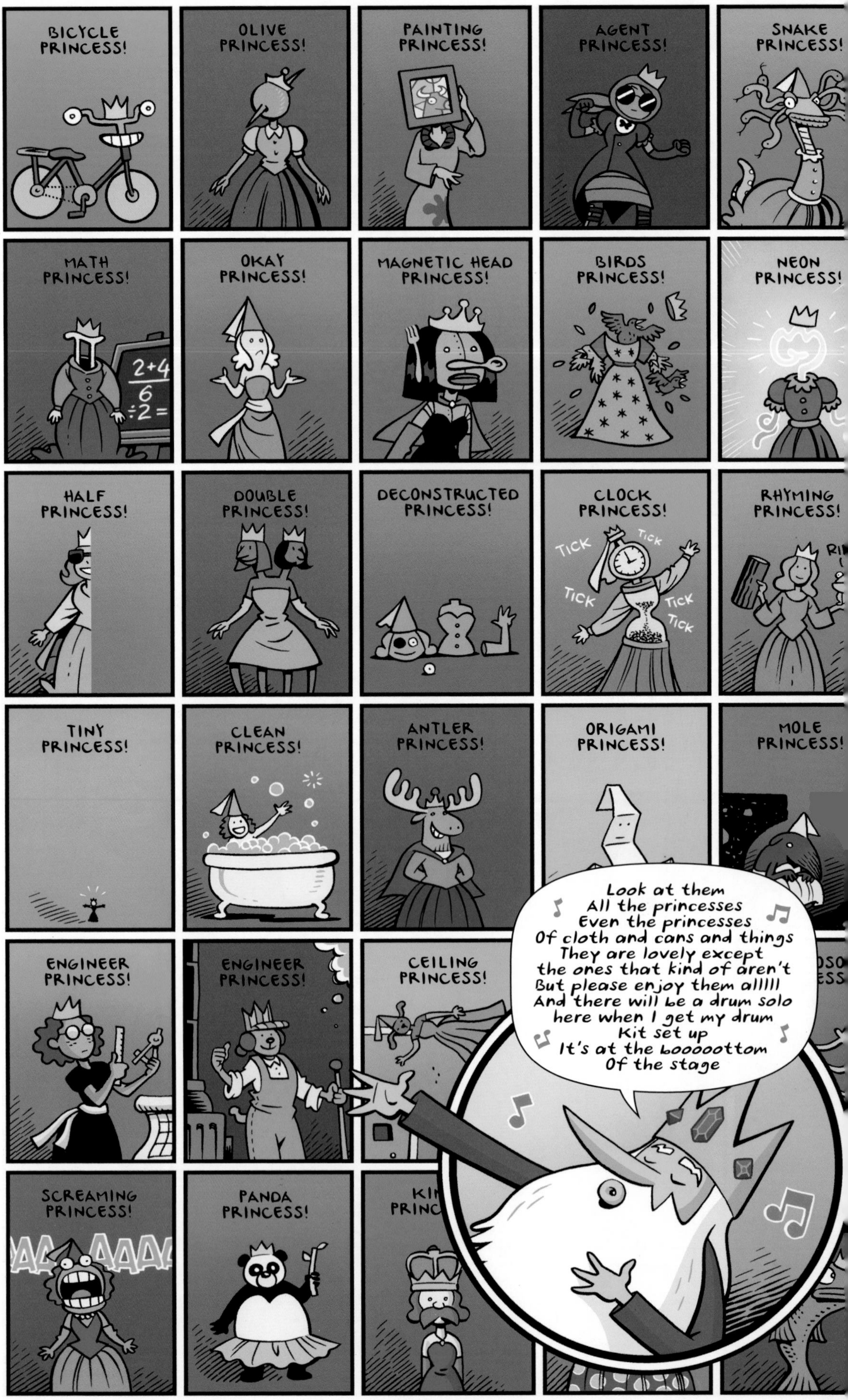

BICYCLE PRINCESS!
OLIVE PRINCESS!
PAINTING PRINCESS!
AGENT PRINCESS!
SNAKE PRINCESS!
MATH PRINCESS!
2+4
6
÷2=
OKAY PRINCESS!
MAGNETIC HEAD PRINCESS!
BIRDS PRINCESS!
NEON PRINCESS!
HALF PRINCESS!
DOUBLE PRINCESS!
DECONSTRUCTED PRINCESS!
CLOCK PRINCESS!
TICK TICK TICK TICK TICK
RHYMING PRINCESS!
TINY PRINCESS!
CLEAN PRINCESS!
ANTLER PRINCESS!
ORIGAMI PRINCESS!
MOLE PRINCESS!
ENGINEER PRINCESS!
ENGINEER PRINCESS!
CEILING PRINCESS!
SCREAMING PRINCESS!
PANDA PRINCESS!
Look at them
All the princesses
Even the princesses
Of cloth and cans and things
They are lovely except
the ones that kind of aren't
But please enjoy them alllll
And there will be a drum solo
here when I get my drum
Kit set up
It's at the boooottom
Of the stage

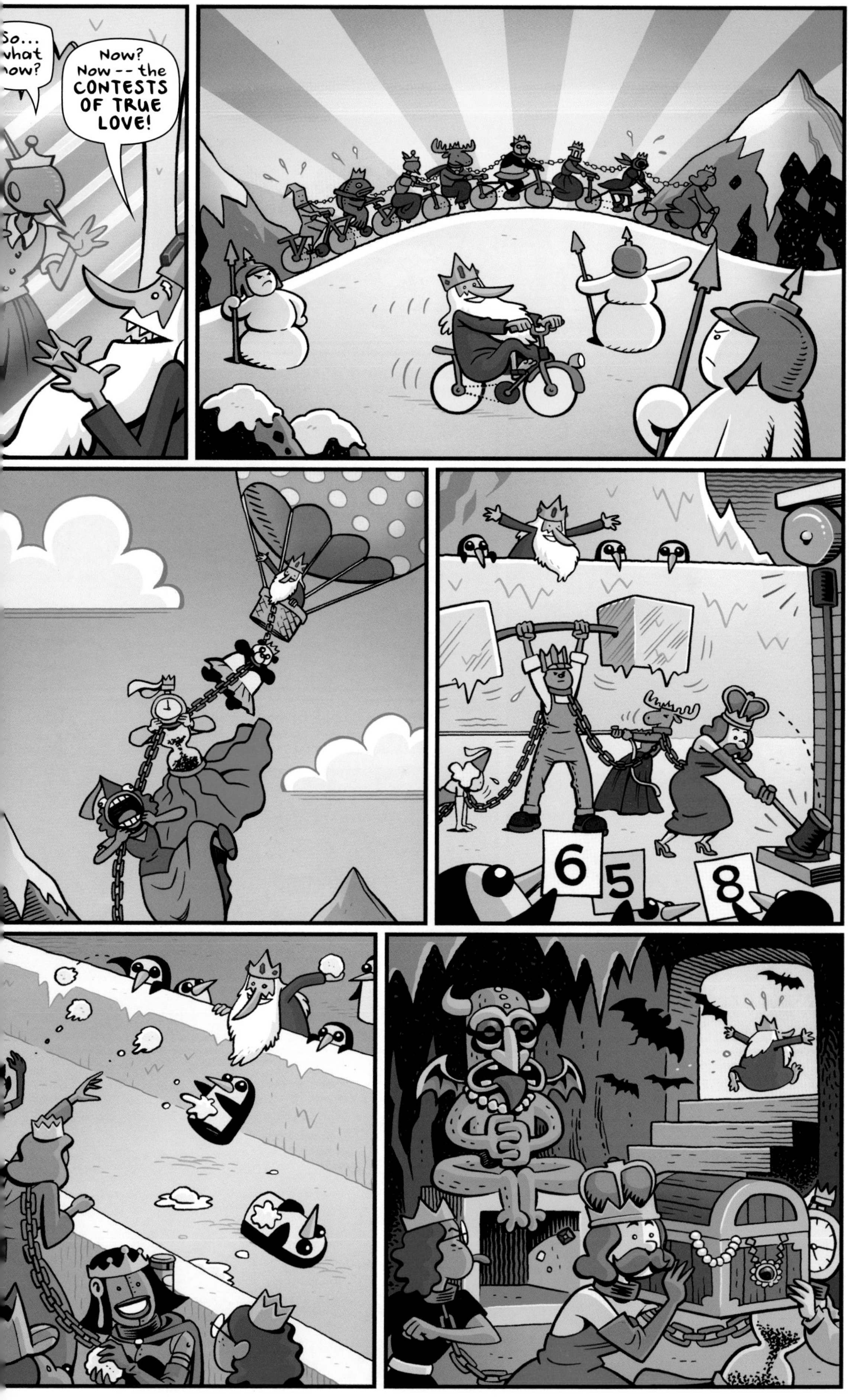
So... what now?
Now? Now -- the CONTESTS OF TRUE LOVE!
6
5
8

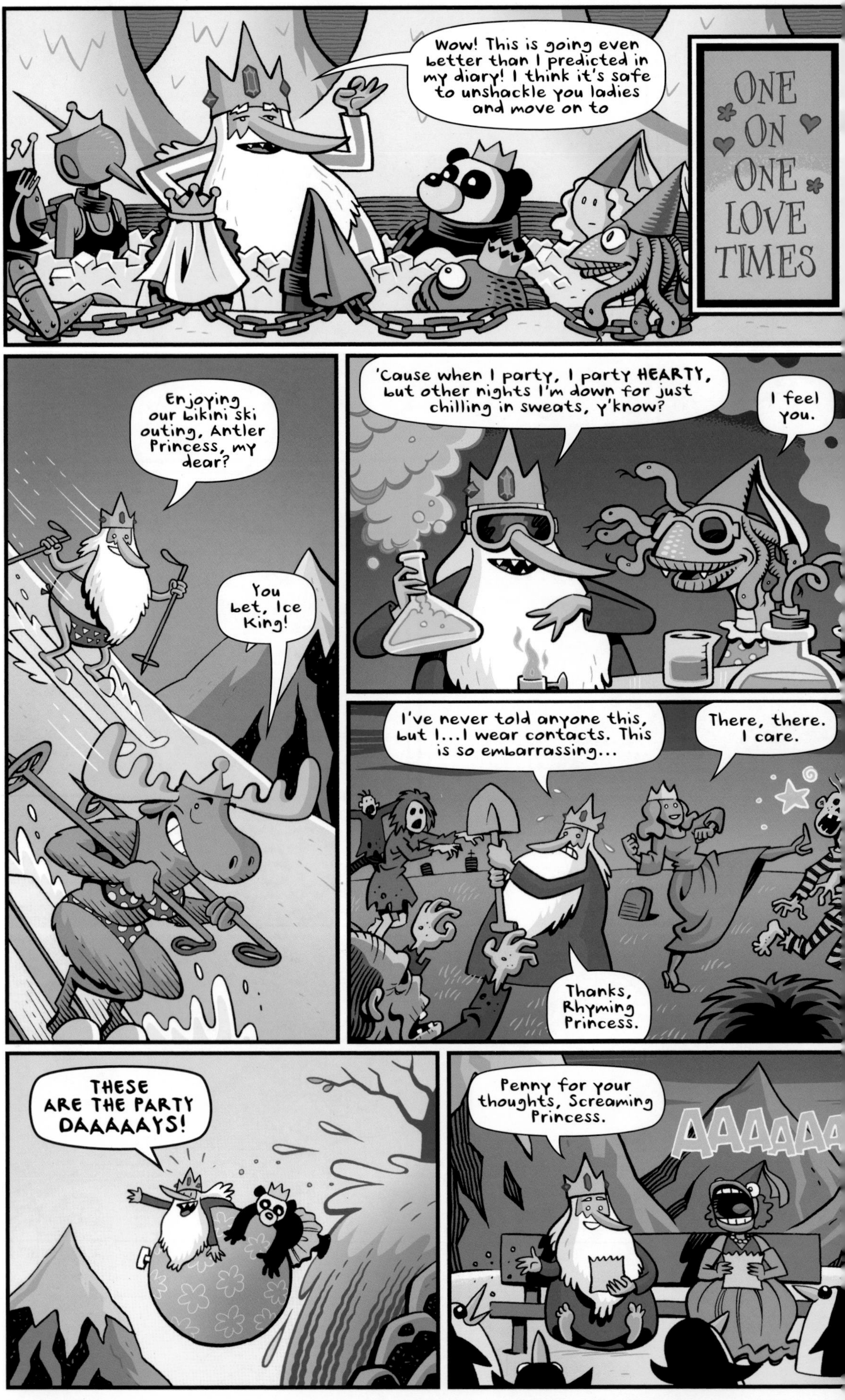

Wow! This is going even better than I predicted in my diary! I think it's safe to unshackle you ladies and move on to
ONE ON ONE LOVE TIMES
Enjoying our bikini ski outing, Antler Princess, my dear?
You bet, Ice King!
'Cause when I party, I party HEARTY, but other nights I'm down for just chilling in sweats, y'know?
I feel you.
I've never told anyone this, but I...I wear contacts. This is so embarrassing...
There, there. I care.
Thanks, Rhyming Princess.
THESE ARE THE PARTY DAAAAAYS!
Penny for your thoughts, Screaming Princess.
AAAAAA

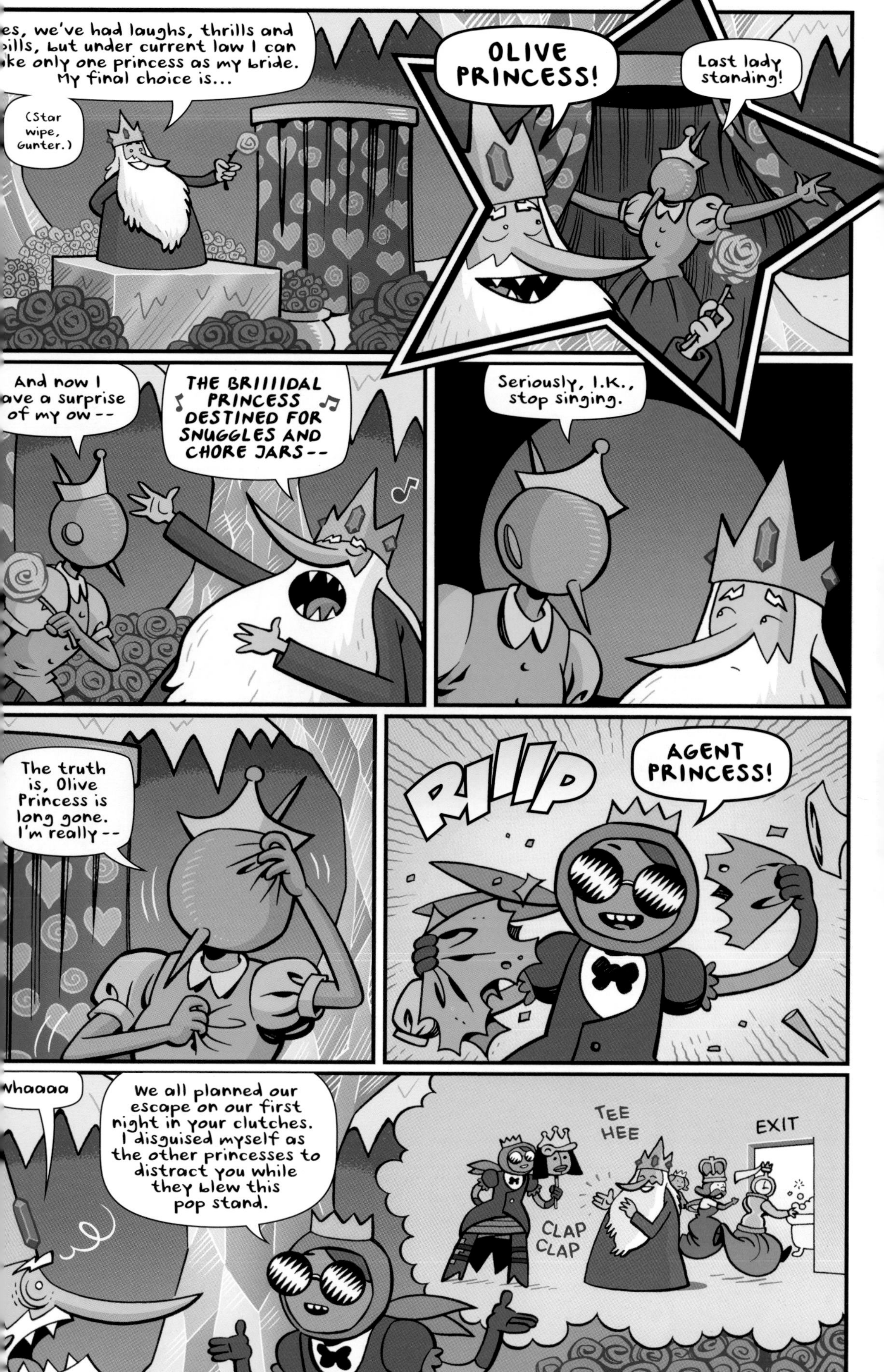
es, we've had laughs, thrills and
pills, but under current law I can
ke only one princess as my bride.
My final choice is...
(Star wipe, Gunter.)
OLIVE PRINCESS!
Last lady standing!
And now I ave a surprise of my ow--
THE BRIIIIDAL PRINCESS DESTINED FOR SNUGGLES AND CHORE JARS--
Seriously, I.K., stop singing.
The truth is, Olive Princess is long gone. I'm really--
RIIIP
AGENT PRINCESS!
whaaaa
We all planned our escape on our first night in your clutches. I disguised myself as the other princesses to distract you while they blew this pop stand.
TEE HEE
EXIT
CLAP CLAP

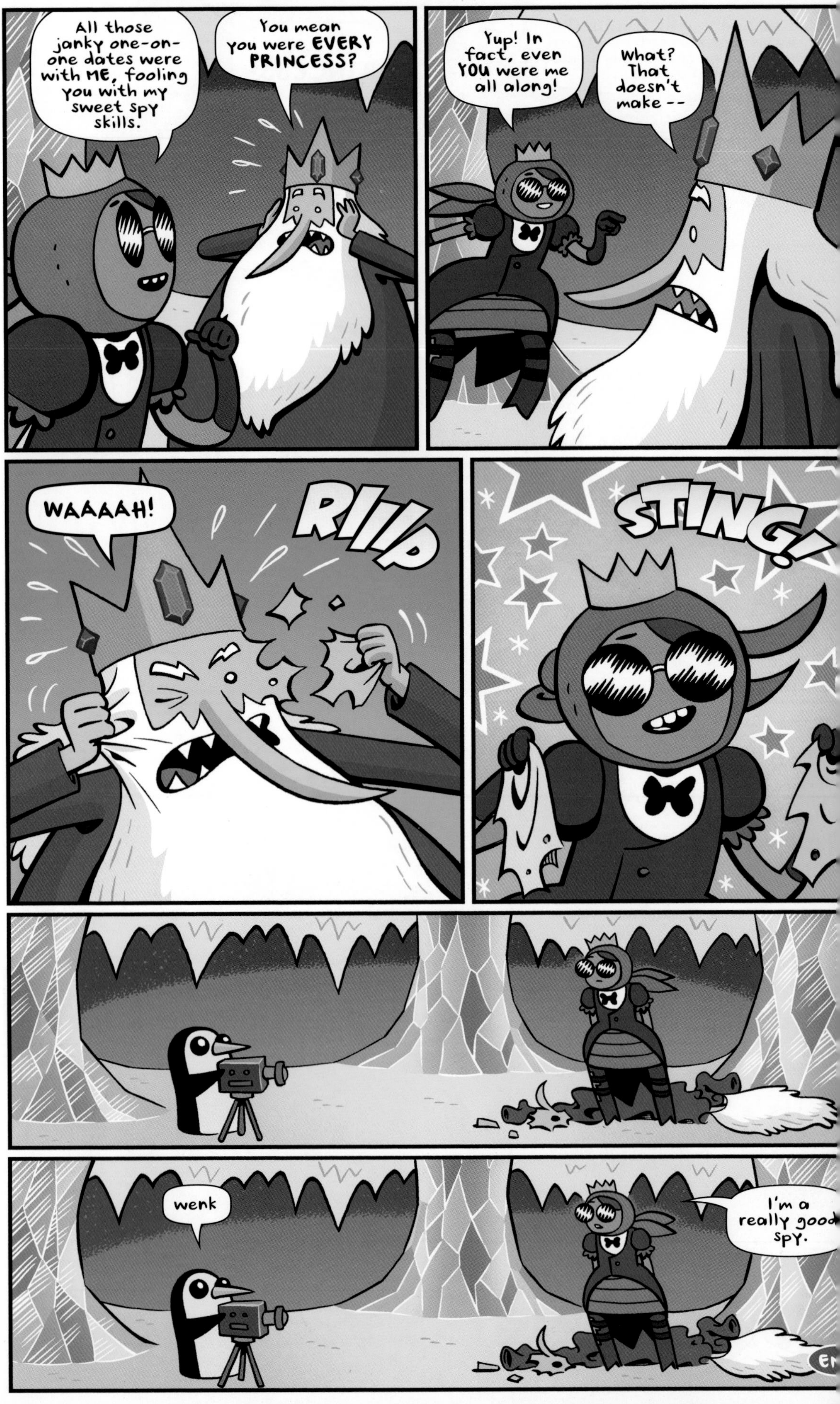
All those janky one-on-one dates were with ME, fooling you with my sweet spy skills.
You mean you were EVERY PRINCESS?
Yup! In fact, even YOU were me all along!
What? That doesn't make --
WAAAAH!
RIIIP
STING!
wenk
I'm a really good spy.

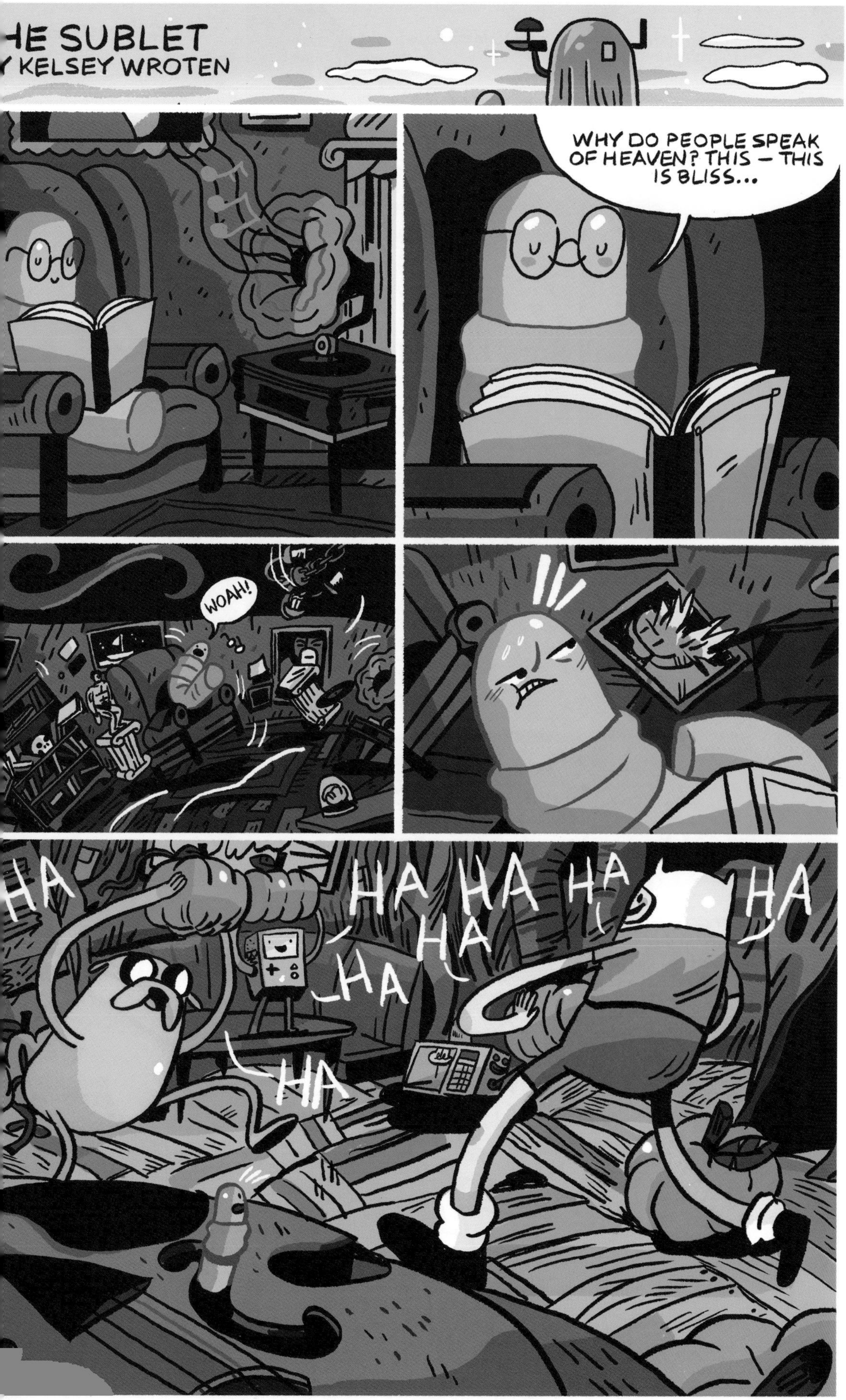

HE SUBLET
Y KELSEY WROTEN
WHY DO PEOPLE SPEAK OF HEAVEN? THIS — THIS IS BLISS...
WOAH!
HA
HA HA HA HA HA
HA
HA
HA

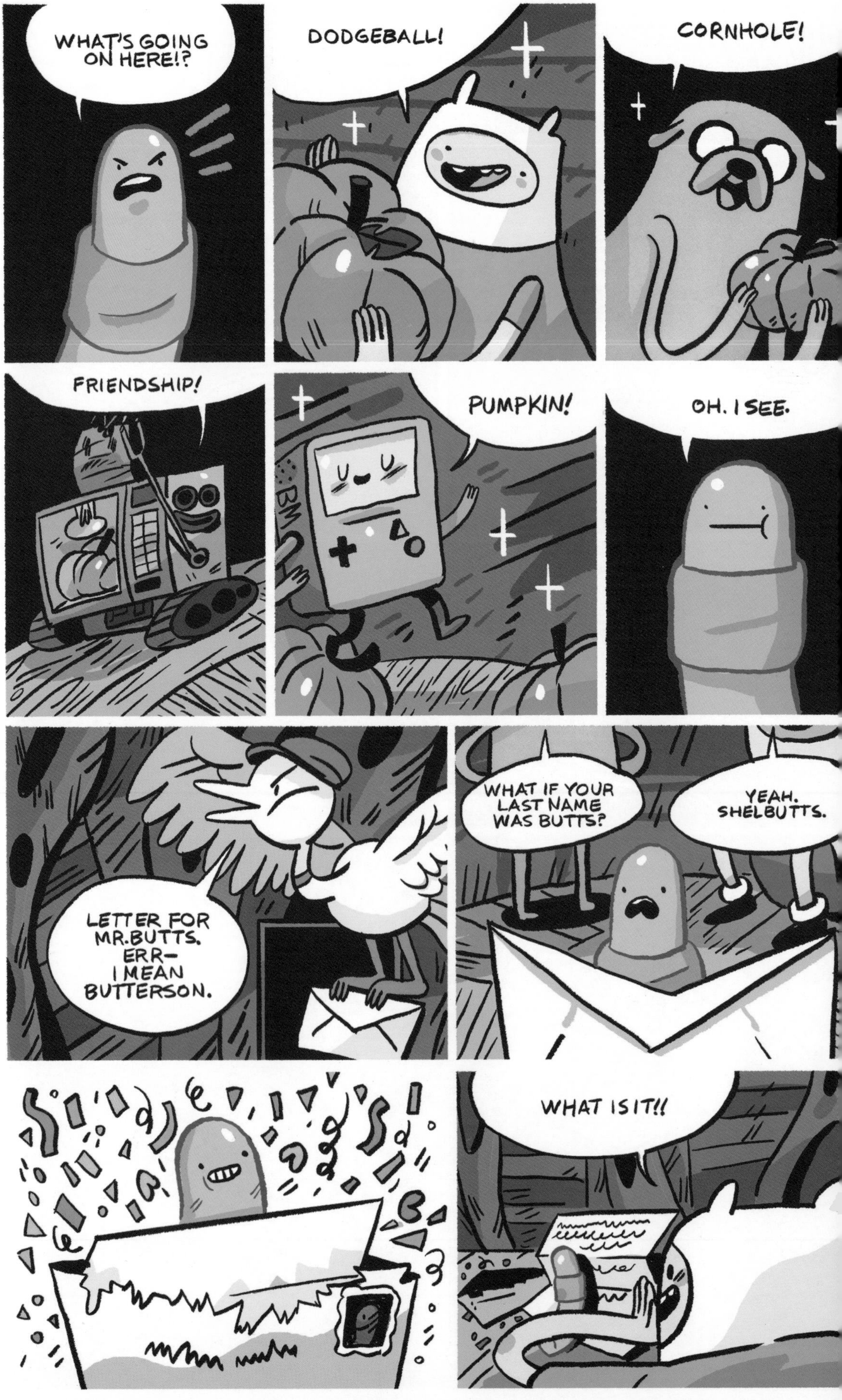
WHAT'S GOING ON HERE!?
DODGEBALL!
CORNHOLE!
FRIENDSHIP!
PUMPKIN!
OH. I SEE.
LETTER FOR MR.BUTTS. ERR– I MEAN BUTTERSON.
WHAT IF YOUR LAST NAME WAS BUTTS?
YEAH. SHELBUTTS.
WHAT IS IT!!

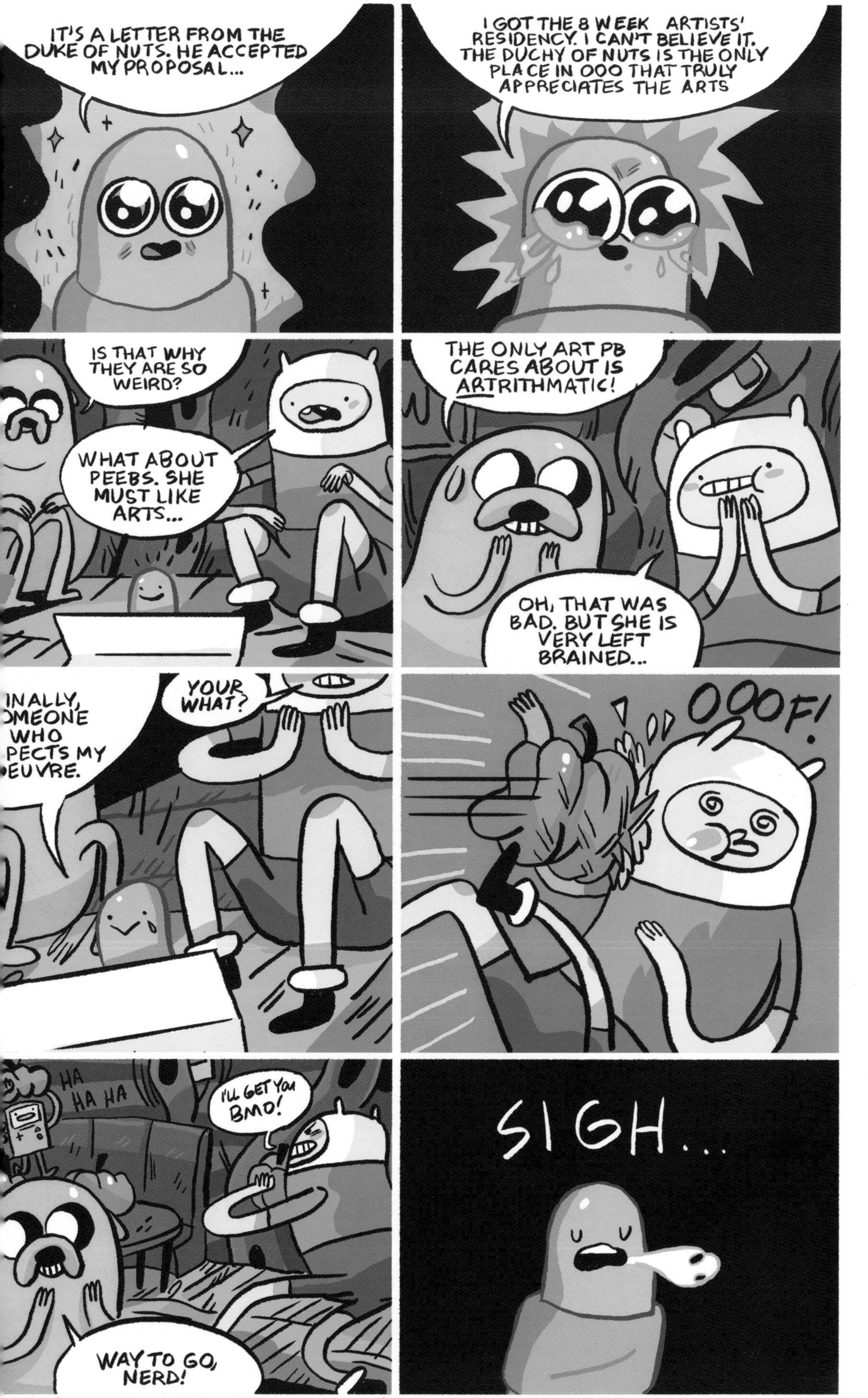
IT'S A LETTER FROM THE DUKE OF NUTS. HE ACCEPTED MY PROPOSAL...
I GOT THE 8 WEEK ARTISTS' RESIDENCY. I CAN'T BELIEVE IT. THE DUCHY OF NUTS IS THE ONLY PLACE IN OOO THAT TRULY APPRECIATES THE ARTS
IS THAT WHY THEY ARE SO WEIRD?
WHAT ABOUT PEEBS. SHE MUST LIKE ARTS...
THE ONLY ART PB CARES ABOUT IS ARTRITHMATIC!
OH, THAT WAS BAD. BUT SHE IS VERY LEFT BRAINED...
INALLY, OMEONE WHO PECTS MY EUVRE.
YOUR WHAT?
OOOF!
HA HA HA HA
I'LL GET YOU BMO!
WAY TO GO, NERD!
SIGH...

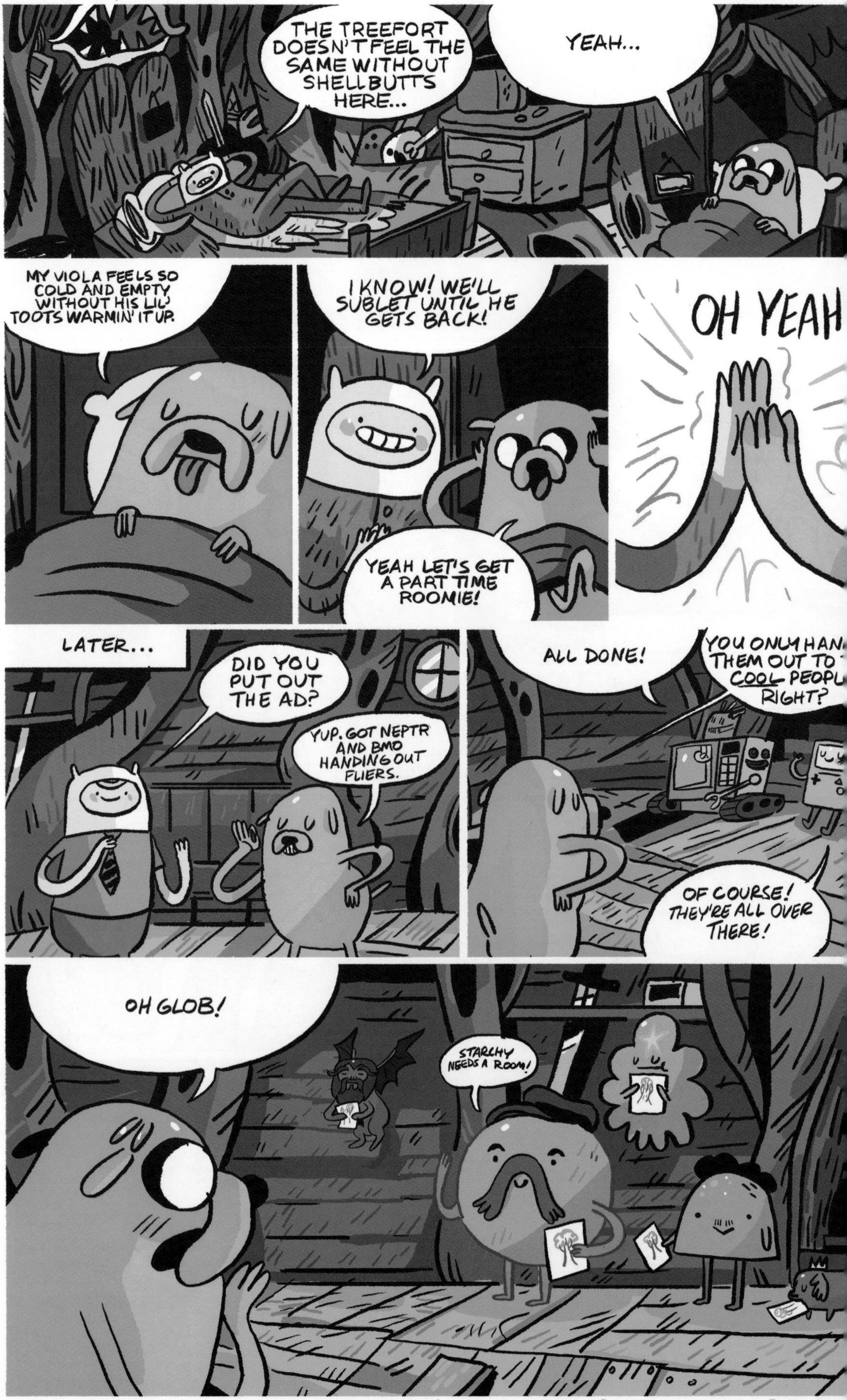
THE TREEFORT DOESN'T FEEL THE SAME WITHOUT SHELLBUTTS HERE...
YEAH...
MY VIOLA FEELS SO COLD AND EMPTY WITHOUT HIS LIL' TOOTS WARMIN' IT UP.
I KNOW! WE'LL SUBLET UNTIL HE GETS BACK!
YEAH LET'S GET A PART TIME ROOMIE!
OH YEAH
LATER...
DID YOU PUT OUT THE AD?
YUP. GOT NEPTR AND BMO HANDING OUT FLIERS.
ALL DONE!
OF COURSE! THEY'RE ALL OVER THERE!
OH GLOB!
STARCHY NEEDS A ROOM!

THE INTERVIEWS!

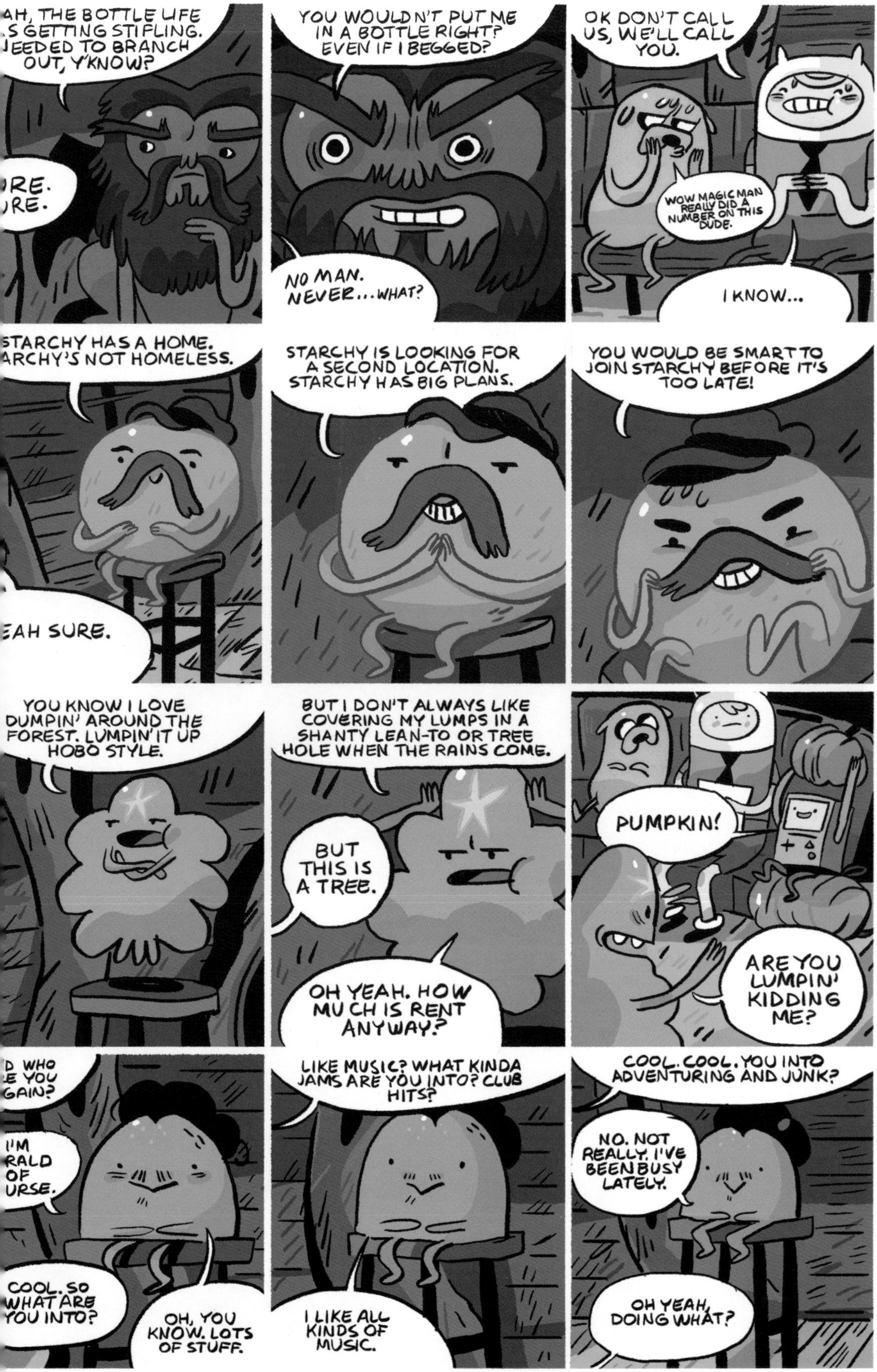

AH, THE BOTTLE LIFE
S GETTING STIFLING.
IEEDED TO BRANCH
OUT, Y'KNOW?
RE.
RE.
YOU WOULDN'T PUT ME IN A BOTTLE RIGHT? EVEN IF I BEGGED?
NO MAN. NEVER... WHAT?
OK DON'T CALL US, WE'LL CALL YOU.
WOW MAGIC MAN REALLY DID A NUMBER ON THIS DUDE.
I KNOW...
STARCHY HAS A HOME.
ARCHY'S NOT HOMELESS.
EAH SURE.
STARCHY IS LOOKING FOR A SECOND LOCATION. STARCHY HAS BIG PLANS.
YOU WOULD BE SMART TO JOIN STARCHY BEFORE IT'S TOO LATE!
YOU KNOW I LOVE DUMPIN' AROUND THE FOREST. LUMPIN' IT UP HOBO STYLE.
BUT I DON'T ALWAYS LIKE COVERING MY LUMPS IN A SHANTY LEAN-TO OR TREE HOLE WHEN THE RAINS COME.
BUT THIS IS A TREE.
OH YEAH. HOW MUCH IS RENT ANYWAY?
PUMPKIN!
ARE YOU LUMPIN' KIDDING ME?
D WHO
E YOU
GAIN?
I'M
RALD
OF
URSE.
COOL. SO WHAT ARE YOU INTO?
OH, YOU KNOW. LOTS OF STUFF.
LIKE MUSIC? WHAT KINDA JAMS ARE YOU INTO? CLUB HITS?
I LIKE ALL KINDS OF MUSIC.
COOL. COOL. YOU INTO ADVENTURING AND JUNK?
NO. NOT REALLY. I'VE BEEN BUSY LATELY.
OH YEAH, DOING WHAT?

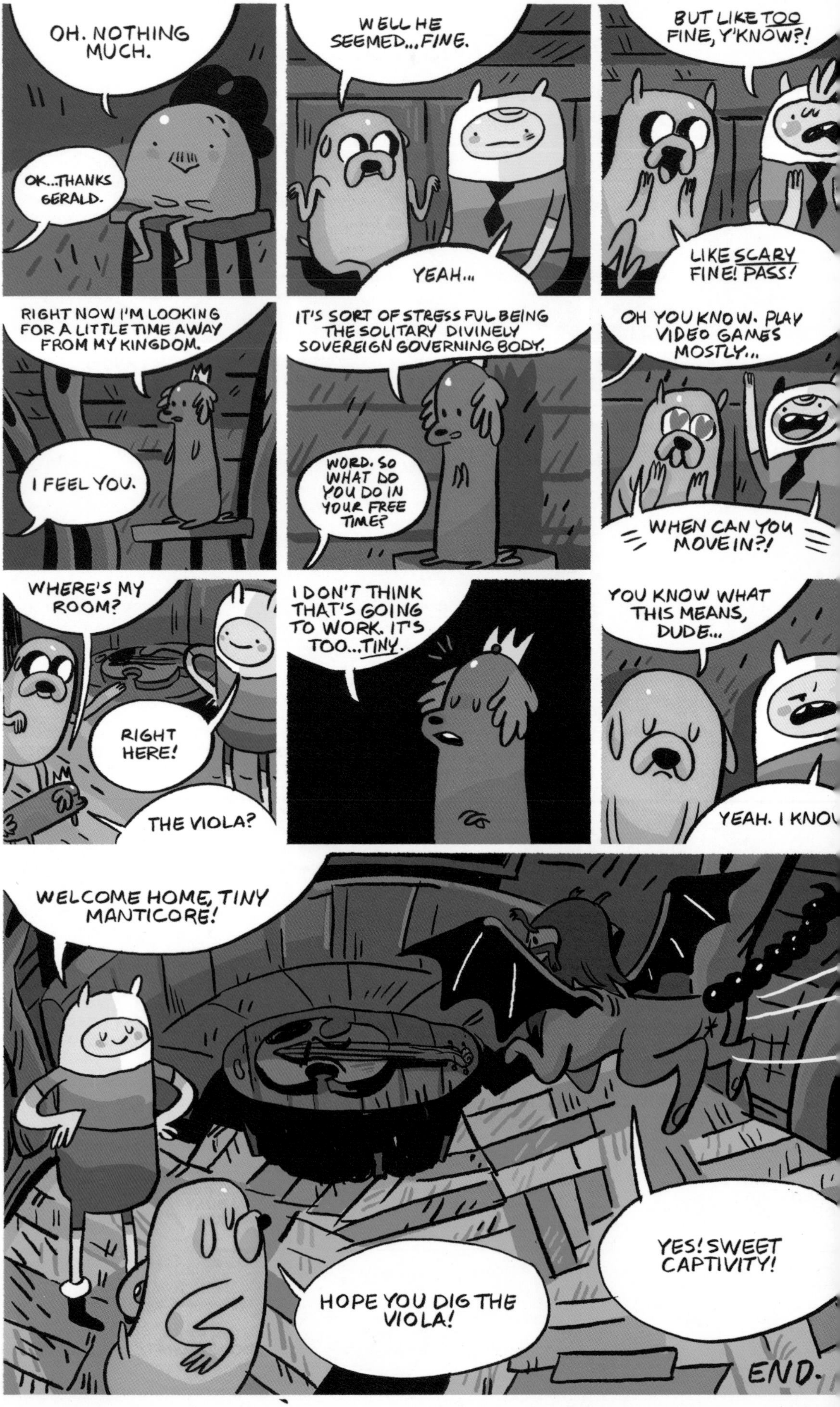
OH. NOTHING MUCH.
OK...THANKS GERALD.
WELL HE SEEMED...FINE.
YEAH...
BUT LIKE TOO FINE, Y'KNOW?!
LIKE SCARY FINE! PASS!
RIGHT NOW I'M LOOKING FOR A LITTLE TIME AWAY FROM MY KINGDOM.
I FEEL YOU.
IT'S SORT OF STRESSFUL BEING THE SOLITARY DIVINELY SOVEREIGN GOVERNING BODY.
WORD. SO WHAT DO YOU DO IN YOUR FREE TIME?
OH YOU KNOW. PLAY VIDEO GAMES MOSTLY...
WHEN CAN YOU MOVE IN?!
WHERE'S MY ROOM?
RIGHT HERE!
THE VIOLA?
I DON'T THINK THAT'S GOING TO WORK. IT'S TOO...TINY.
YOU KNOW WHAT THIS MEANS, DUDE...
YEAH. I KNOW
WELCOME HOME, TINY MANTICORE!
HOPE YOU DIG THE VIOLA!
YES! SWEET CAPTIVITY!
END.

"NO CHILL"

By Annie Mok and Rachel Dukes

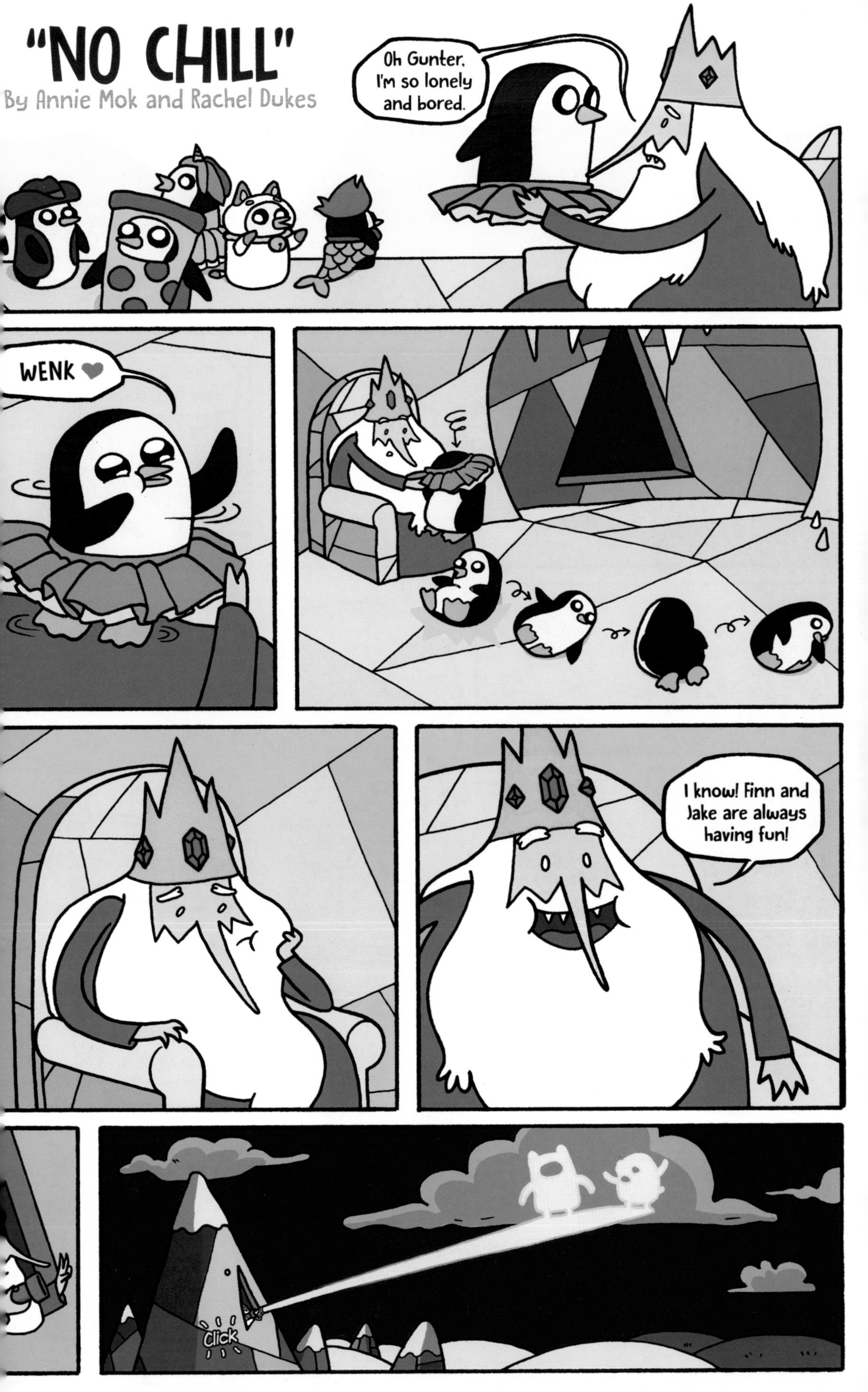

Oh Gunter, I'm so lonely and bored.
WENK
I know! Finn and Jake are always having fun!
Click

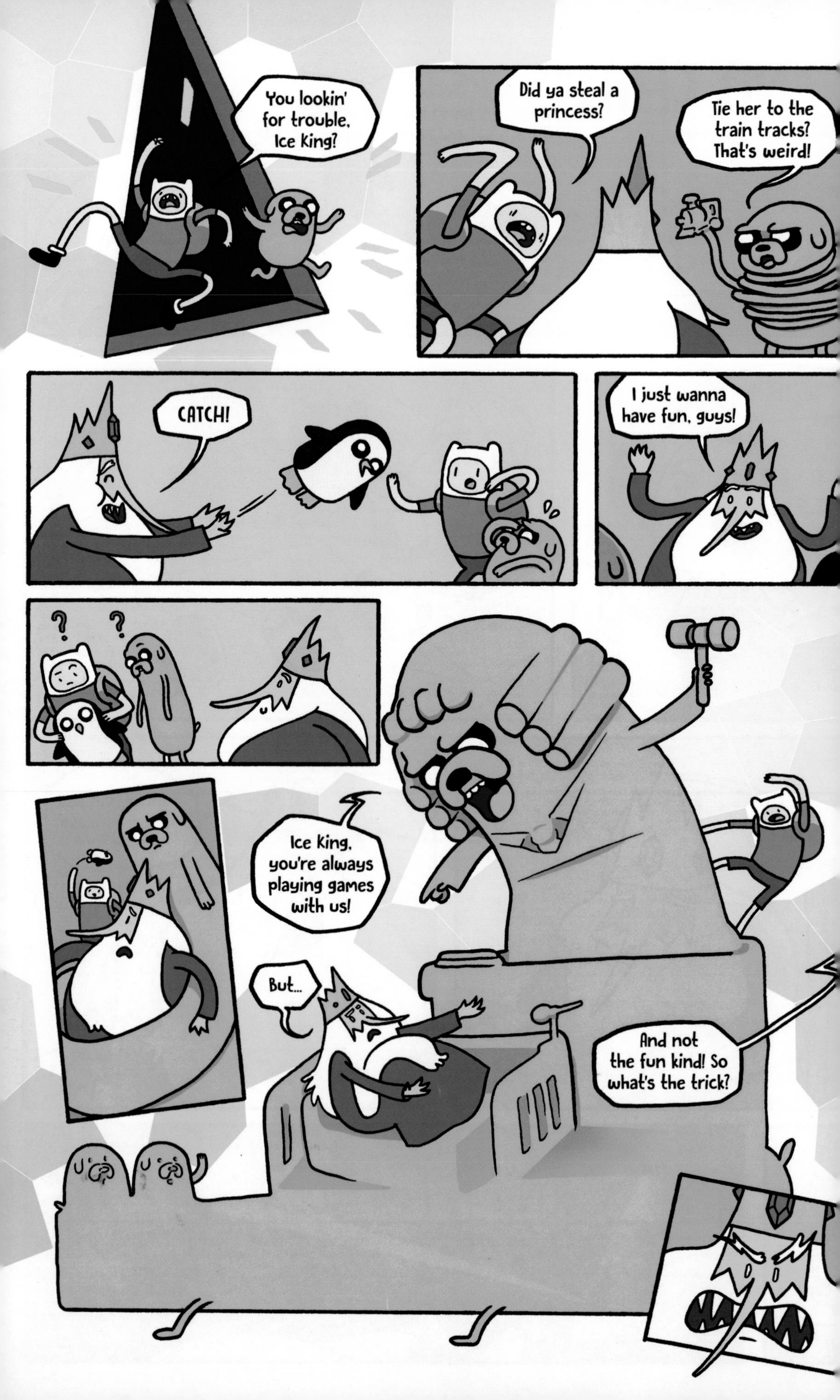
You lookin' for trouble, Ice King?
Did ya steal a princess?
Tie her to the train tracks? That's weird!
CATCH!
I just wanna have fun, guys!
?
?
Ice King, you're always playing games with us!
But...
And not the fun kind! So what's the trick?

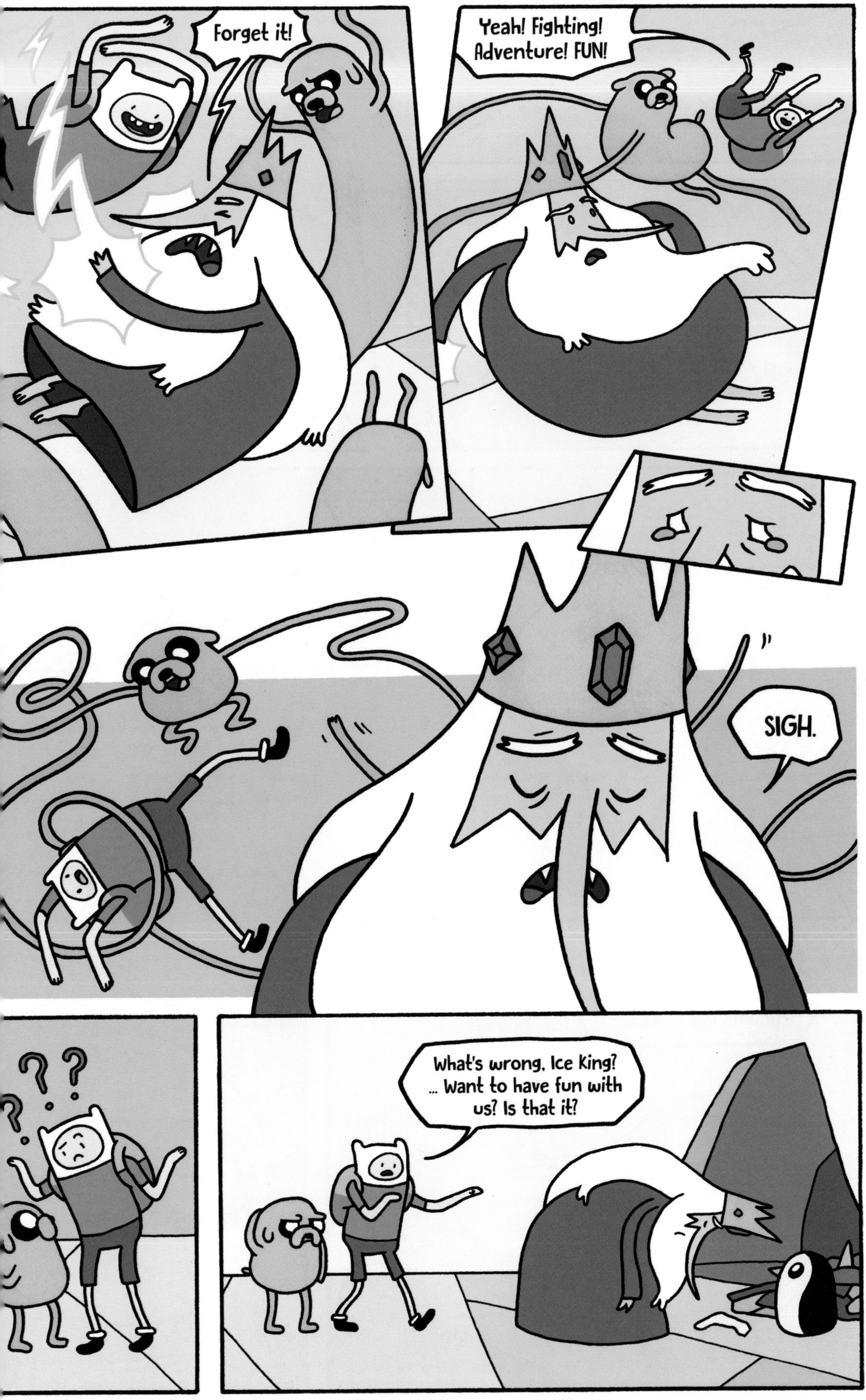
Forget it!
Yeah! Fighting! Adventure! FUN!
SIGH.
What's wrong, Ice King? ... Want to have fun with us? Is that it?

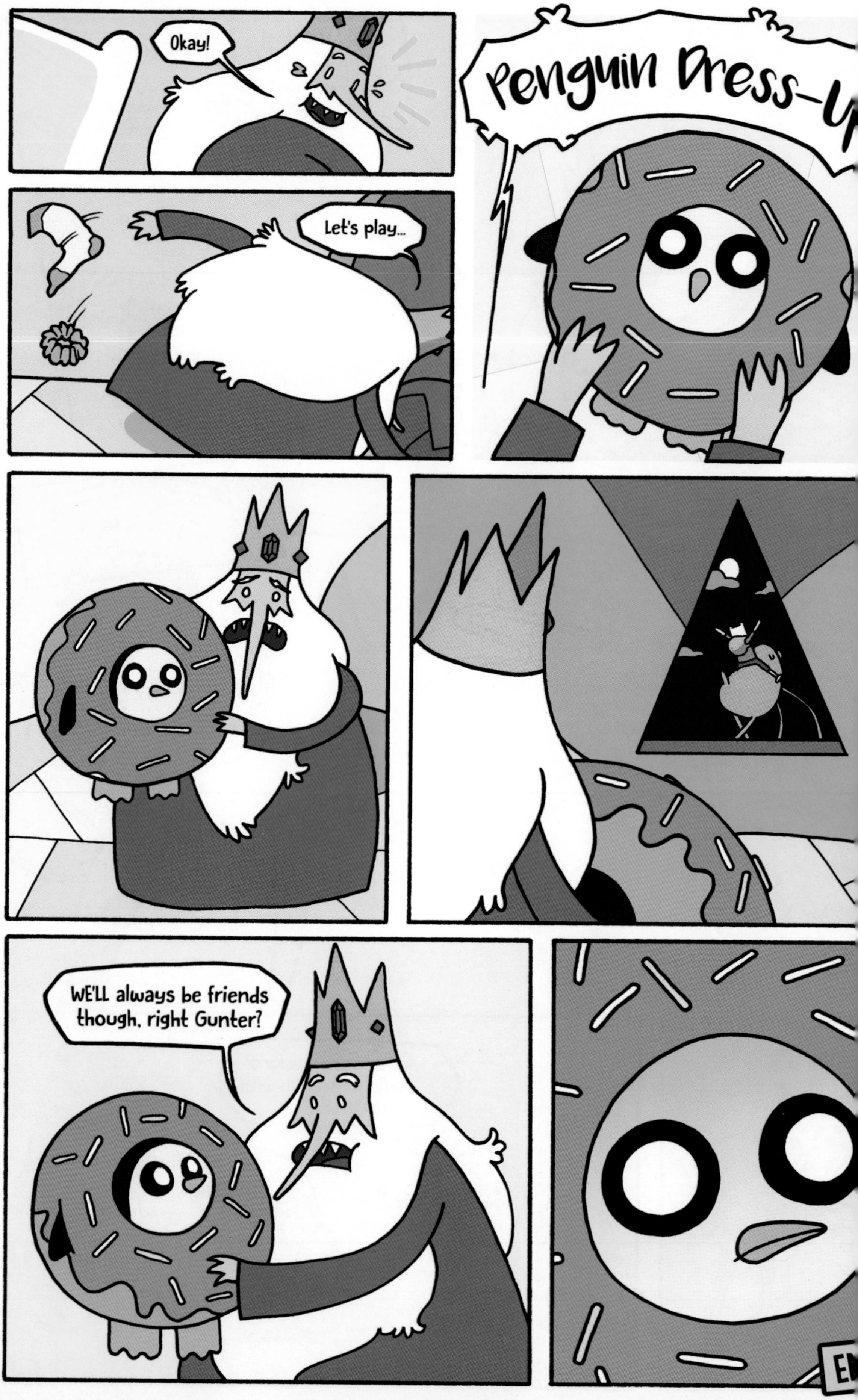
Okay!
Let's play...
Penguin Dress-U
WE'LL always be friends
though, right Gunter?

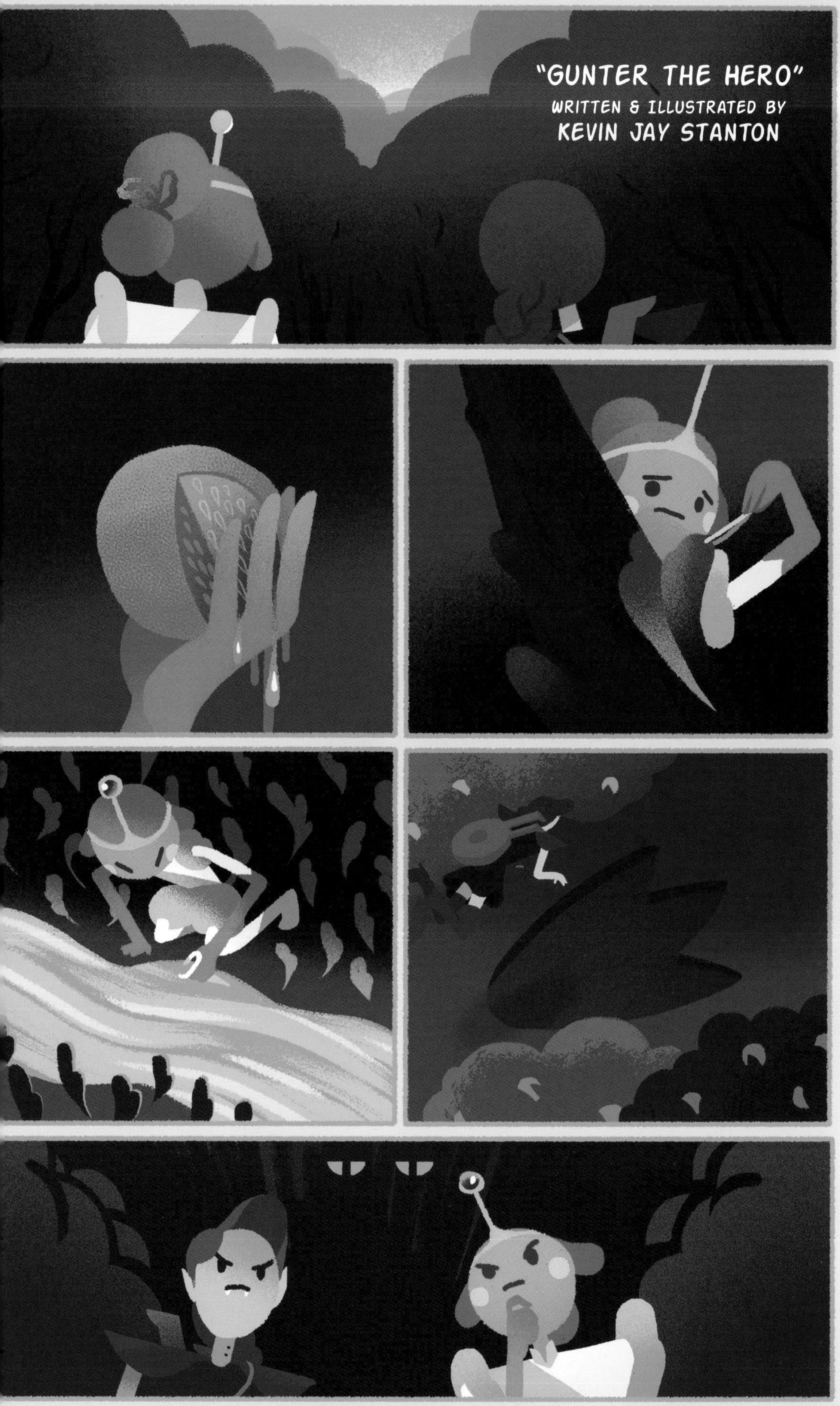
"GUNTER THE HERO"
WRITTEN & ILLUSTRATED BY
KEVIN JAY STANTON

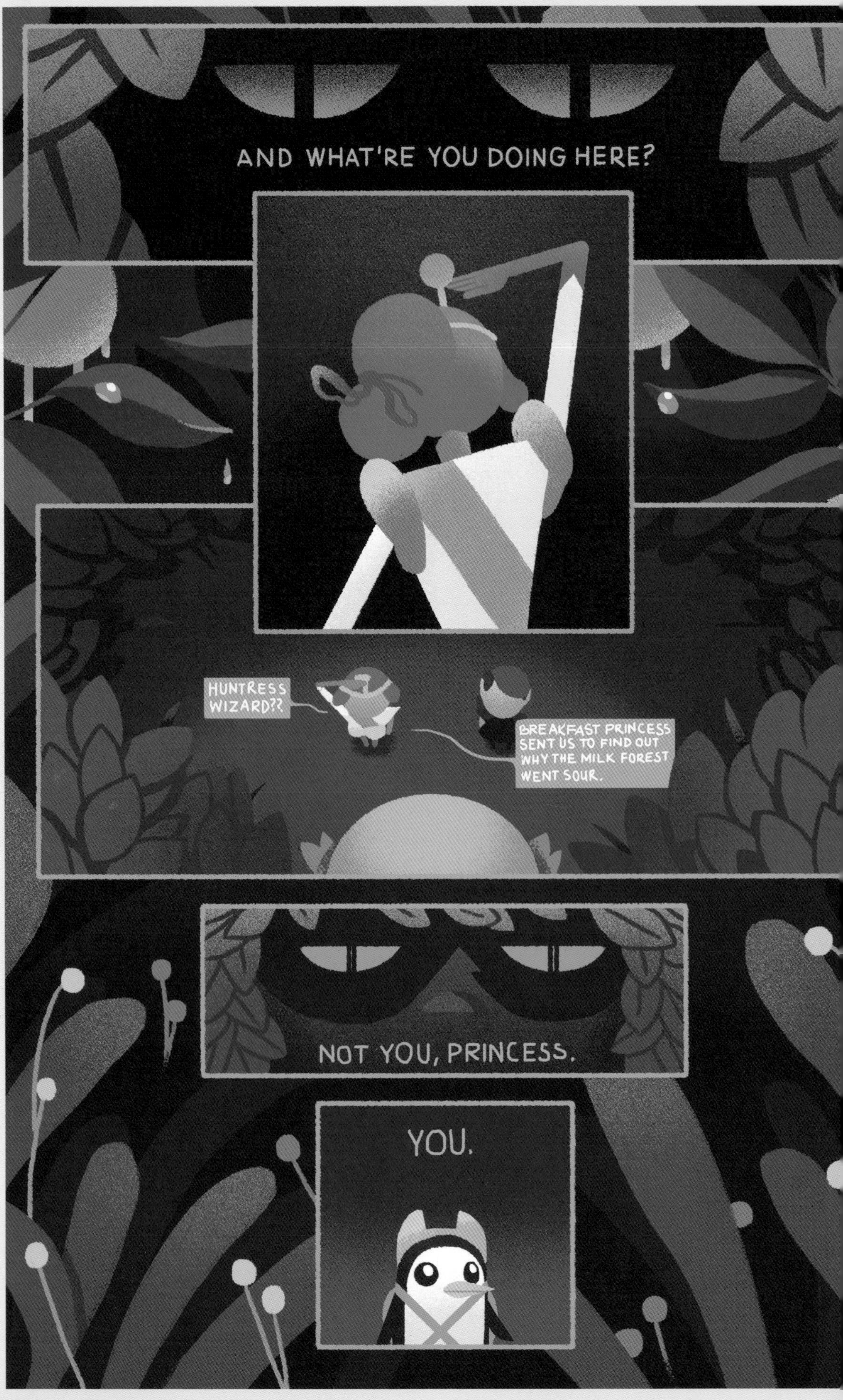
AND WHAT'RE YOU DOING HERE?
HUNTRESS WIZARD??
BREAKFAST PRINCESS SENT US TO FIND OUT WHY THE MILK FOREST WENT SOUR.
NOT YOU, PRINCESS.
YOU.

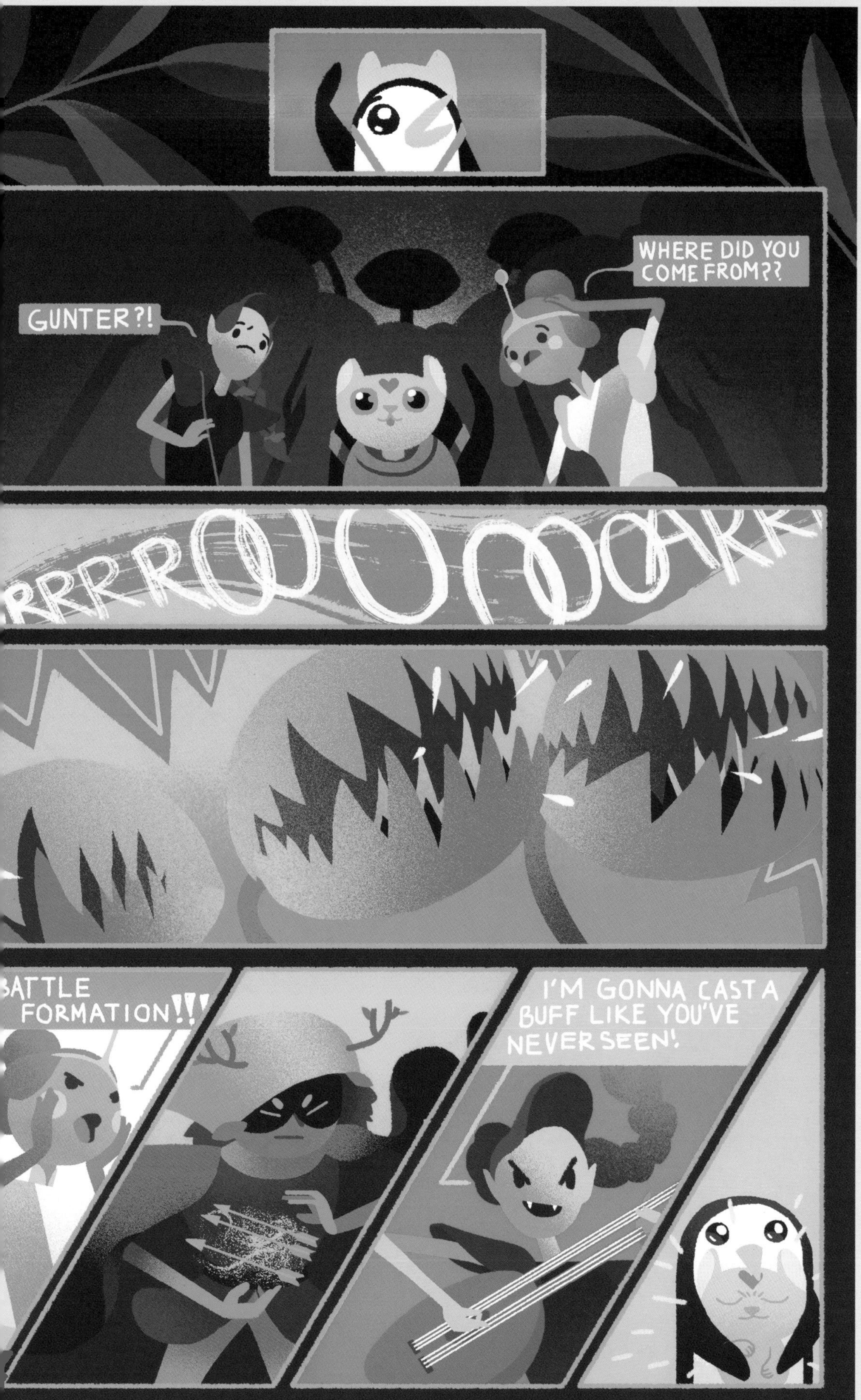
GUNTER?!
WHERE DID YOU COME FROM??
RRRRROOOOOOARR
ATTLE FORMATION!!!
I'M GONNA CAST A BUFF LIKE YOU'VE NEVER SEEN!

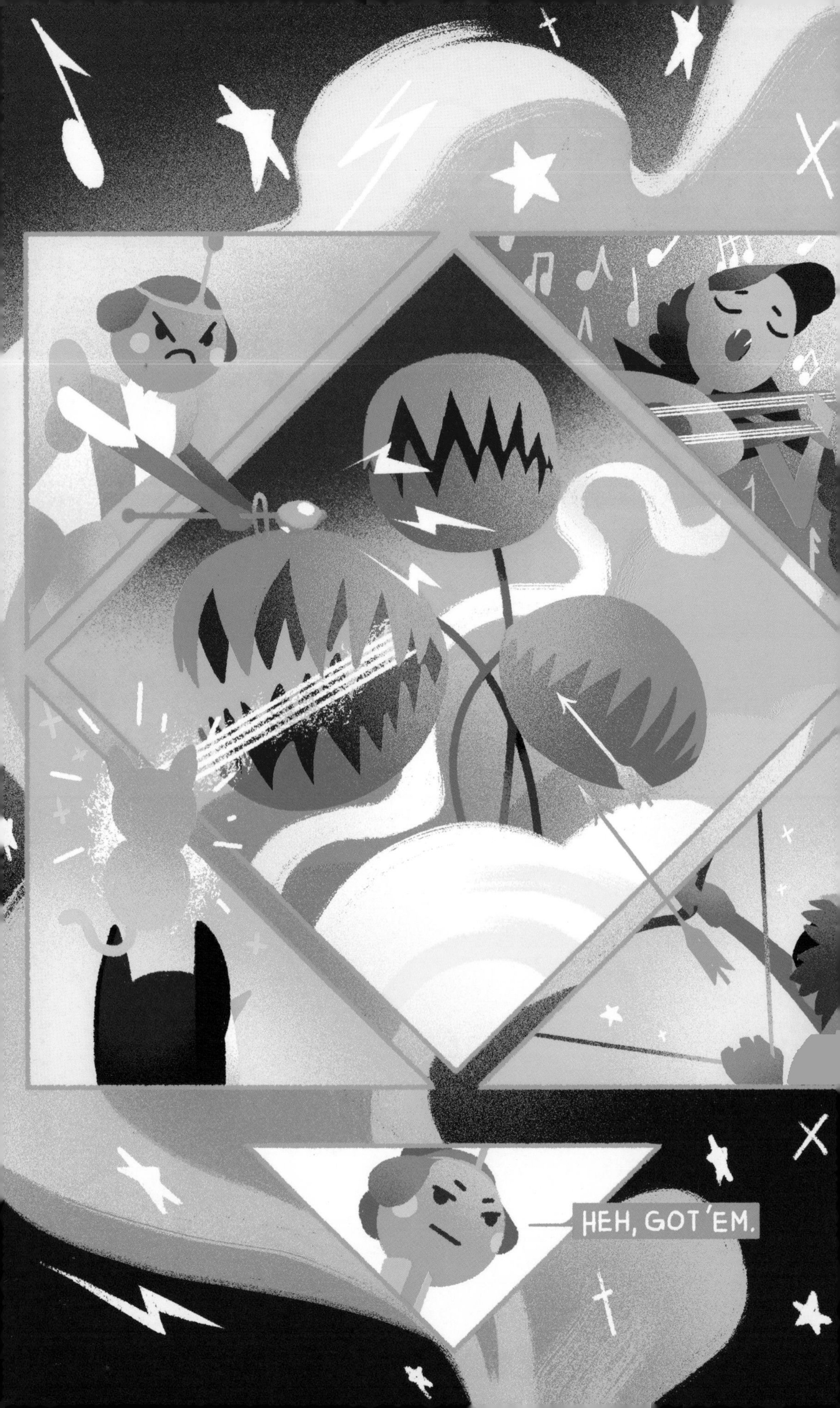
HEH, GOT 'EM.

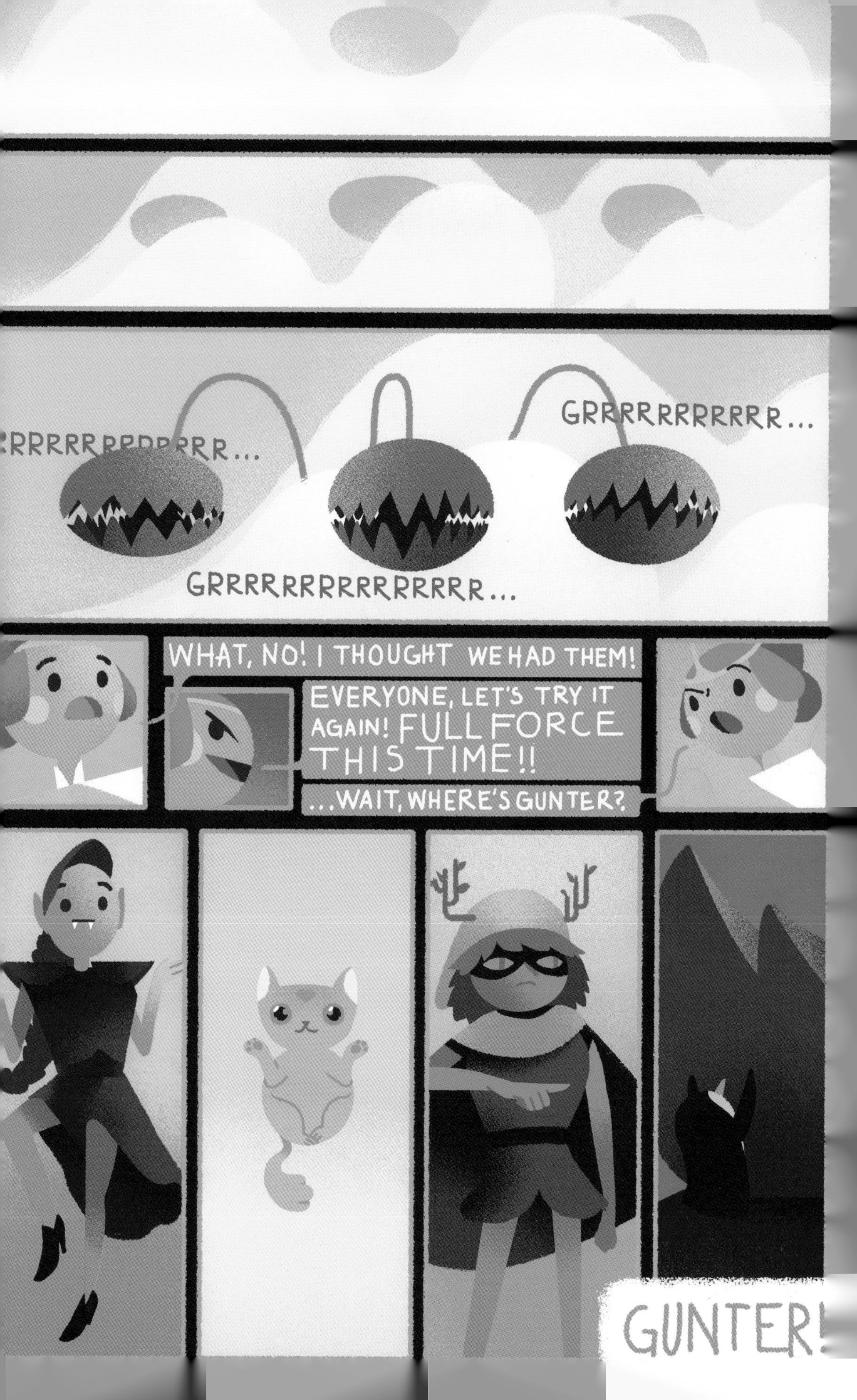

GRRRRRRRRRRR...
GRRRRRRRRRRRRRR...
GRRRRRRRRRRRR...
WHAT, NO! I THOUGHT WE HAD THEM!
EVERYONE, LET'S TRY IT AGAIN! FULL FORCE THIS TIME!!
...WAIT, WHERE'S GUNTER?
GUNTER!

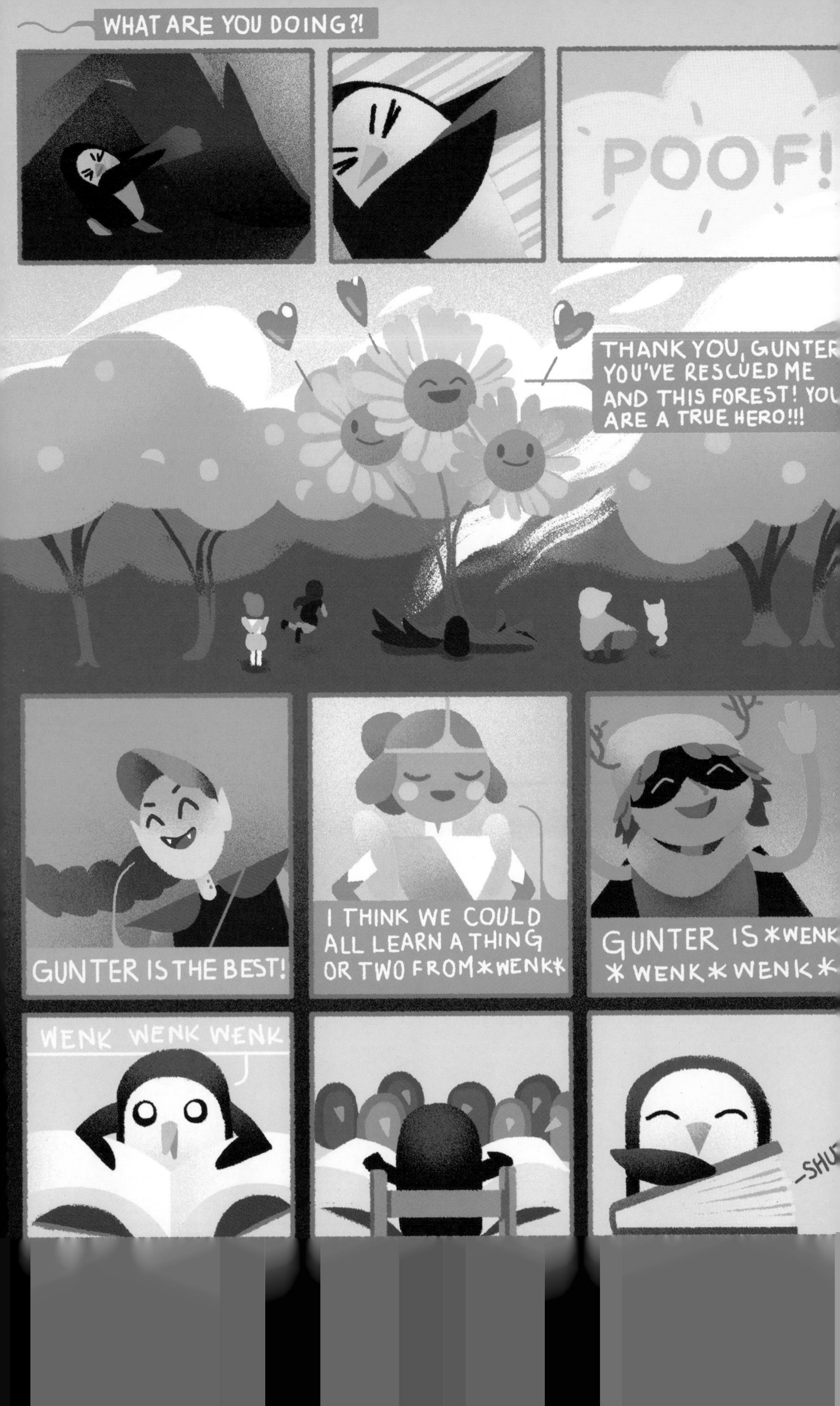
WHAT ARE YOU DOING?!
POOF!
THANK YOU, GUNTER YOU'VE RESCUED ME AND THIS FOREST! YOU ARE A TRUE HERO!!!
GUNTER IS THE BEST!
I THINK WE COULD ALL LEARN A THING OR TWO FROM *WENK*
GUNTER IS *WENK* *WENK* WENK*
WENK WENK WENK

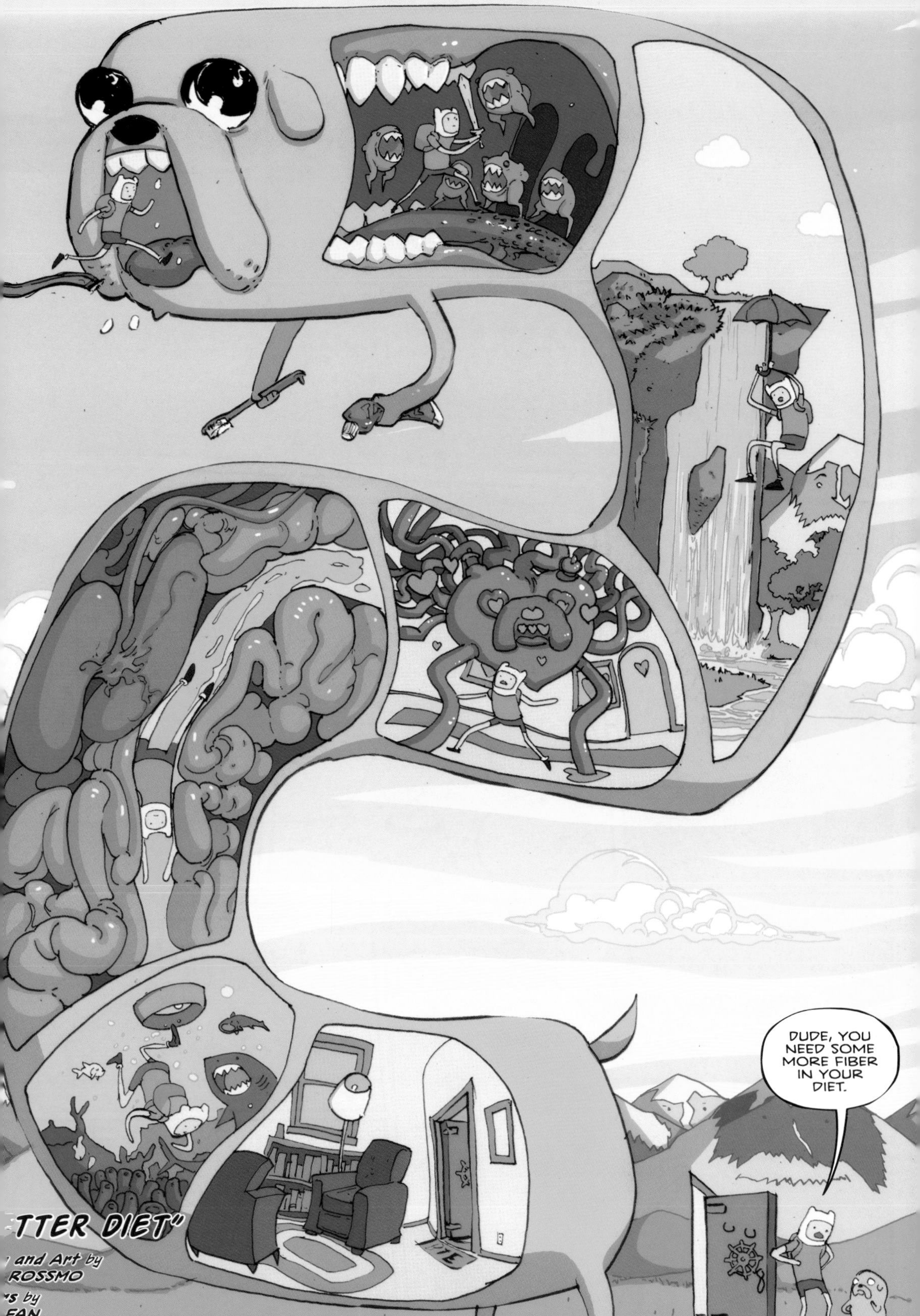
TTER DIET"
and Art by
ROSSMO
rs by
FAN
rs by
CAMPBELL
DUDE, YOU NEED SOME MORE FIBER IN YOUR DIET.

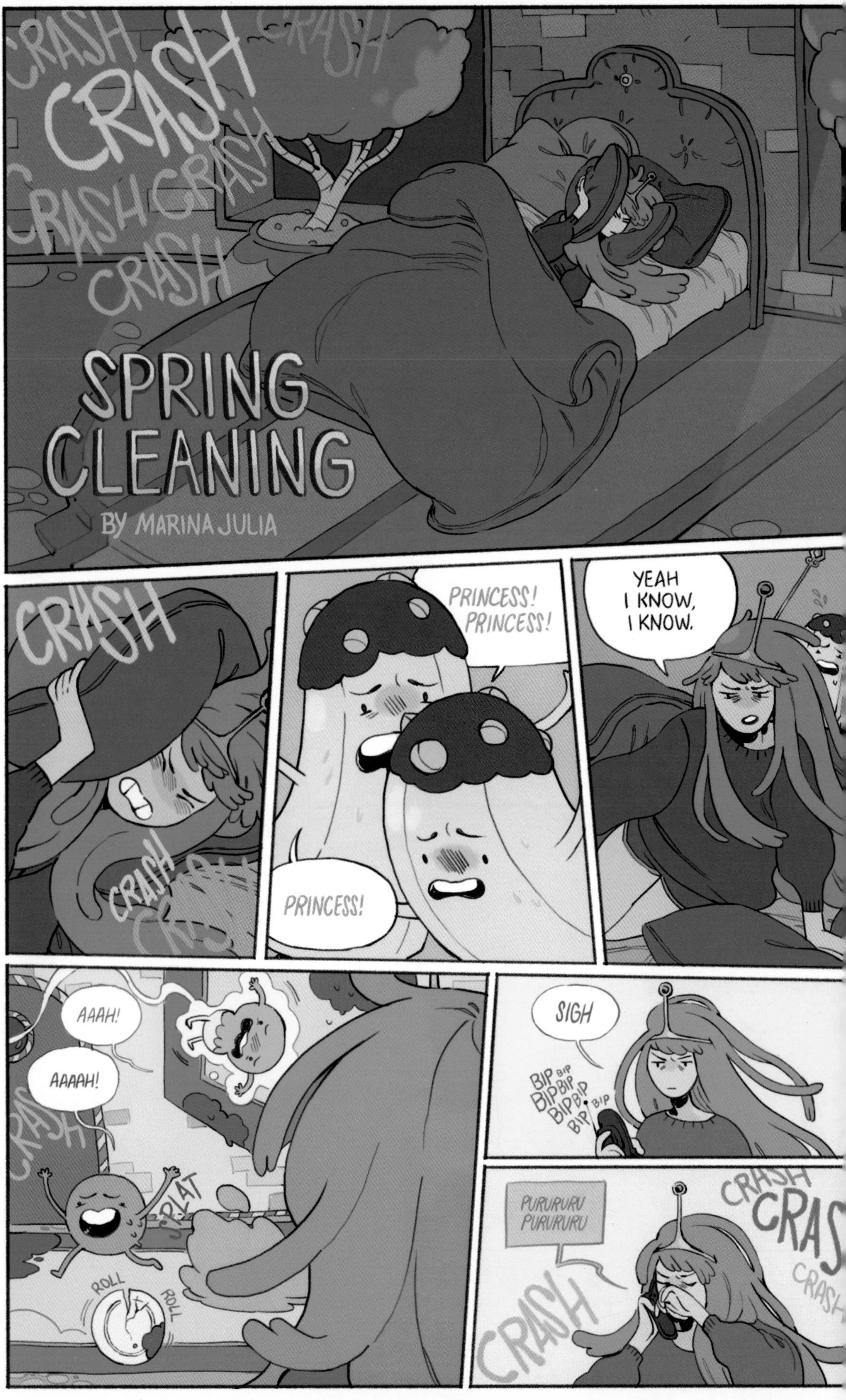
CRASH
CRASH
CRASH
CRASH CRASH
CRASH
SPRING CLEANING
BY MARINA JULIA
CRASH
CRASH
PRINCESS! PRINCESS!
PRINCESS!
YEAH I KNOW, I KNOW.
AAAH!
AAAAH!
SPLAT
ROLL
ROLL
SIGH
BIP BIP BIP BIP BIP BIP BIP BIP
PURURURU PURURURU
CRASH
CRASH
CRASH
CRASH

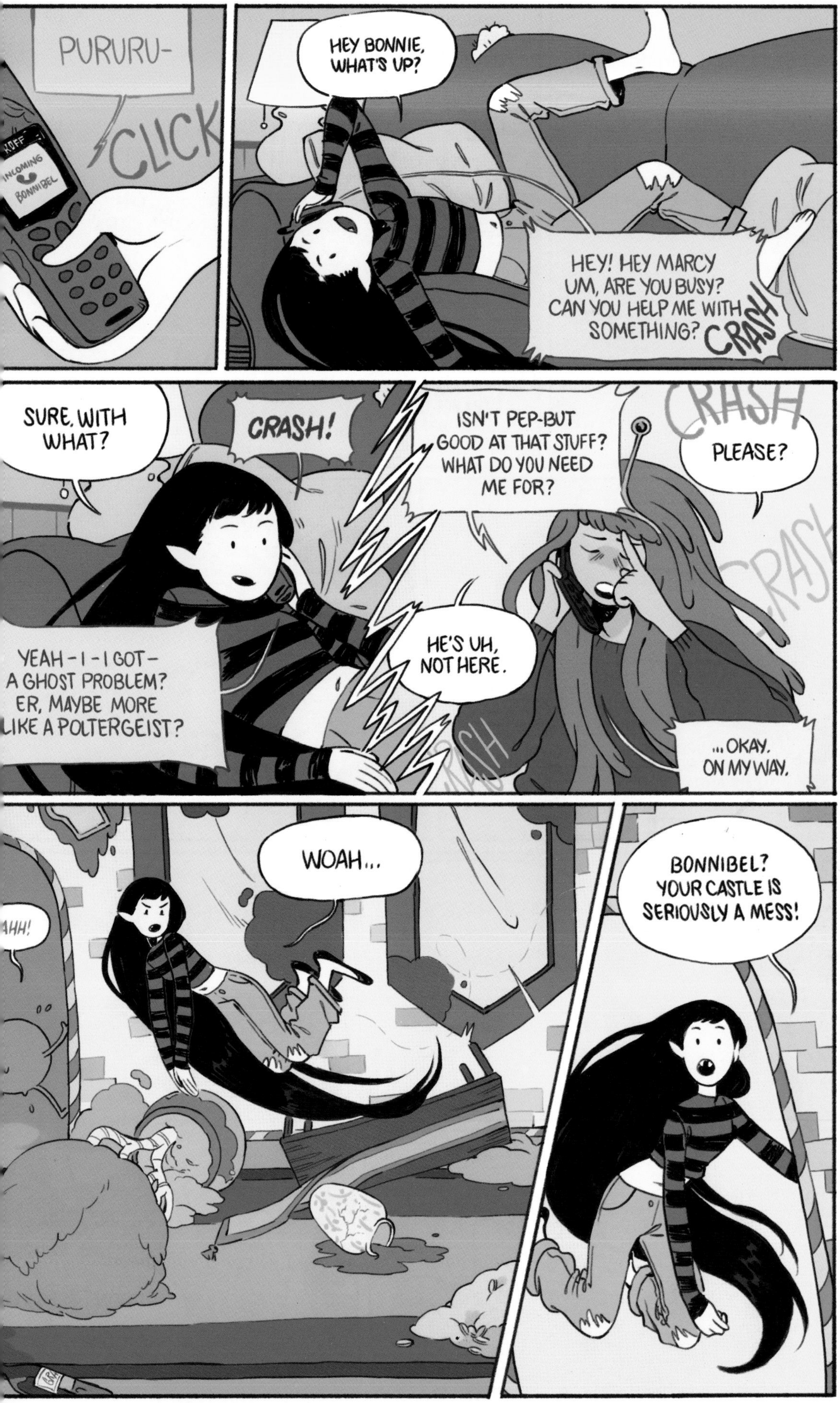
PURURU-
CLICK
KOFF
INCOMING
BONNIBEL
HEY BONNIE, WHAT'S UP?
HEY! HEY MARCY UM, ARE YOU BUSY? CAN YOU HELP ME WITH SOMETHING?
CRASH
SURE, WITH WHAT?
CRASH!
ISN'T PEP-BUT GOOD AT THAT STUFF? WHAT DO YOU NEED ME FOR?
CRASH
PLEASE?
CRASH
YEAH - I - I GOT - A GHOST PROBLEM? ER, MAYBE MORE LIKE A POLTERGEIST?
HE'S UH, NOT HERE.
...OKAY. ON MY WAY.
WOAH...
BONNIBEL? YOUR CASTLE IS SERIOUSLY A MESS!

MARCELINE!

YIKES, WHEN WAS THE LAST TIME YOU SLEPT?

NOT IMPORTANT.

SO, PEP LEFT THIS LIST OF WHAT TO DO IN CASE OF...

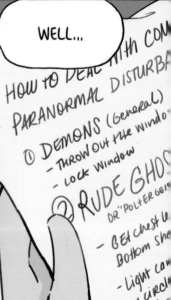

WELL...

HOW TO DEAL WITH COM
PARANORMAL DISTURBA

① DEMONS (General)
— THROW OUT THE WINDO
— LOCK WINDOW

② RUDE GHOS
OR "POLTERGEI

— GET chest u
Bottom she

— Light ca
a circle
sh

BUT IT'S ALL LIGHT SIX CANDLES IN A CIRCLE CHANT SOME NONSENSE!

LURE IT INTO A BOX WITH SALT AND WAX! HOW IS THIS JUNK SUPPOSED TO WORK?

HAVE YOU TRIED IT?

... UGH, NO.

WHAT HAVE YOU BEEN DOING UNTIL NOW?

HEH

OKAY, WELL LET'S TRY PEP'S WEIRD CANDLES THEN.

I DON'T SEE HOW *CANDLES* ARE GOING TO DO ANYTHING...

... TRYING TO WAIT IT OUT.

CRASH

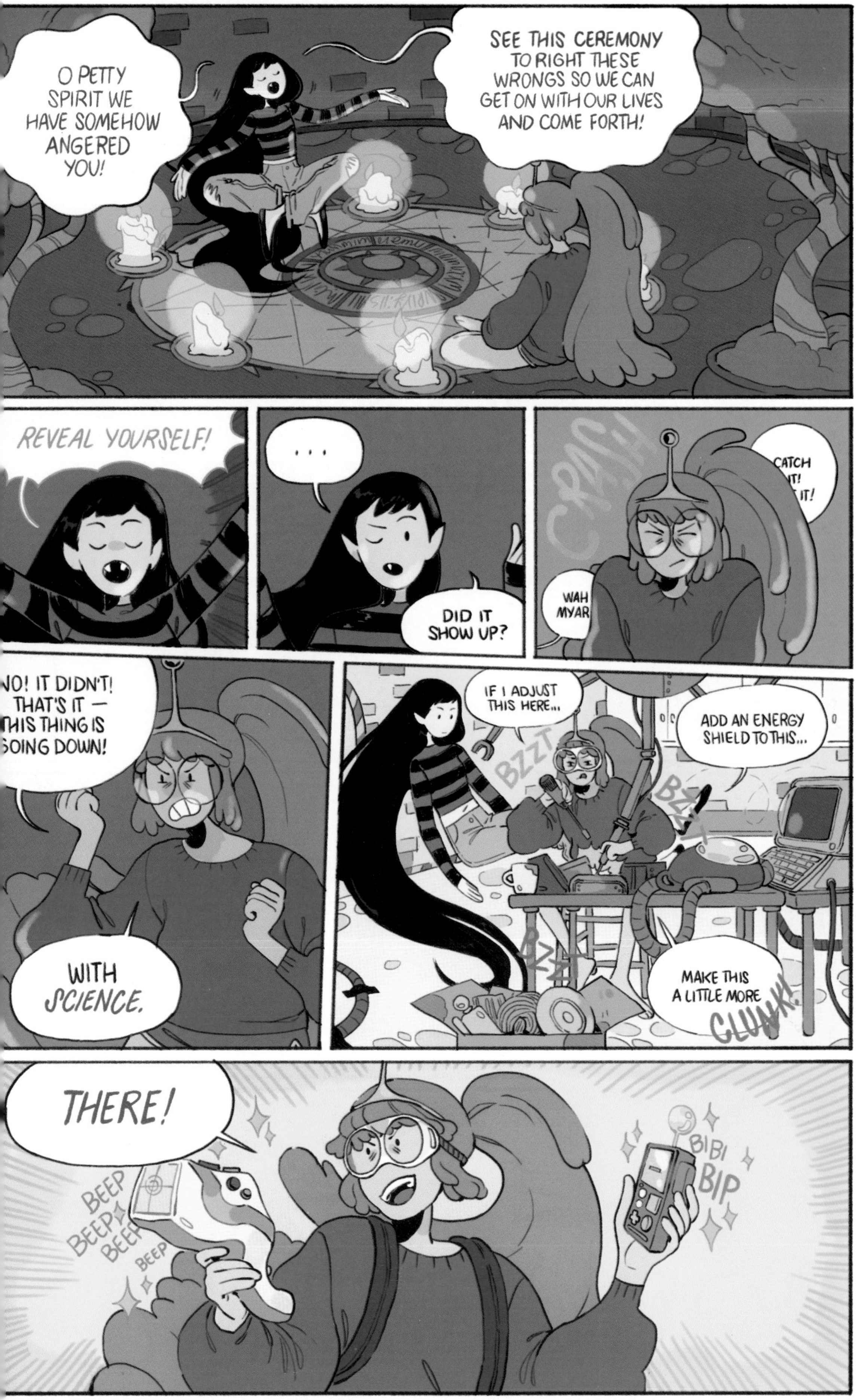

O PETTY SPIRIT WE HAVE SOMEHOW ANGERED YOU!
SEE THIS CEREMONY TO RIGHT THESE WRONGS SO WE CAN GET ON WITH OUR LIVES AND COME FORTH!
REVEAL YOURSELF!
. . .
DID IT SHOW UP?
CATCH IT!
WAH MYAR
NO! IT DIDN'T! THAT'S IT — THIS THING IS GOING DOWN!
WITH SCIENCE.
IF I ADJUST THIS HERE...
BZZT
ADD AN ENERGY SHIELD TO THIS...
BZZT
MAKE THIS A LITTLE MORE
CLUNK!
THERE!
BEEP BEEP BEEP
BEEP
BIBI BIP

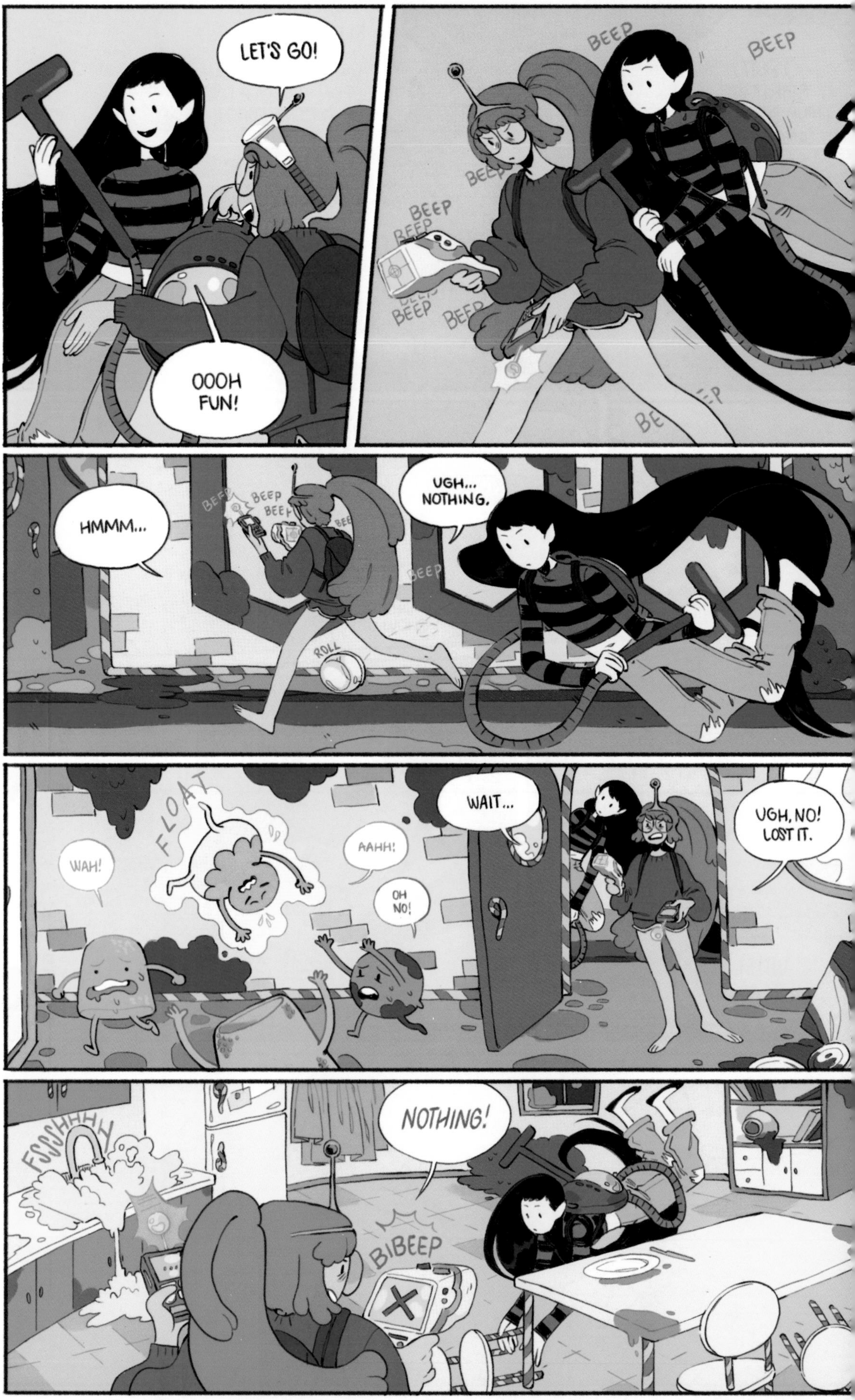
LET'S GO!
OOOH FUN!
BEEP
BEEP
BEEP
BEEP
BEEP
BEEP
BEEP
HMMM...
BEEP
BEEP
BEEP
UGH... NOTHING.
BEEP
ROLL
FLOAT
WAH!
AAHH!
OH NO!
WAIT...
UGH, NO! LOST IT.
FSSSHHHH
NOTHING!
BIBEEP

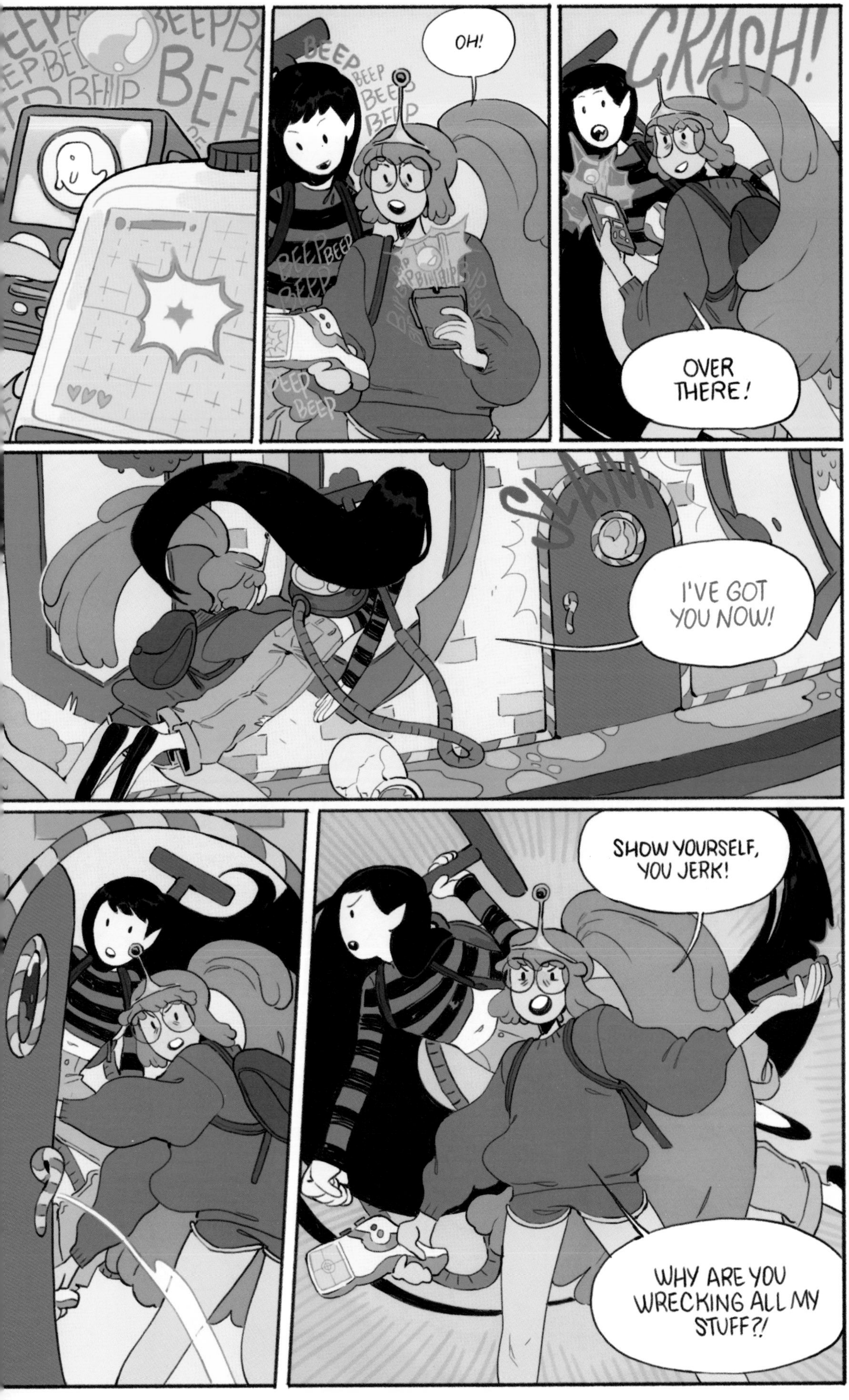
BEEP BEEP BEEP BEEP BEEP
OH!
BEEP BEEP BEEP BEEP
CRASH!
OVER THERE!
SLAM
I'VE GOT YOU NOW!
SHOW YOURSELF, YOU JERK!
WHY ARE YOU WRECKING ALL MY STUFF?!

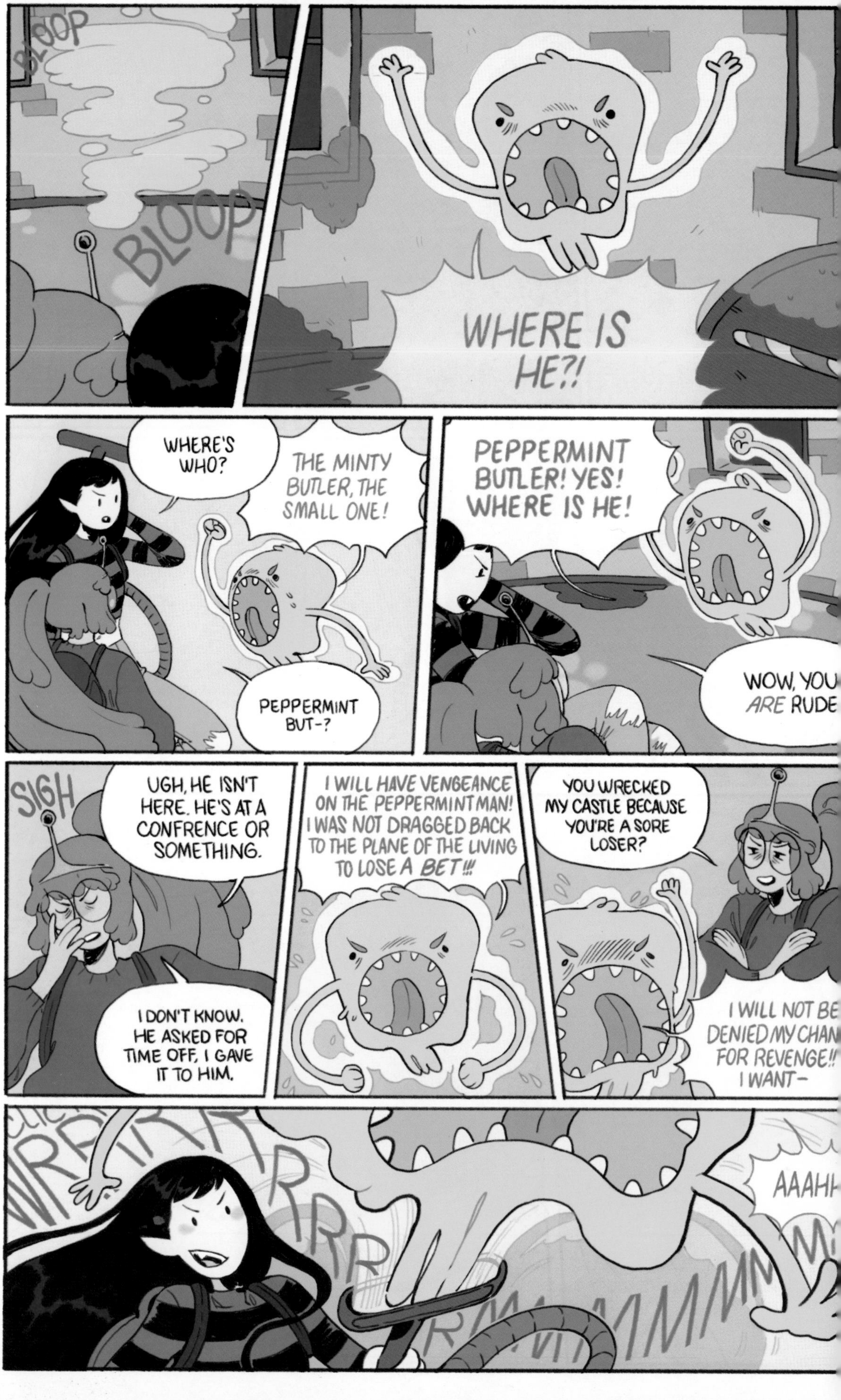
BLOOP
BLOOP
WHERE IS HE?!
WHERE'S WHO?
THE MINTY BUTLER, THE SMALL ONE!
PEPPERMINT BUT-?
PEPPERMINT BUTLER! YES! WHERE IS HE!
WOW, YOU ARE RUDE
SIGH
UGH, HE ISN'T HERE. HE'S AT A CONFRENCE OR SOMETHING.
I DON'T KNOW. HE ASKED FOR TIME OFF, I GAVE IT TO HIM.
I WILL HAVE VENGEANCE ON THE PEPPERMINT MAN! I WAS NOT DRAGGED BACK TO THE PLANE OF THE LIVING TO LOSE A BET!!!
YOU WRECKED MY CASTLE BECAUSE YOU'RE A SORE LOSER?
I WILL NOT BE DENIED MY CHAN FOR REVENGE!! I WANT-
WRRRRRRRR
RMMMMMM
AAAH

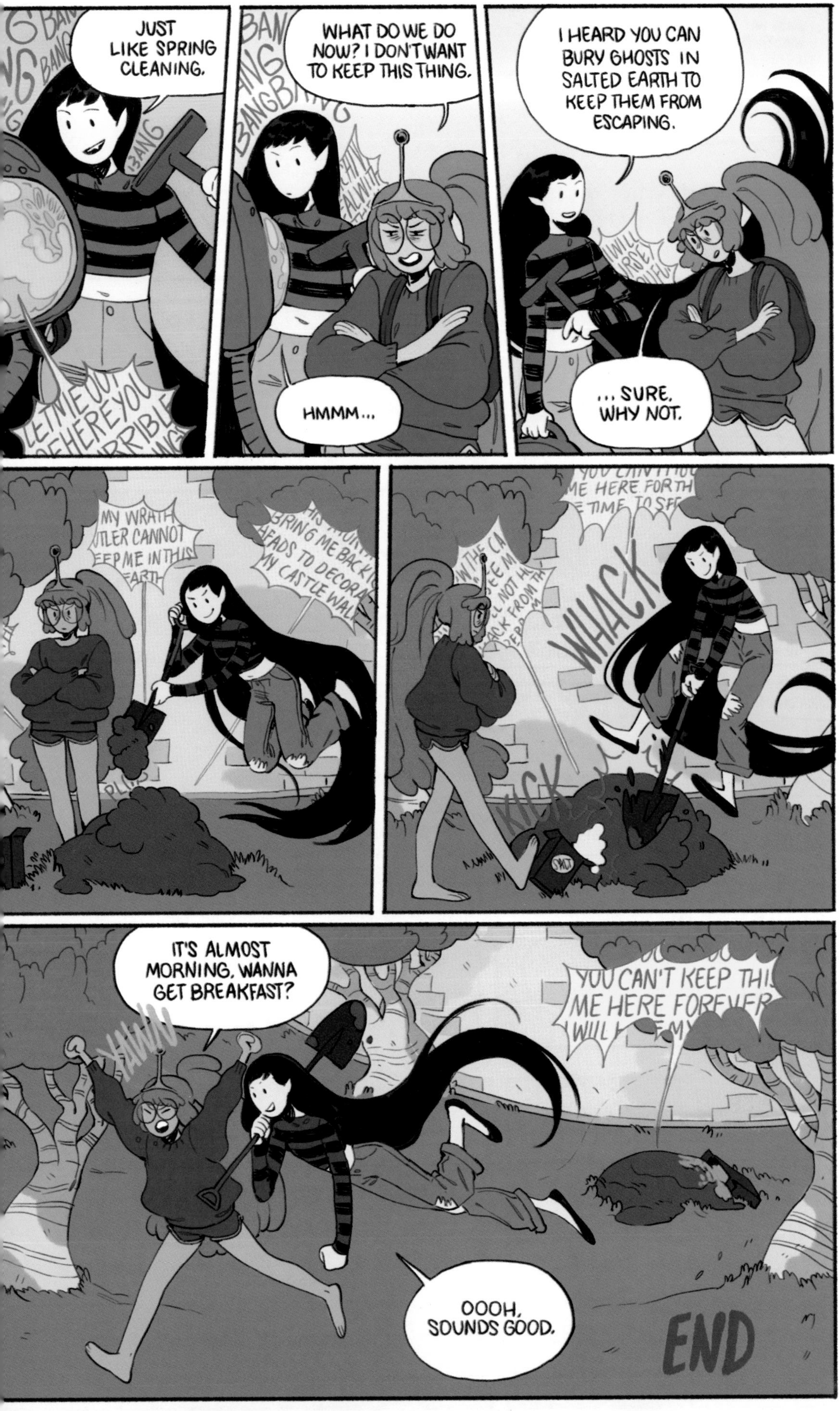
BANG
JUST LIKE SPRING CLEANING.
WHAT DO WE DO NOW? I DON'T WANT TO KEEP THIS THING.
HMMM...
I HEARD YOU CAN BURY GHOSTS IN SALTED EARTH TO KEEP THEM FROM ESCAPING.
... SURE, WHY NOT.
WHACK
KICK
IT'S ALMOST MORNING, WANNA GET BREAKFAST?
YAWN
OOOH, SOUNDS GOOD.
END

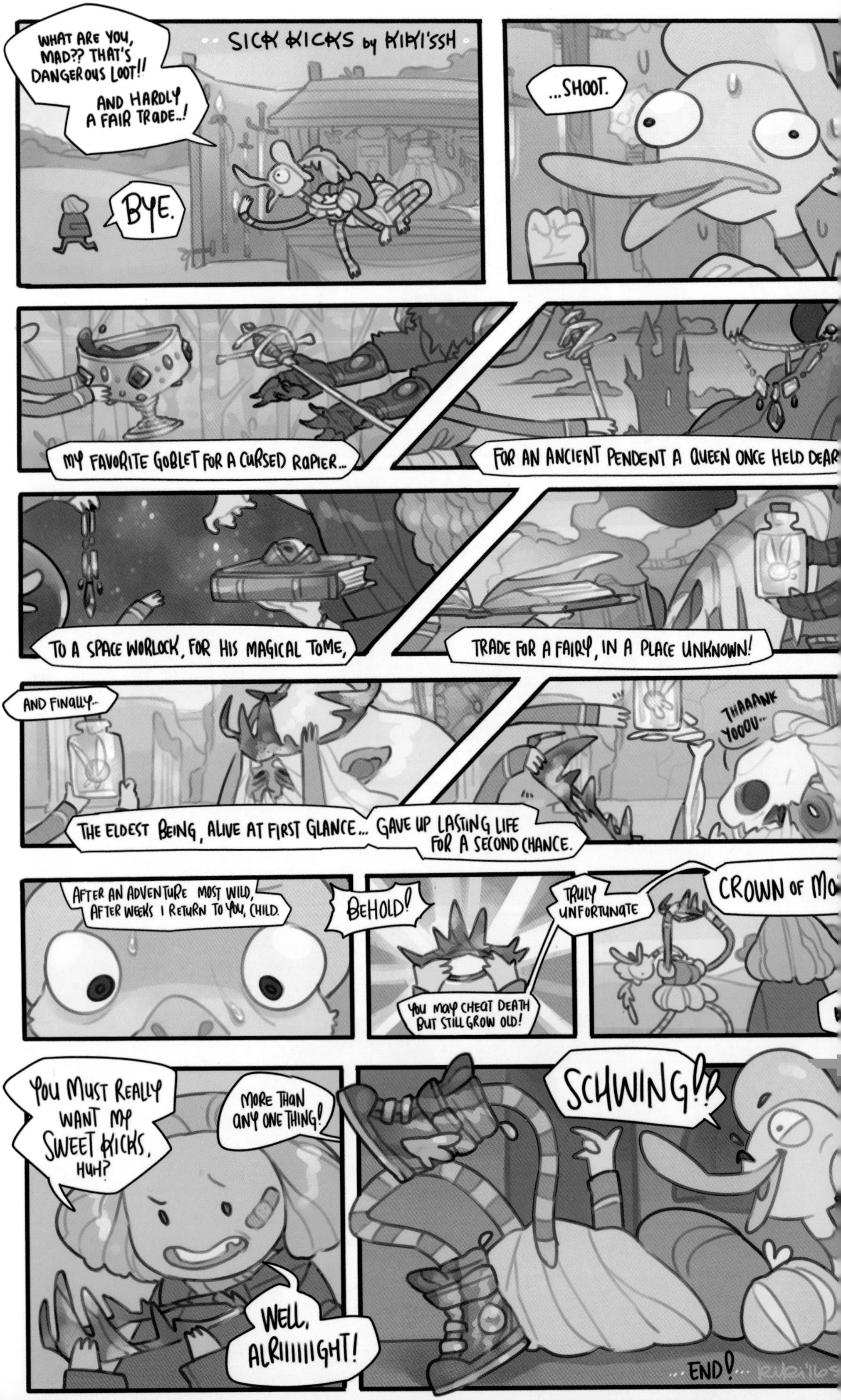

SICK KICKS by KIKI'SSH
WHAT ARE YOU, MAD?? THAT'S DANGEROUS LOOT!!
AND HARDLY A FAIR TRADE..!
BYE.
...SHOOT.
MY FAVORITE GOBLET FOR A CURSED RAPIER...
FOR AN ANCIENT PENDENT A QUEEN ONCE HELD DEAR
TO A SPACE WORLOCK, FOR HIS MAGICAL TOME,
TRADE FOR A FAIRY, IN A PLACE UNKNOWN!
AND FINALLY..
THAAANK YOOOU..
THE ELDEST BEING, ALIVE AT FIRST GLANCE...
GAVE UP LASTING LIFE FOR A SECOND CHANCE.
AFTER AN ADVENTURE MOST WILD, AFTER WEEKS I RETURN TO YOU, CHILD.
BEHOLD!
TRULY UNFORTUNATE
CROWN OF MO
YOU MAY CHEAT DEATH BUT STILL GROW OLD!
YOU MUST REALLY WANT MY SWEET KICKS, HUH?
MORE THAN ANY ONE THING!
SCHWING!!
WELL, ALRIIIIIIGHT!
...END!...

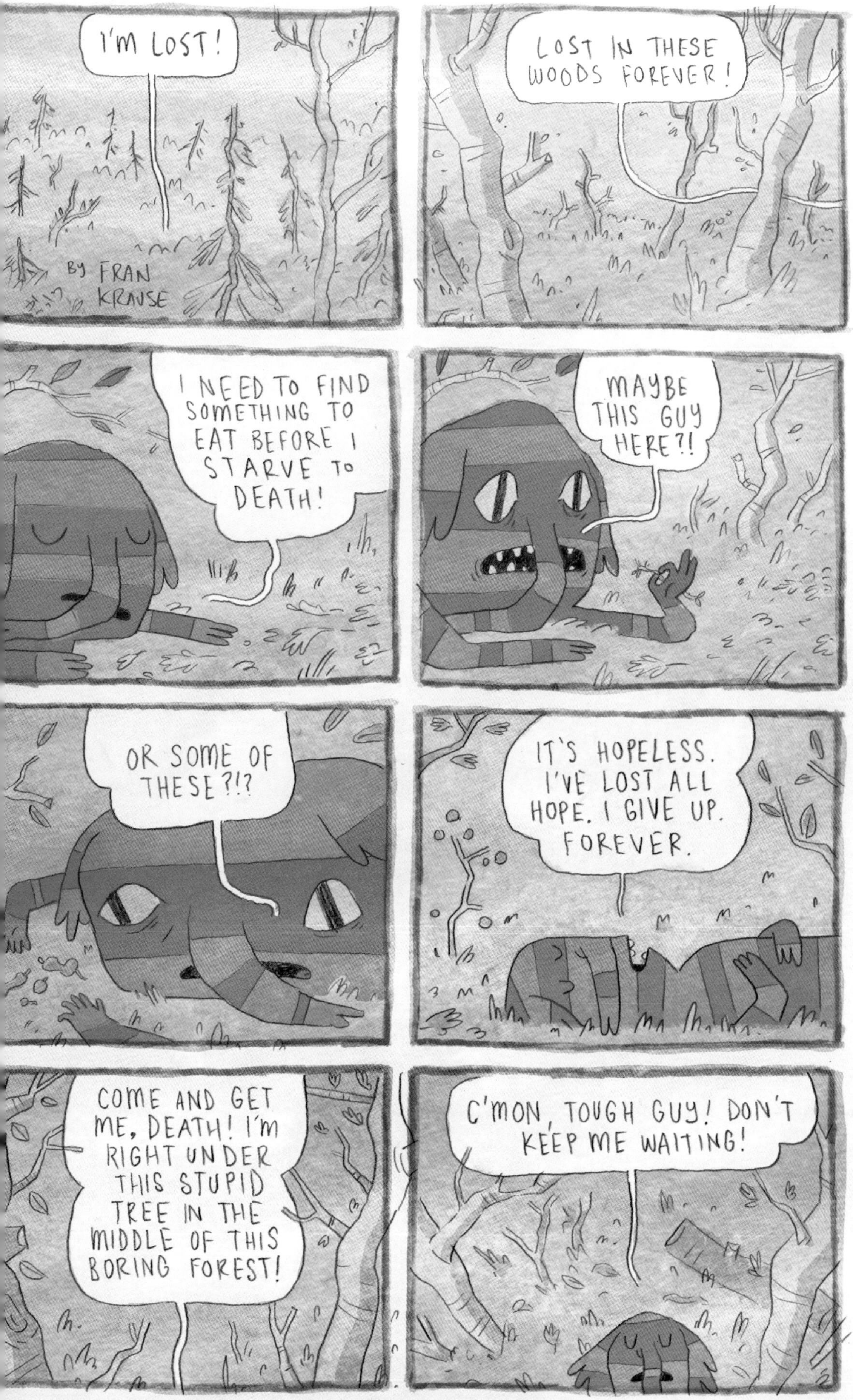
I'M LOST!
BY FRAN KRAUSE
LOST IN THESE WOODS FOREVER!
I NEED TO FIND SOMETHING TO EAT BEFORE I STARVE TO DEATH!
MAYBE THIS GUY HERE?!
OR SOME OF THESE?!?
IT'S HOPELESS. I'VE LOST ALL HOPE. I GIVE UP. FOREVER.
COME AND GET ME, DEATH! I'M RIGHT UNDER THIS STUPID TREE IN THE MIDDLE OF THIS BORING FOREST!
C'MON, TOUGH GUY! DON'T KEEP ME WAITING!

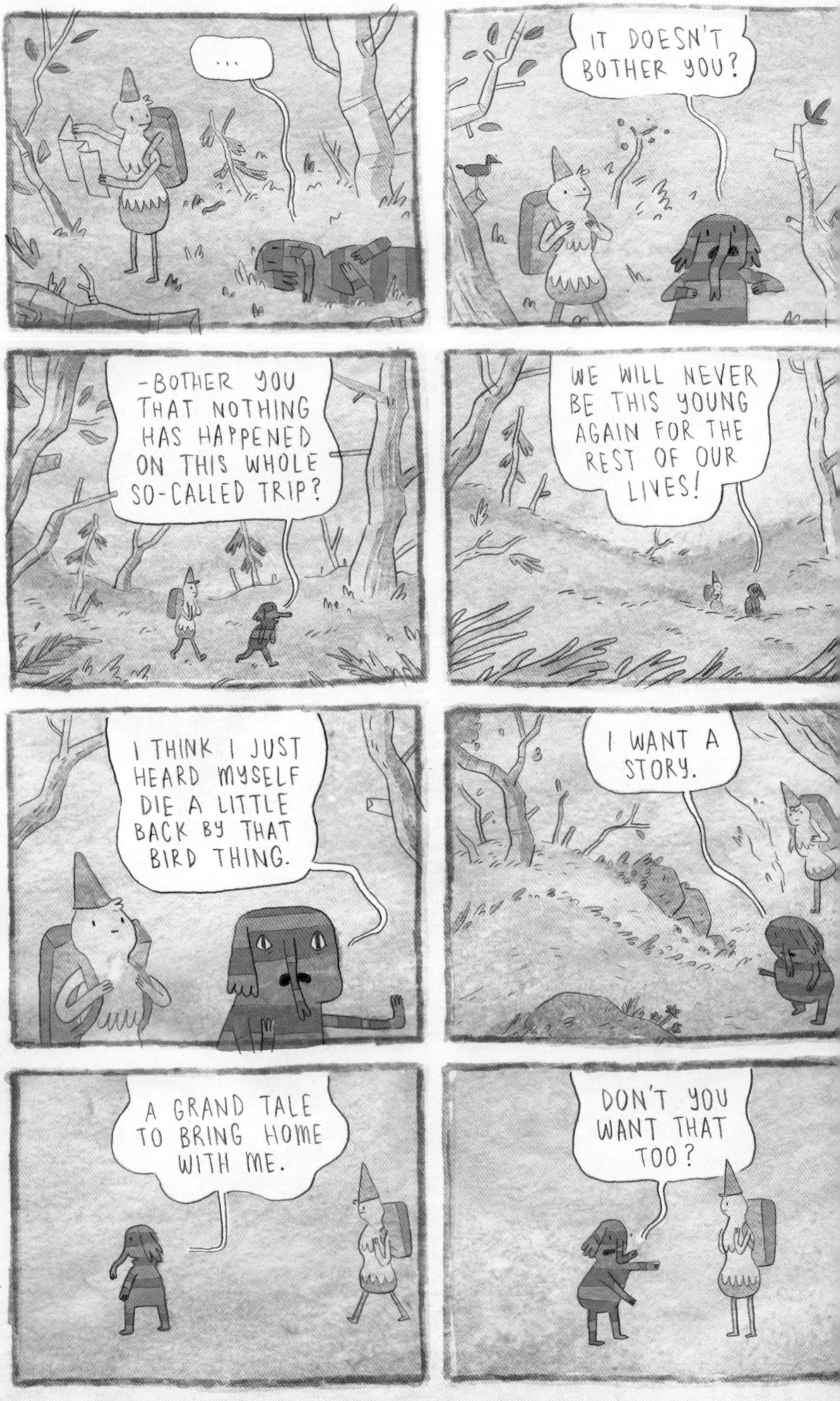
...
IT DOESN'T BOTHER YOU?
-BOTHER YOU THAT NOTHING HAS HAPPENED ON THIS WHOLE SO-CALLED TRIP?
WE WILL NEVER BE THIS YOUNG AGAIN FOR THE REST OF OUR LIVES!
I THINK I JUST HEARD MYSELF DIE A LITTLE BACK BY THAT BIRD THING.
I WANT A STORY.
A GRAND TALE TO BRING HOME WITH ME.
DON'T YOU WANT THAT TOO?

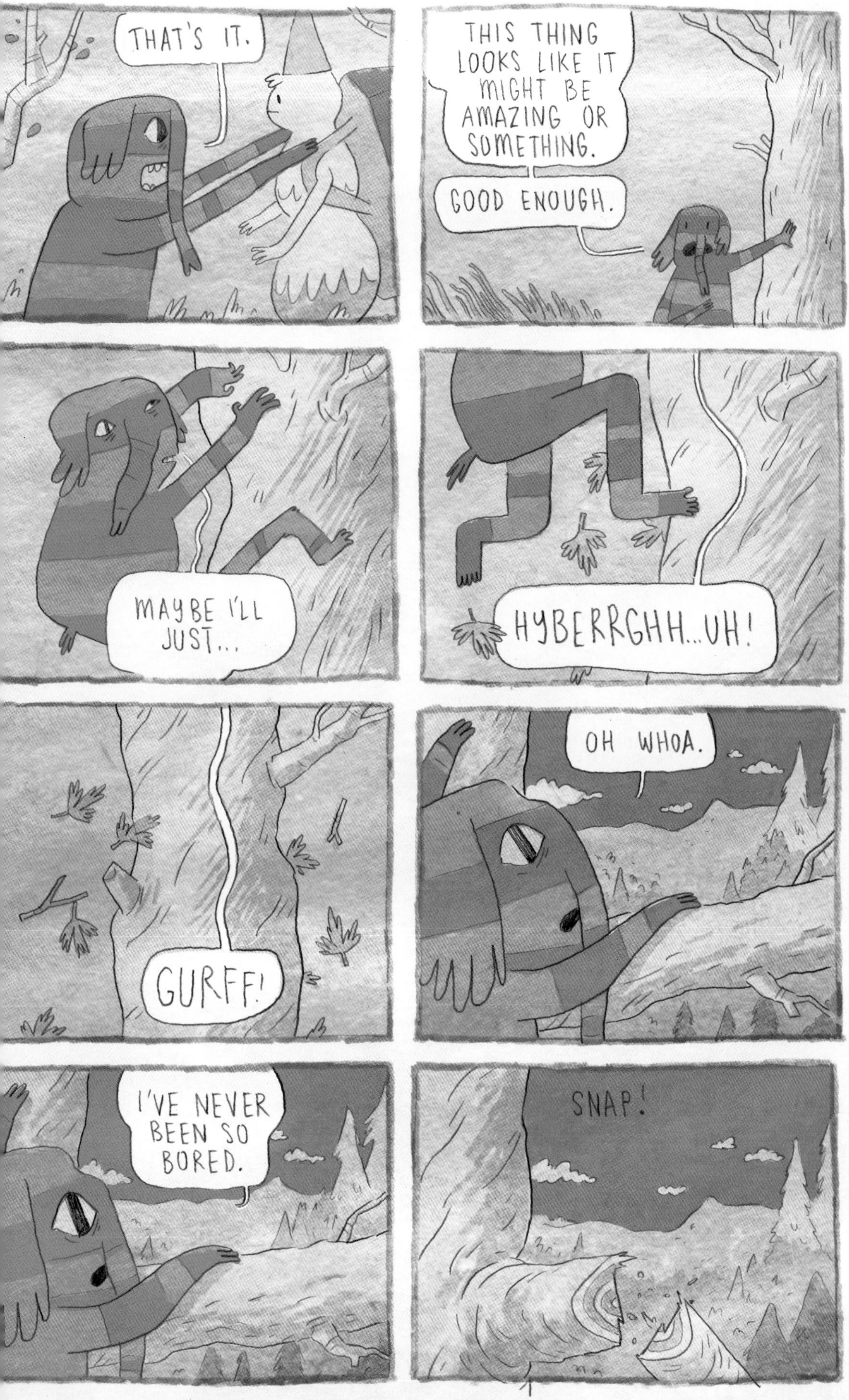
THAT'S IT.
THIS THING LOOKS LIKE IT MIGHT BE AMAZING OR SOMETHING.
GOOD ENOUGH.
MAYBE I'LL JUST...
HYBERRGHH...UH!
GURFF!
OH WHOA.
I'VE NEVER BEEN SO BORED.
SNAP!

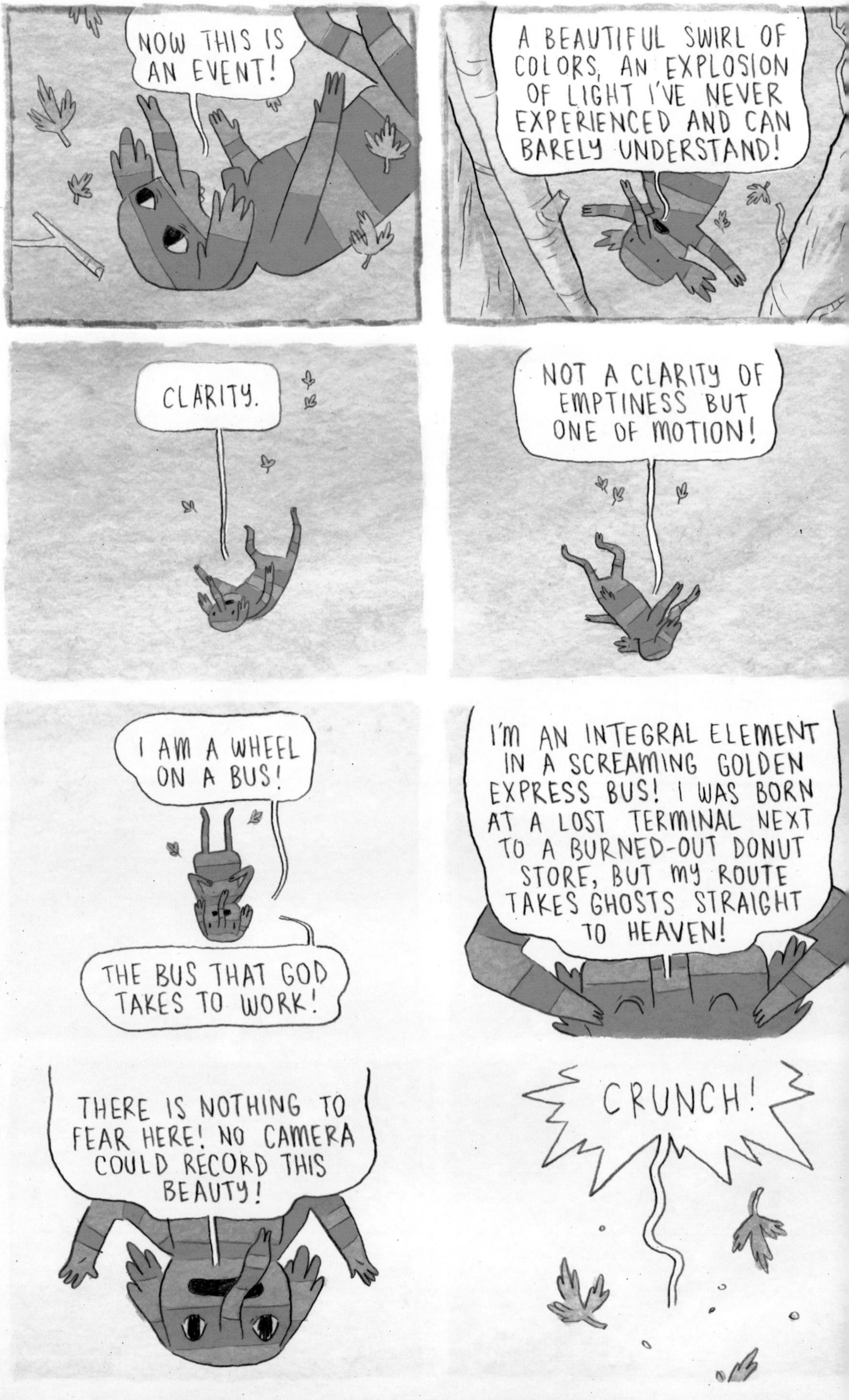
NOW THIS IS AN EVENT!
A BEAUTIFUL SWIRL OF COLORS, AN EXPLOSION OF LIGHT I'VE NEVER EXPERIENCED AND CAN BARELY UNDERSTAND!
CLARITY.
NOT A CLARITY OF EMPTINESS BUT ONE OF MOTION!
I AM A WHEEL ON A BUS!
THE BUS THAT GOD TAKES TO WORK!
I'M AN INTEGRAL ELEMENT IN A SCREAMING GOLDEN EXPRESS BUS! I WAS BORN AT A LOST TERMINAL NEXT TO A BURNED-OUT DONUT STORE, BUT MY ROUTE TAKES GHOSTS STRAIGHT TO HEAVEN!
THERE IS NOTHING TO FEAR HERE! NO CAMERA COULD RECORD THIS BEAUTY!
CRUNCH!

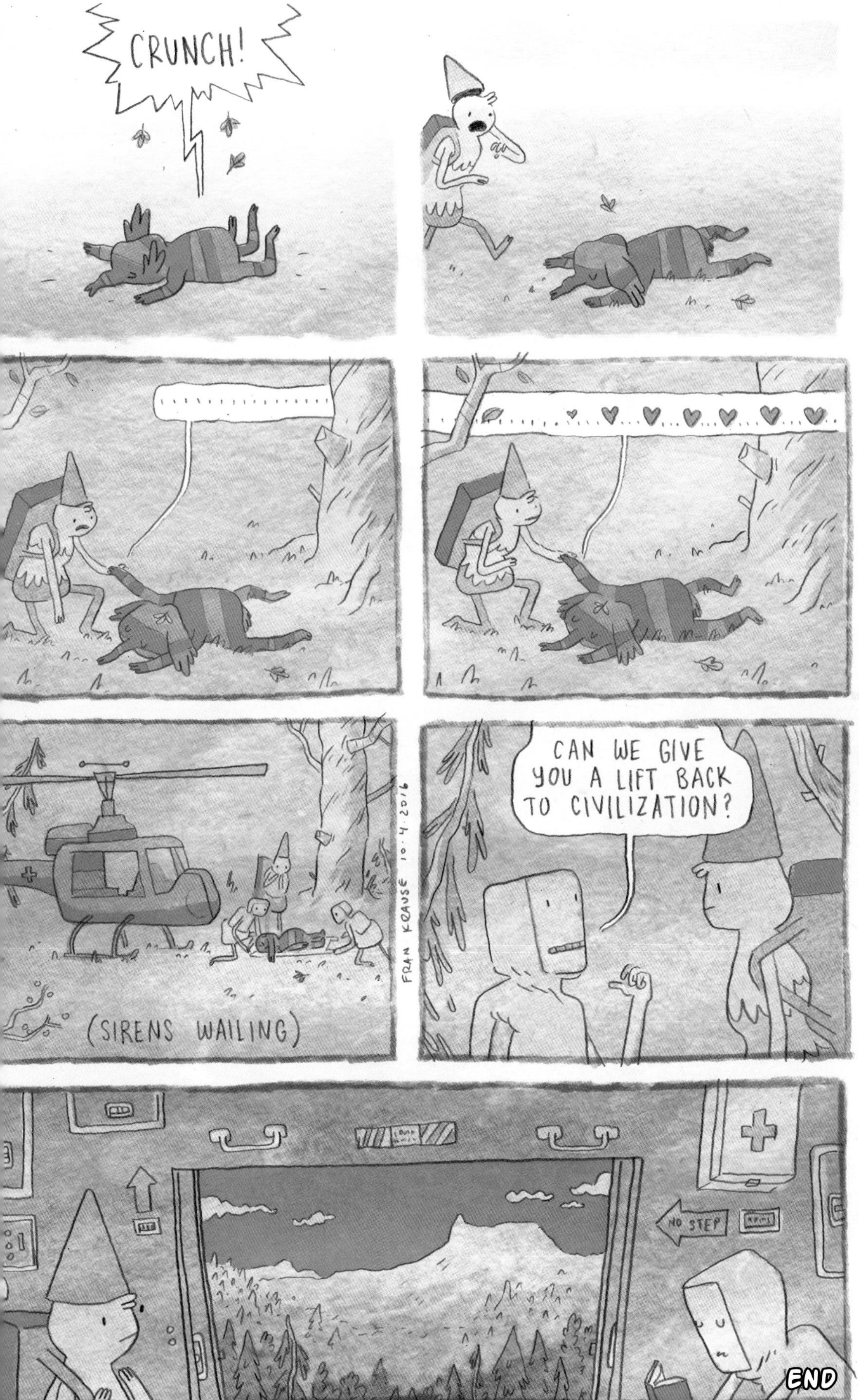
CRUNCH!
(SIRENS WAILING)
FRAN KRAUSE 10.4.2016
CAN WE GIVE YOU A LIFT BACK TO CIVILIZATION?
NO STEP
END

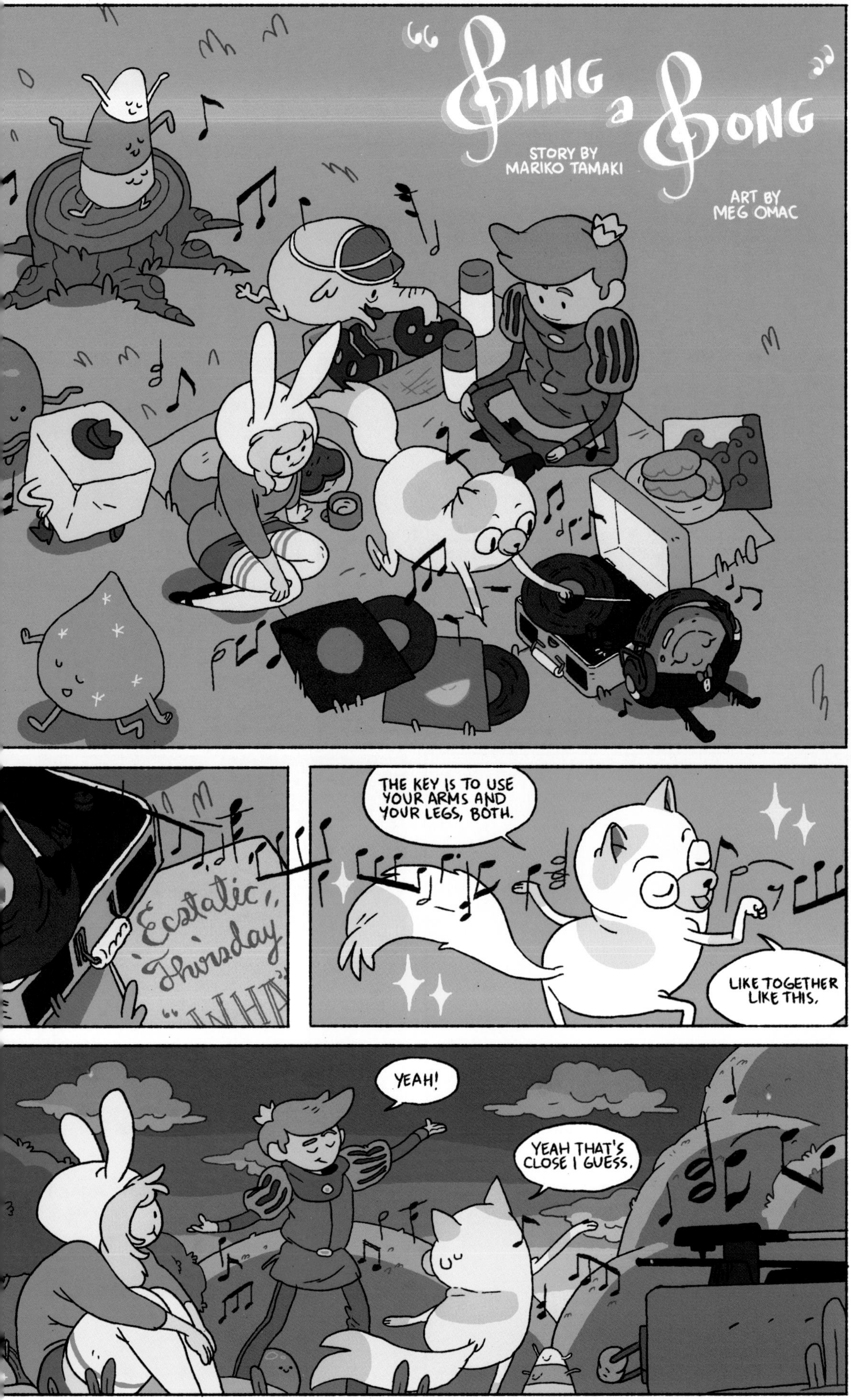
"Sing a Song"
STORY BY
MARIKO TAMAKI
ART BY
MEG OMAC
Ecstatic Thursday
THE KEY IS TO USE YOUR ARMS AND YOUR LEGS, BOTH.
LIKE TOGETHER LIKE THIS,
YEAH!
YEAH THAT'S CLOSE I GUESS.

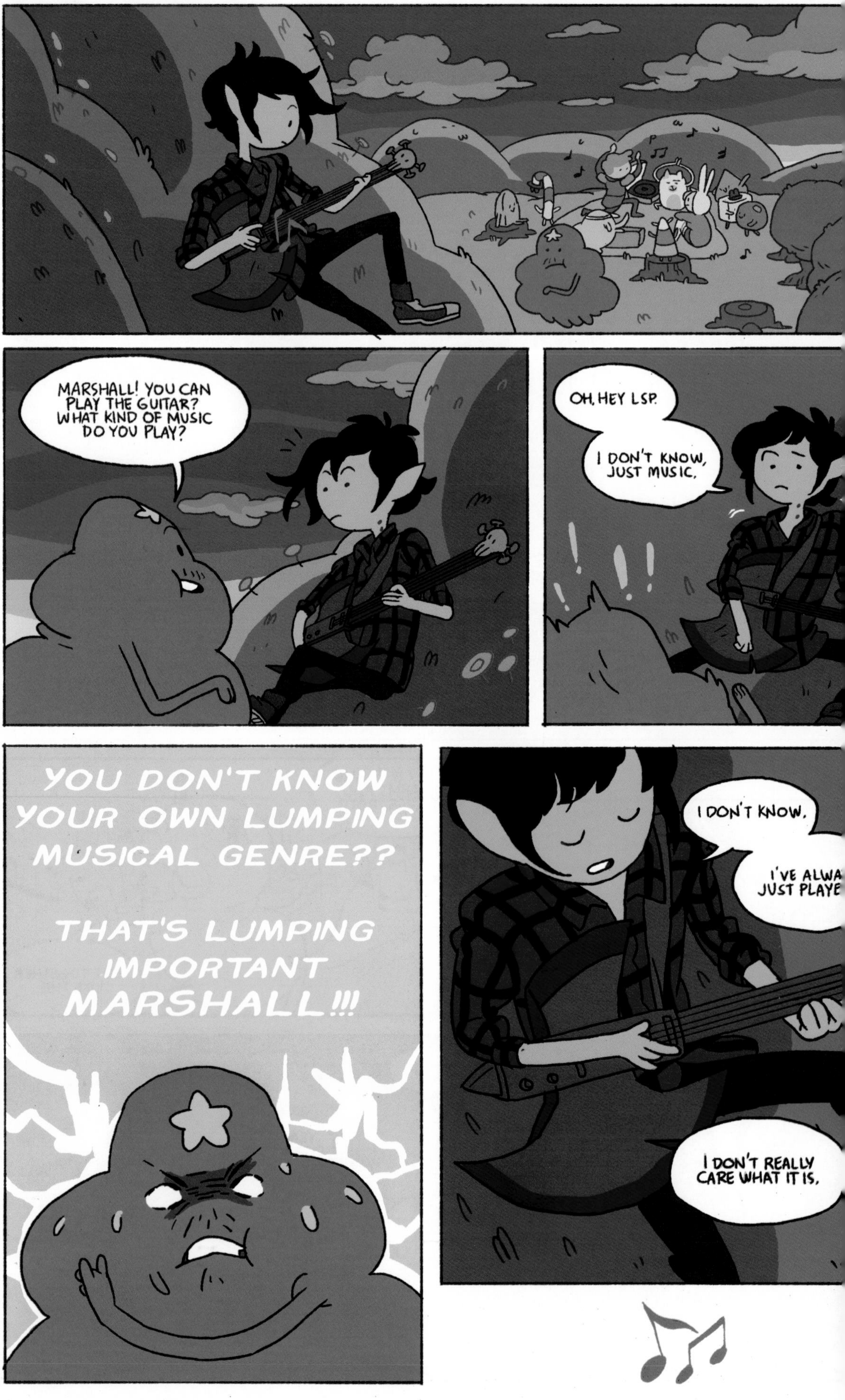
MARSHALL! YOU CAN PLAY THE GUITAR? WHAT KIND OF MUSIC DO YOU PLAY?
OH, HEY LSP.
I DON'T KNOW, JUST MUSIC.
YOU DON'T KNOW YOUR OWN LUMPING MUSICAL GENRE??
THAT'S LUMPING IMPORTANT MARSHALL!!!
I DON'T KNOW.
I'VE ALWA JUST PLAYE
I DON'T REALLY CARE WHAT IT IS.

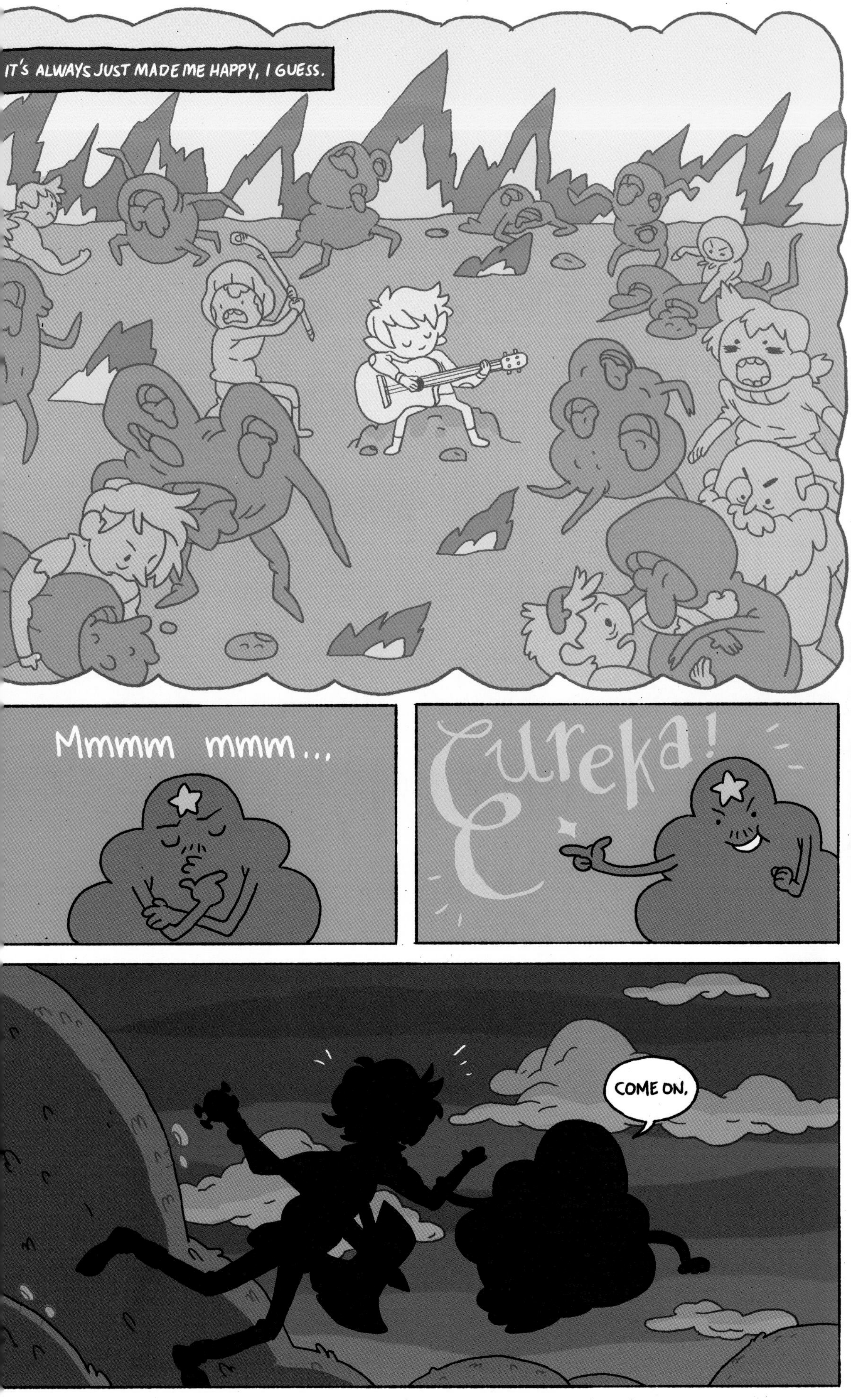
IT'S ALWAYS JUST MADE ME HAPPY, I GUESS.
Mmmm mmm...
Eureka!
COME ON.

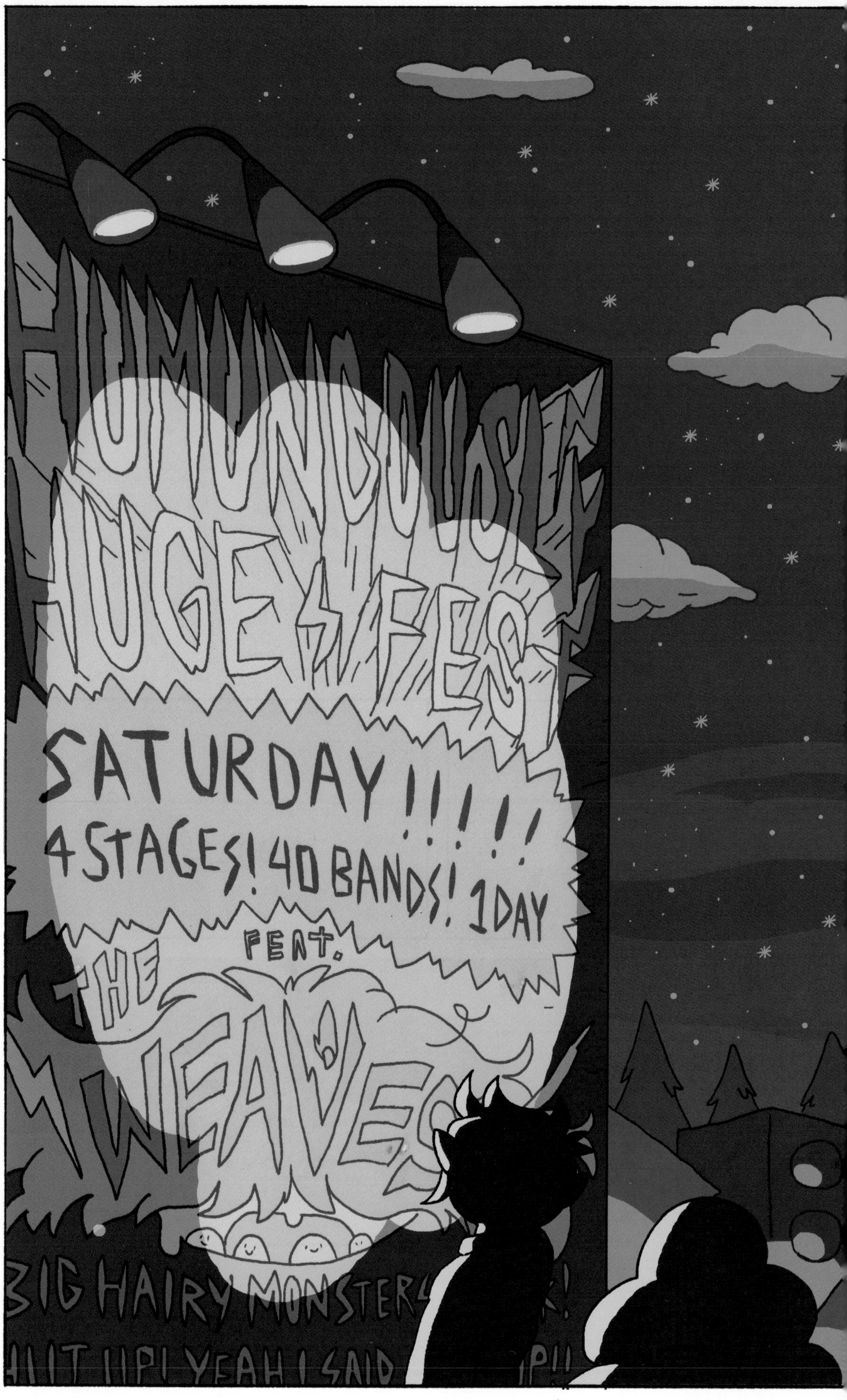
HUGE FEST
SATURDAY!!!!!
4 STAGES! 40 BANDS! 1 DAY
FEAT.
THE WEAVES
BIG HAIRY MONSTERS
YEAH I SAID

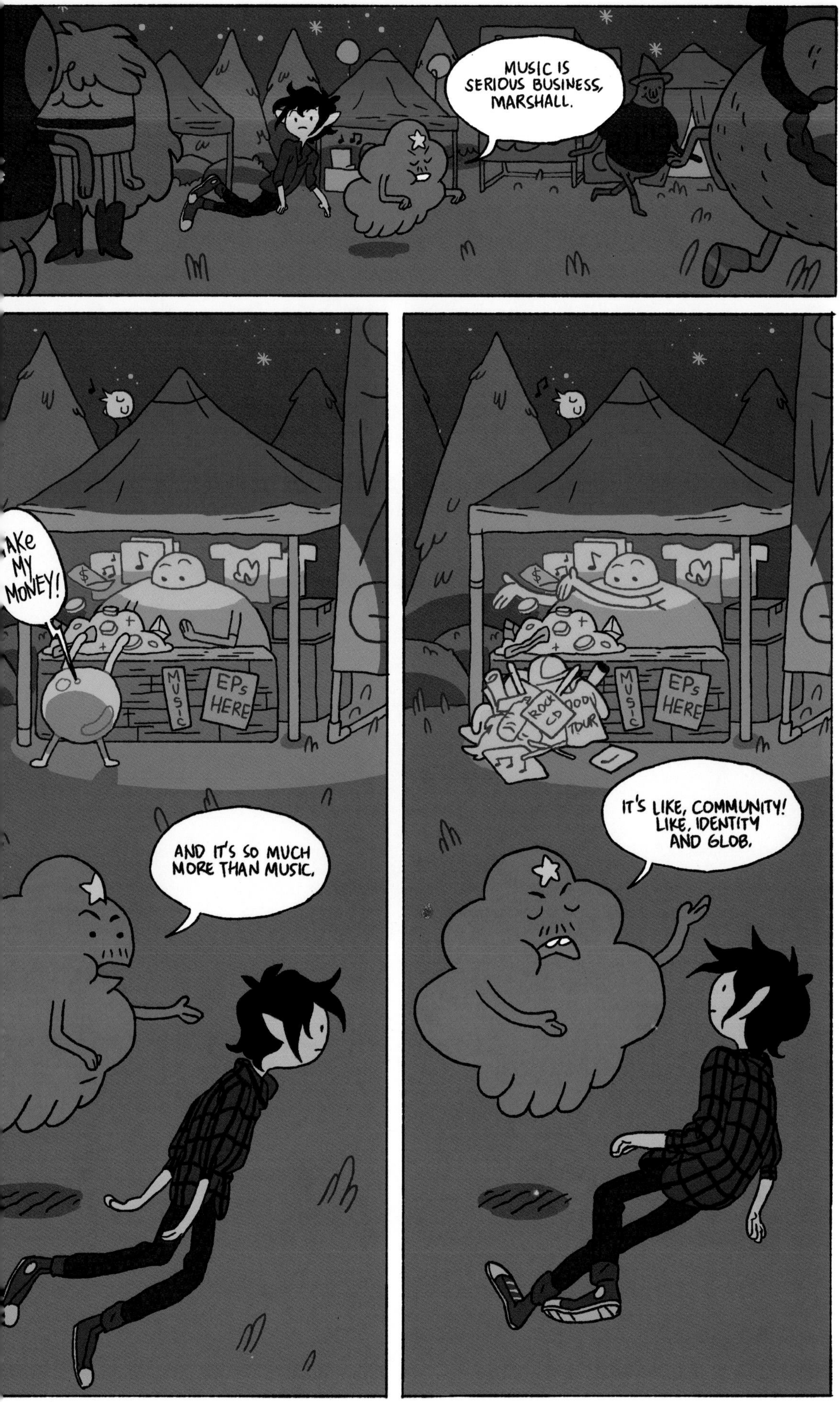
MUSIC IS SERIOUS BUSINESS, MARSHALL.
AKE MY MONEY!
MUSIC
EPs HERE
AND IT'S SO MUCH MORE THAN MUSIC.
ROCK CD
TOUR
IT'S LIKE, COMMUNITY! LIKE, IDENTITY AND GLOB.

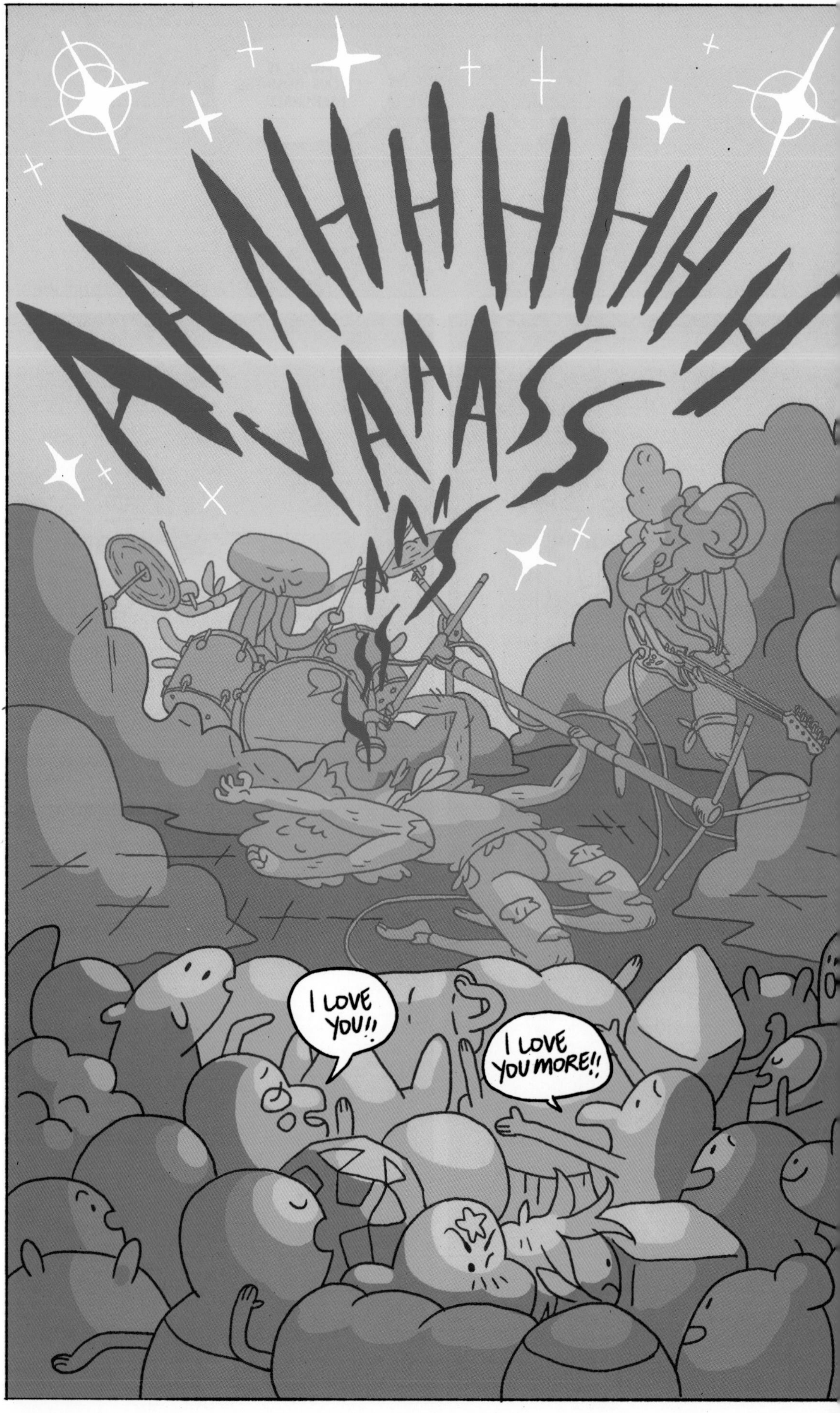

AAAHHHHHHH
YAAASS
AAS
I LOVE YOU!!
I LOVE YOU MORE!!

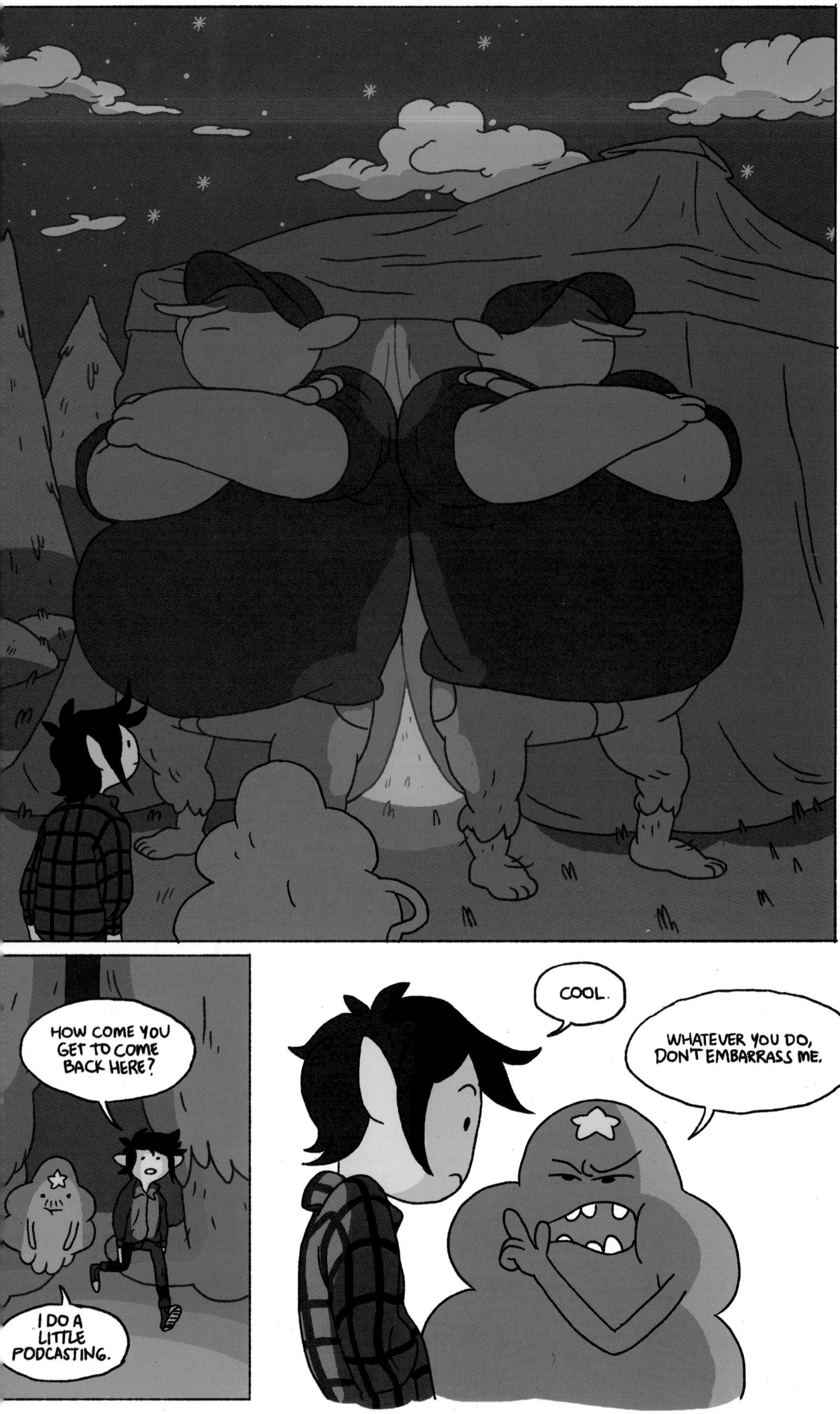
HOW COME YOU GET TO COME BACK HERE?
I DO A LITTLE PODCASTING.
COOL.
WHATEVER YOU DO, DON'T EMBARRASS ME.

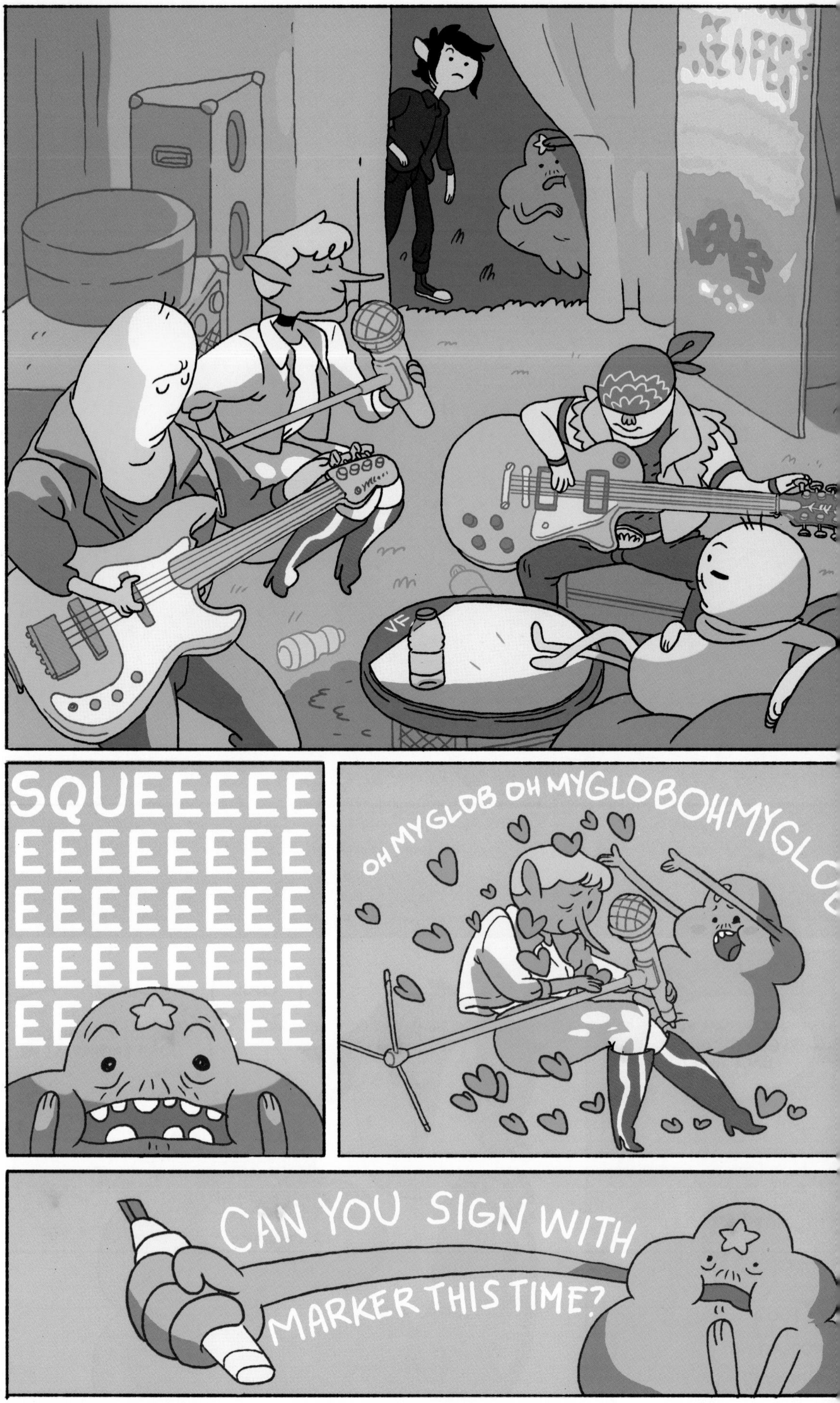
SQUEEEEEEEEEEEEEEEEEEEEEEEEEEEEEEEEEEEEEE
OH MY GLOB OH MY GLOB OH MY GLOB
CAN YOU SIGN WITH MARKER THIS TIME?

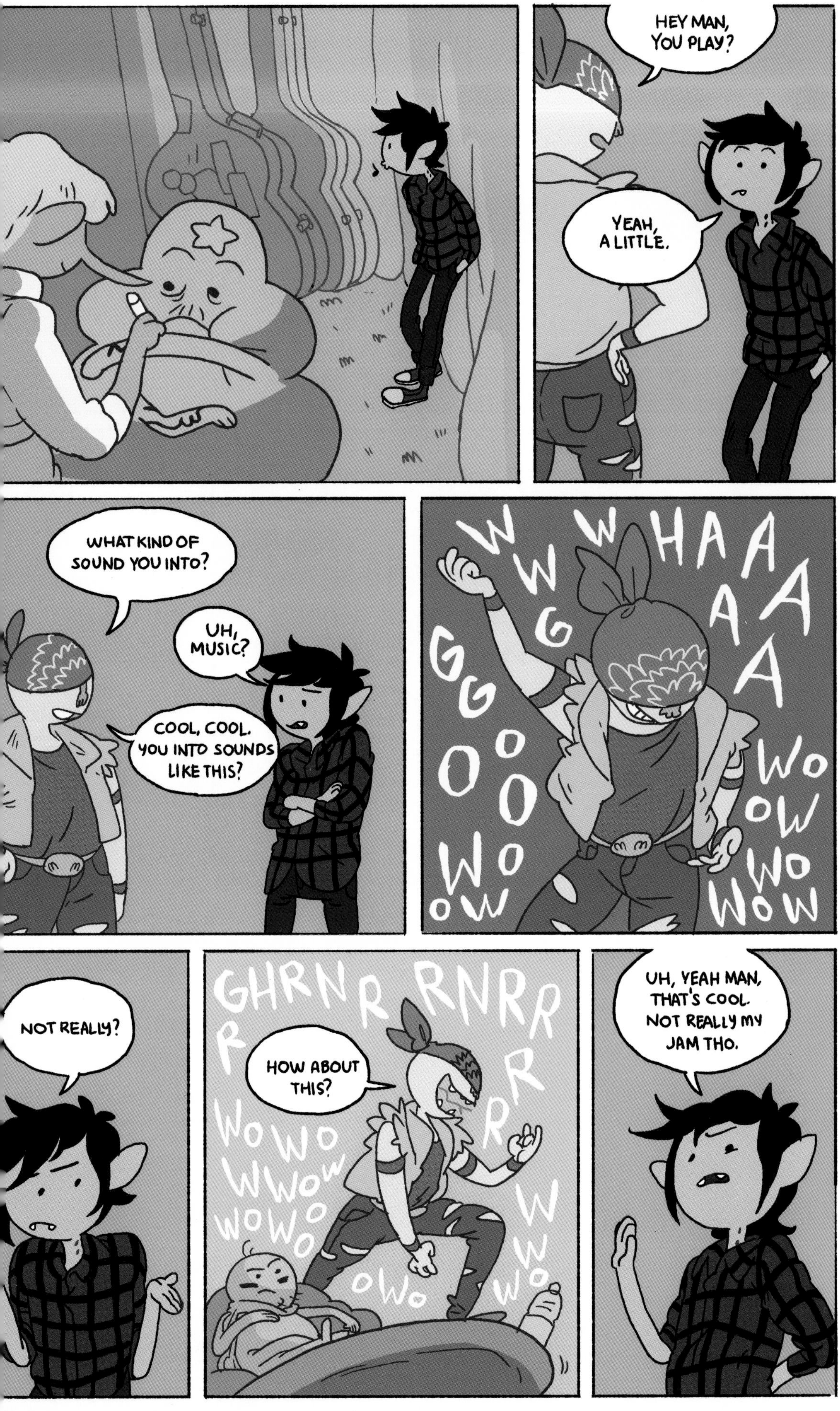
HEY MAN, YOU PLAY?
YEAH, A LITTLE.
WHAT KIND OF SOUND YOU INTO?
UH, MUSIC?
COOL, COOL. YOU INTO SOUNDS LIKE THIS?
WWWHAAAAAAA
GGGOOOOWOOOW
WOOWWOWOW
NOT REALLY?
GHRNR RNRRRRRR
HOW ABOUT THIS?
WOWOWWOWWOWOWOWO
WWOWOWO
UH, YEAH MAN, THAT'S COOL. NOT REALLY MY JAM THO.

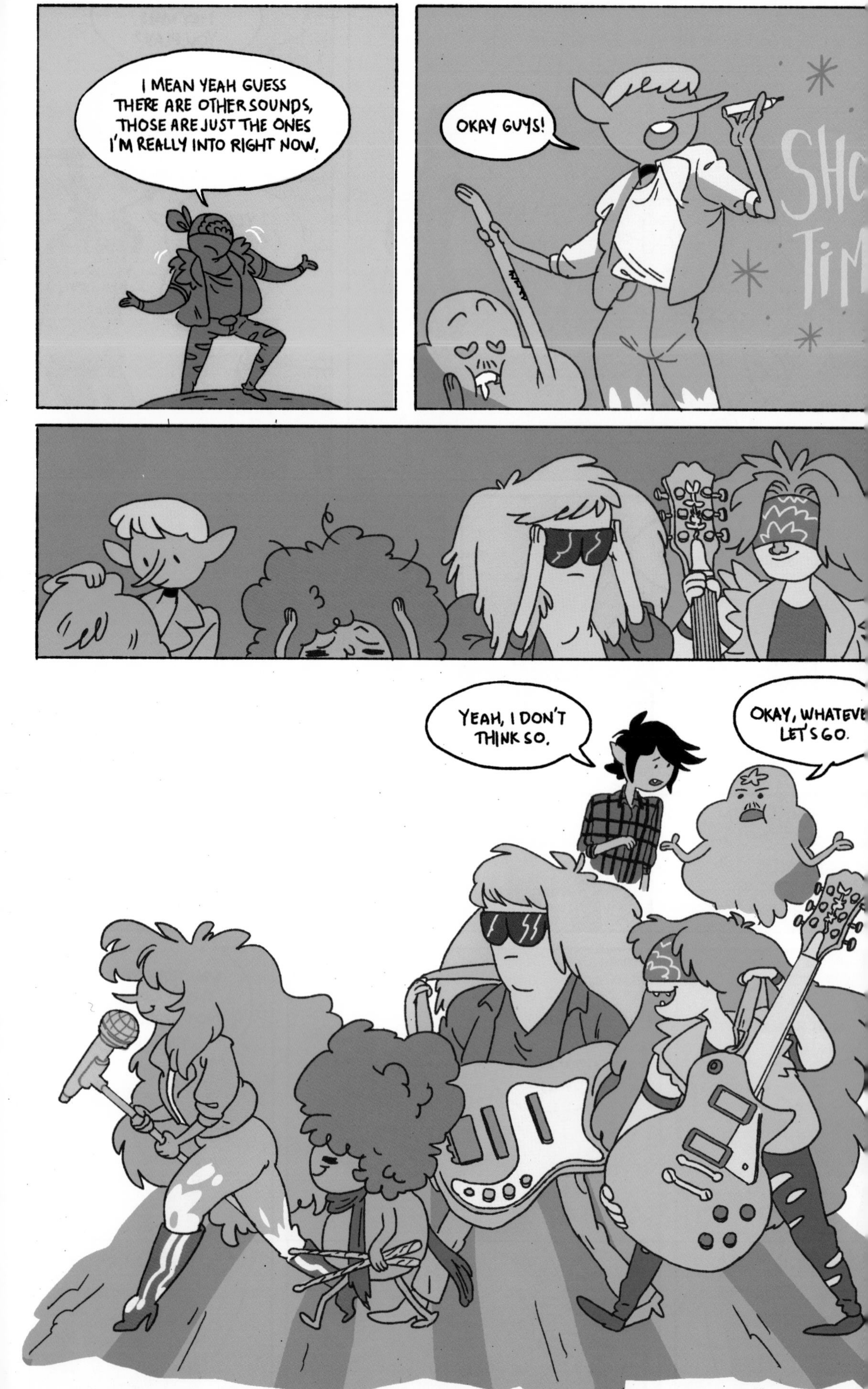
I MEAN YEAH GUESS THERE ARE OTHER SOUNDS, THOSE ARE JUST THE ONES I'M REALLY INTO RIGHT NOW.
OKAY GUYS!
YEAH, I DON'T THINK SO.
OKAY, WHATEVE
LET'S GO.

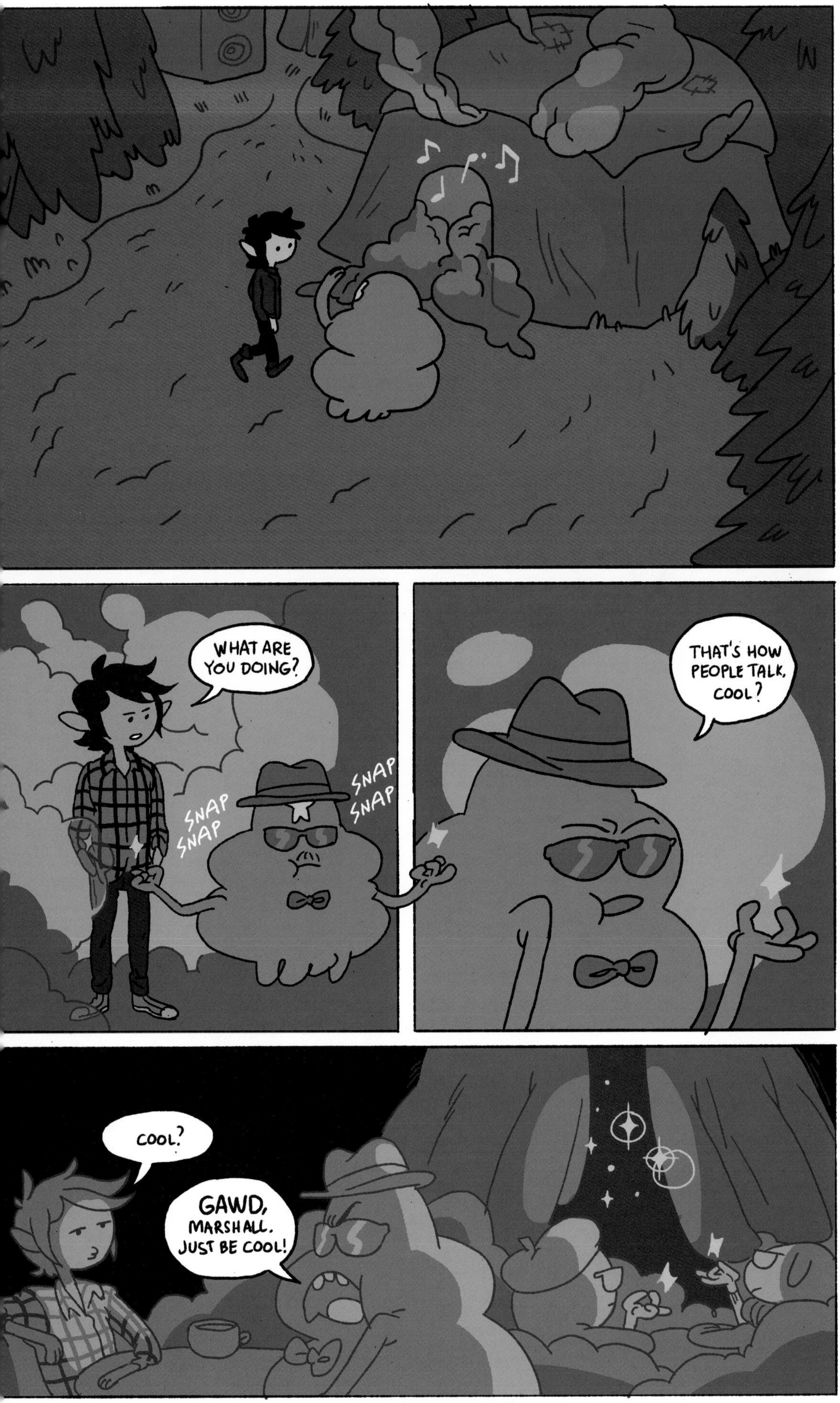
WHAT ARE YOU DOING?
SNAP SNAP
SNAP SNAP
THAT'S HOW PEOPLE TALK, COOL?
COOL?
GAWD, MARSHALL. JUST BE COOL!

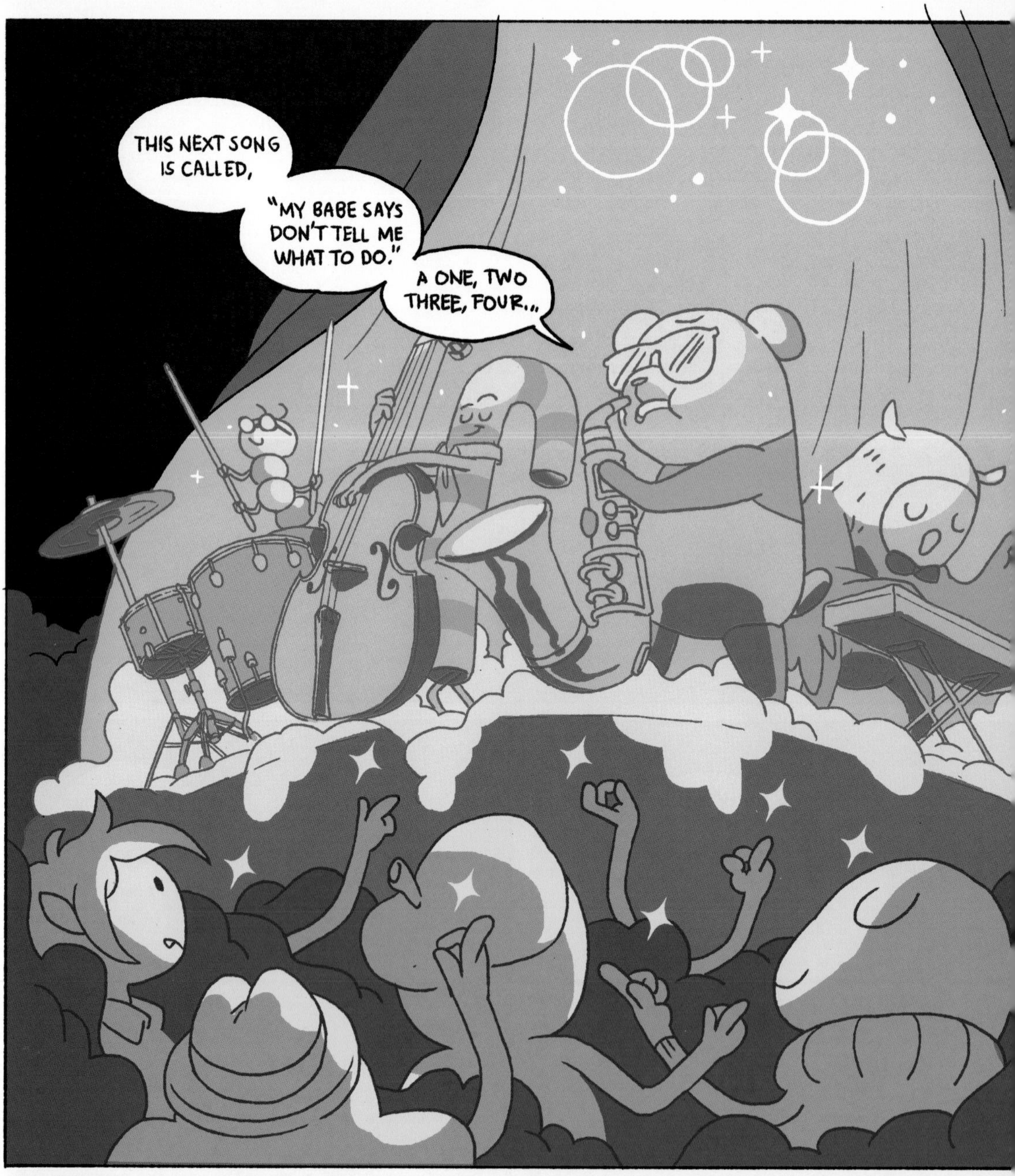
THIS NEXT SONG IS CALLED,
"MY BABE SAYS DON'T TELL ME WHAT TO DO."
A ONE, TWO THREE, FOUR...

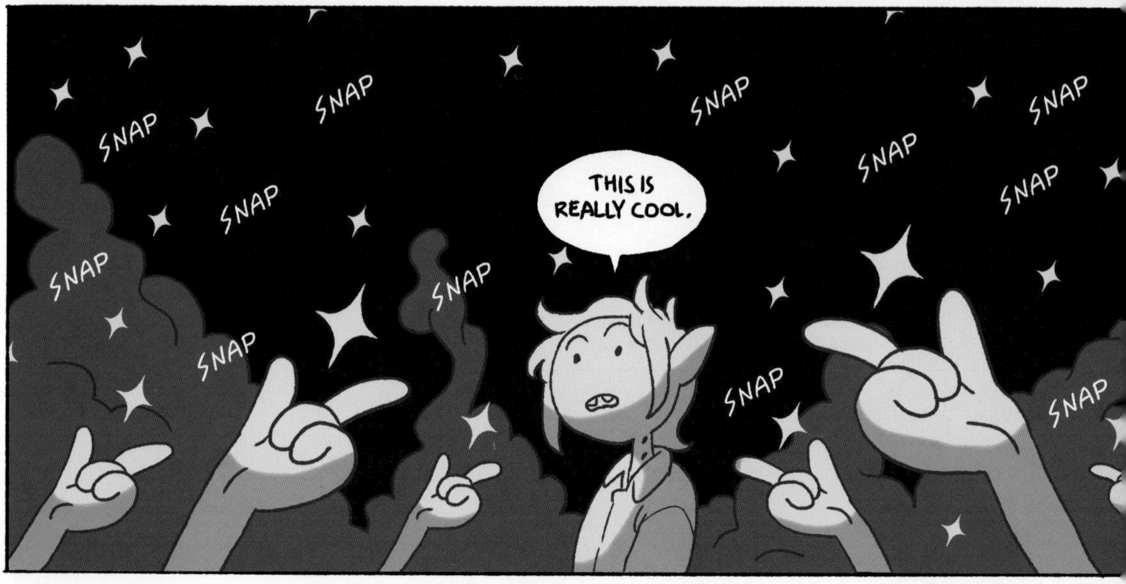
SNAP
SNAP
SNAP
SNAP
SNAP
SNAP
SNAP
THIS IS REALLY COOL.
SNAP
SNAP
SNAP
SNAP
SNAP

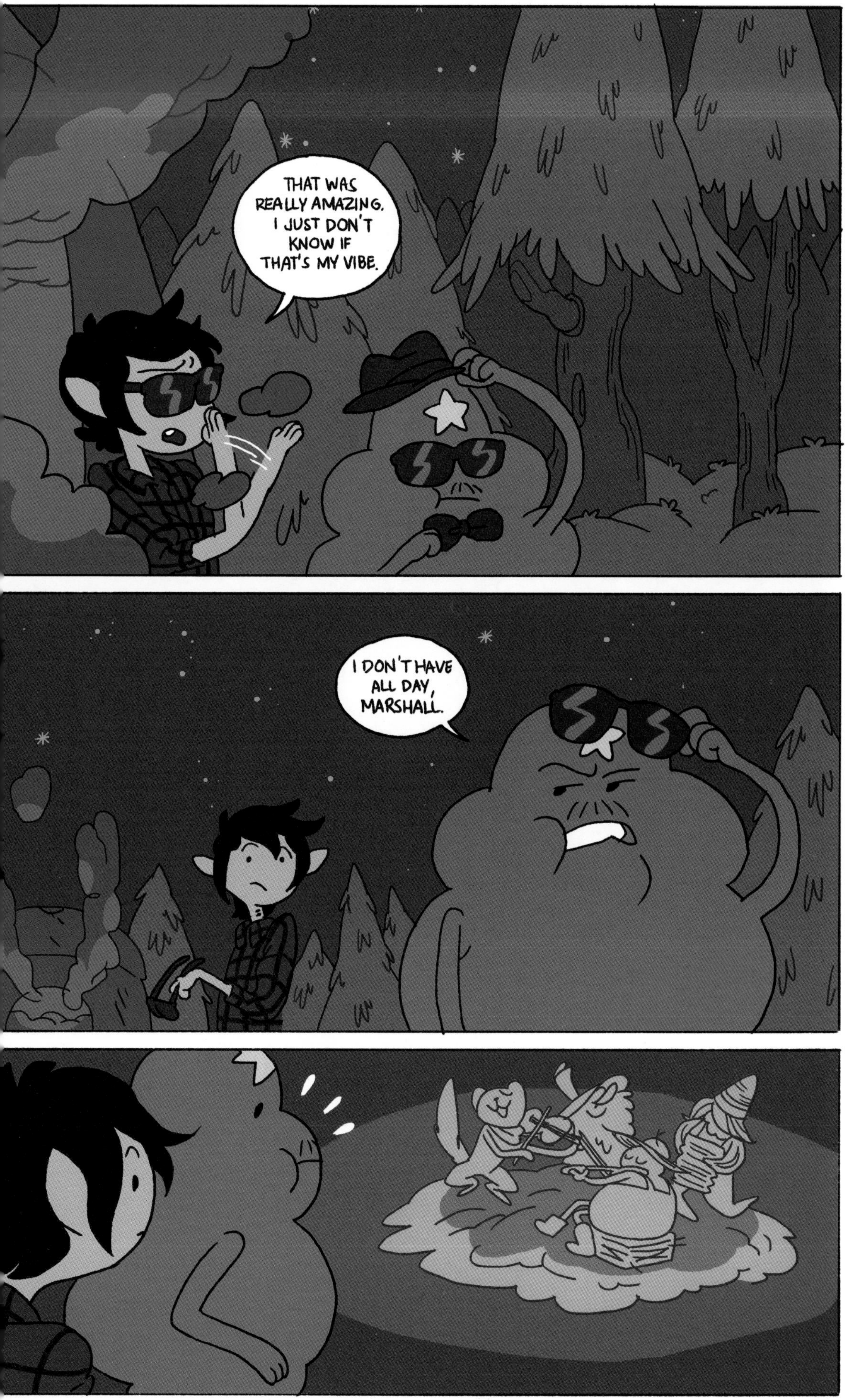
THAT WAS REALLY AMAZING. I JUST DON'T KNOW IF THAT'S MY VIBE.
I DON'T HAVE ALL DAY, MARSHALL.

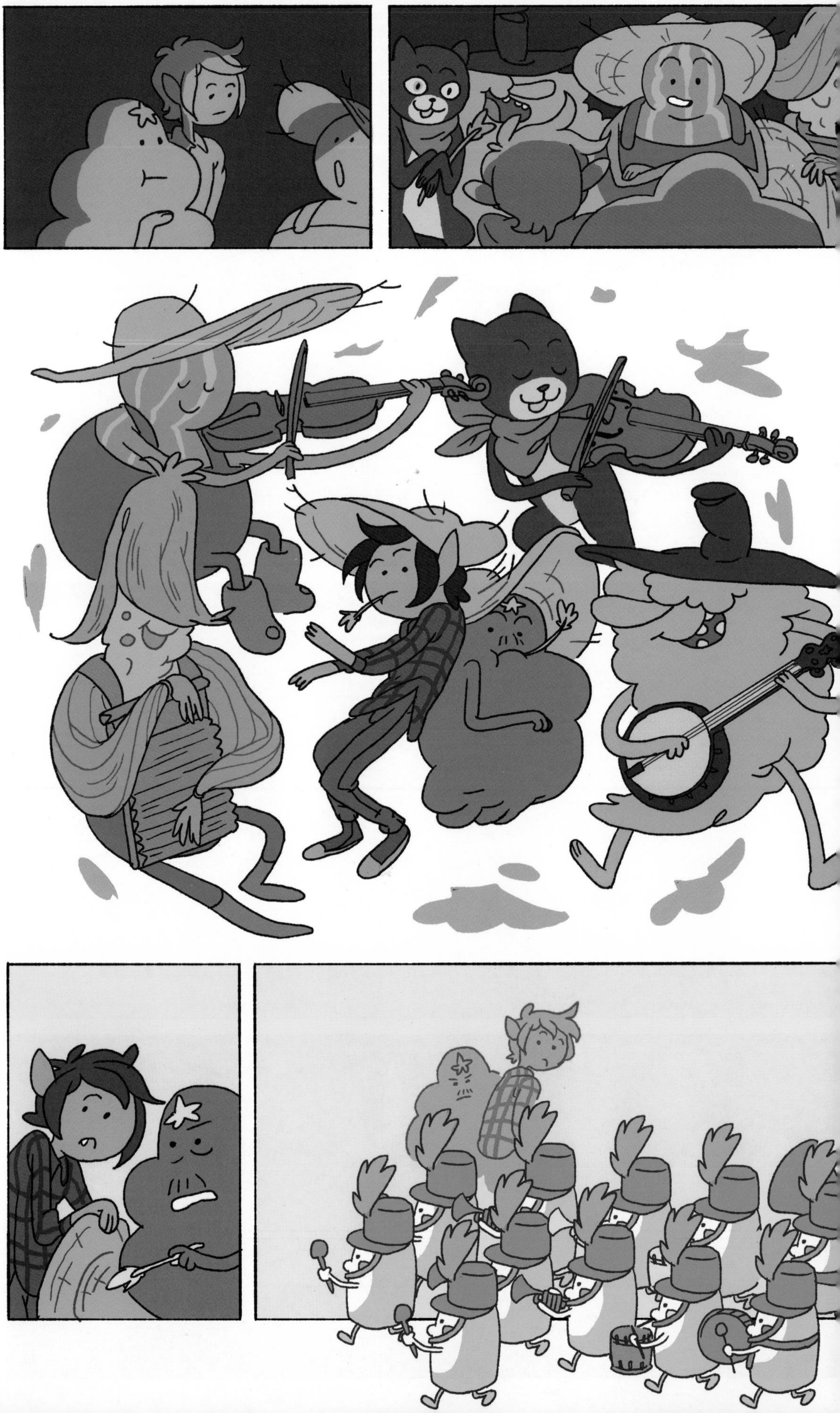

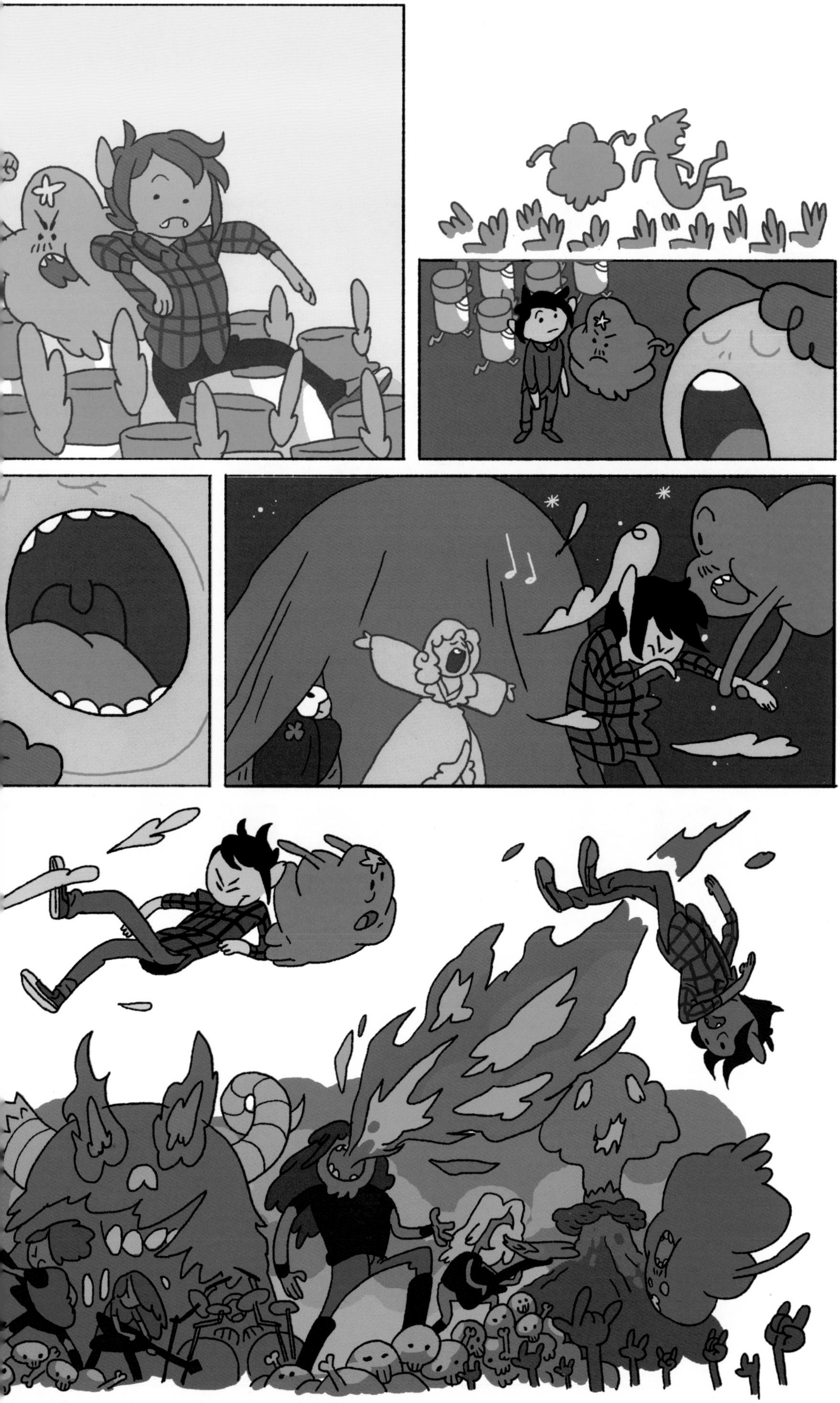

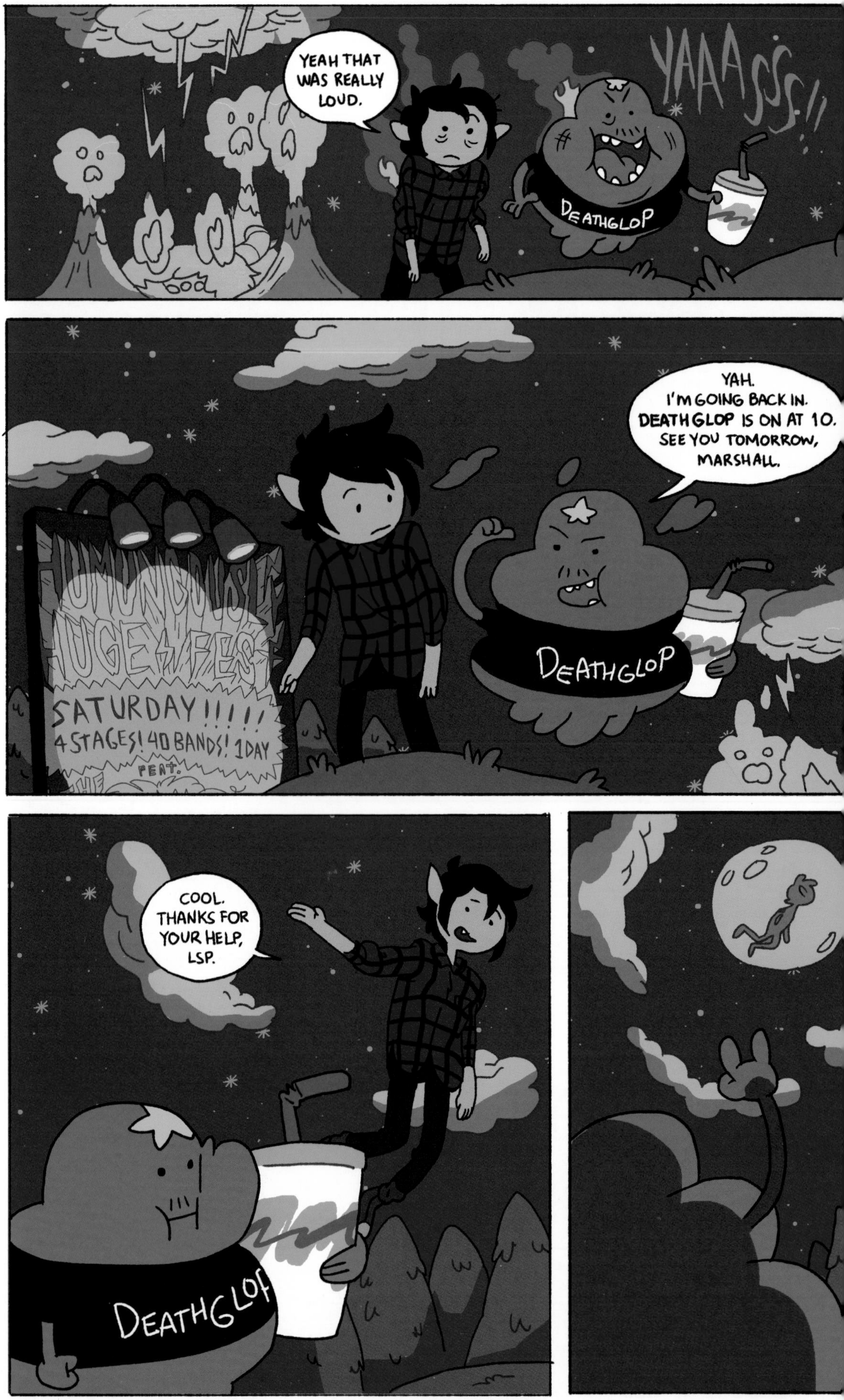
YEAH THAT WAS REALLY LOUD.
YAAASSS!!
DEATHGLOP
YAH. I'M GOING BACK IN. DEATHGLOP IS ON AT 10. SEE YOU TOMORROW, MARSHALL.
HUMUNGOUS HUGE FEST
SATURDAY!!!!!
4 STAGES! 40 BANDS! 1 DAY
FEAT.
DEATHGLOP
COOL. THANKS FOR YOUR HELP, LSP.
DEATHGLOP

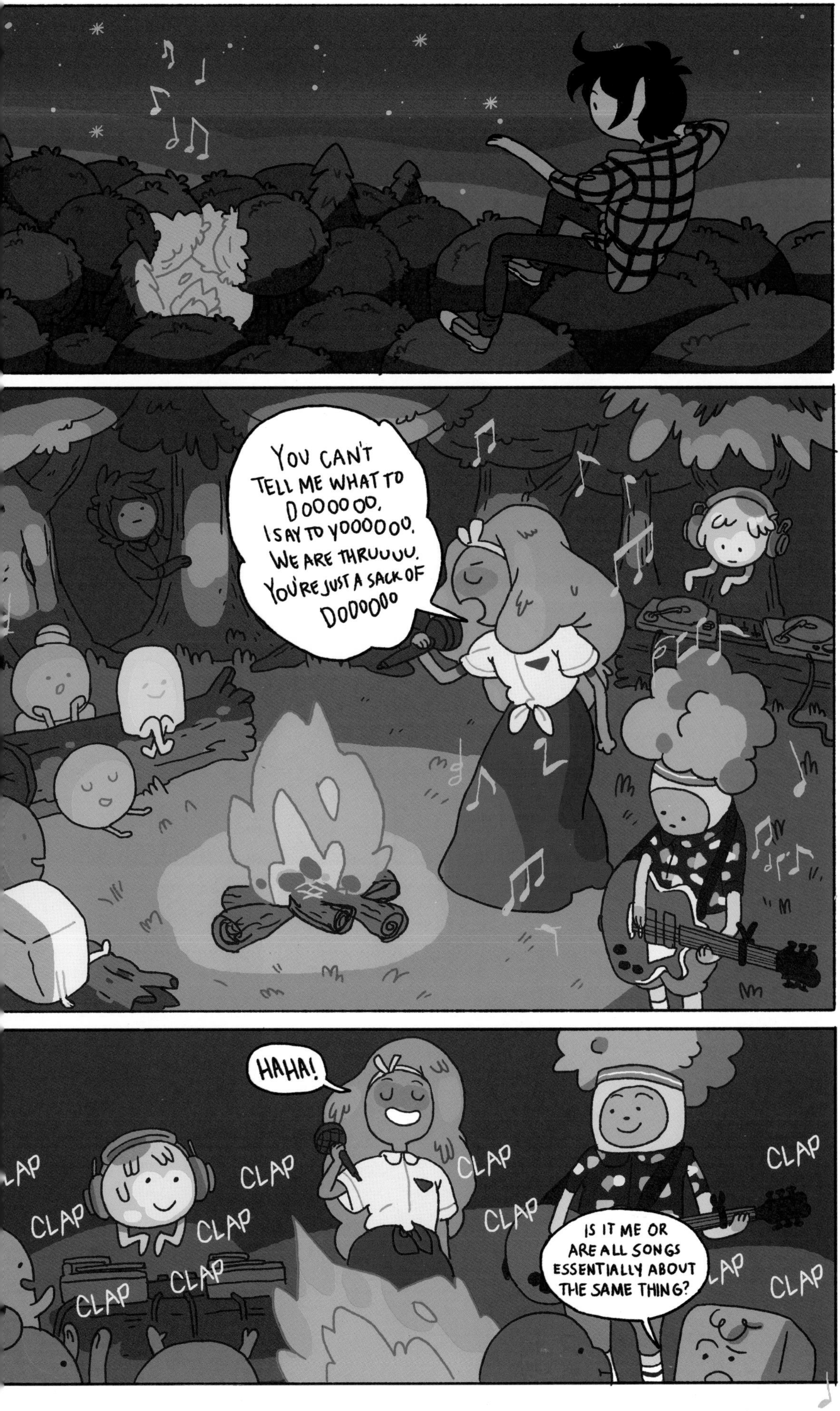
YOU CAN'T TELL ME WHAT TO DOOOOOO, I SAY TO YOOOOOO. WE ARE THRUUUU. YOU'RE JUST A SACK OF DOOOOOO
HAHA!
CLAP
CLAP
CLAP
CLAP
CLAP
CLAP
CLAP
CLAP
CLAP
CLAP
CLAP
IS IT ME OR ARE ALL SONGS ESSENTIALLY ABOUT THE SAME THING?

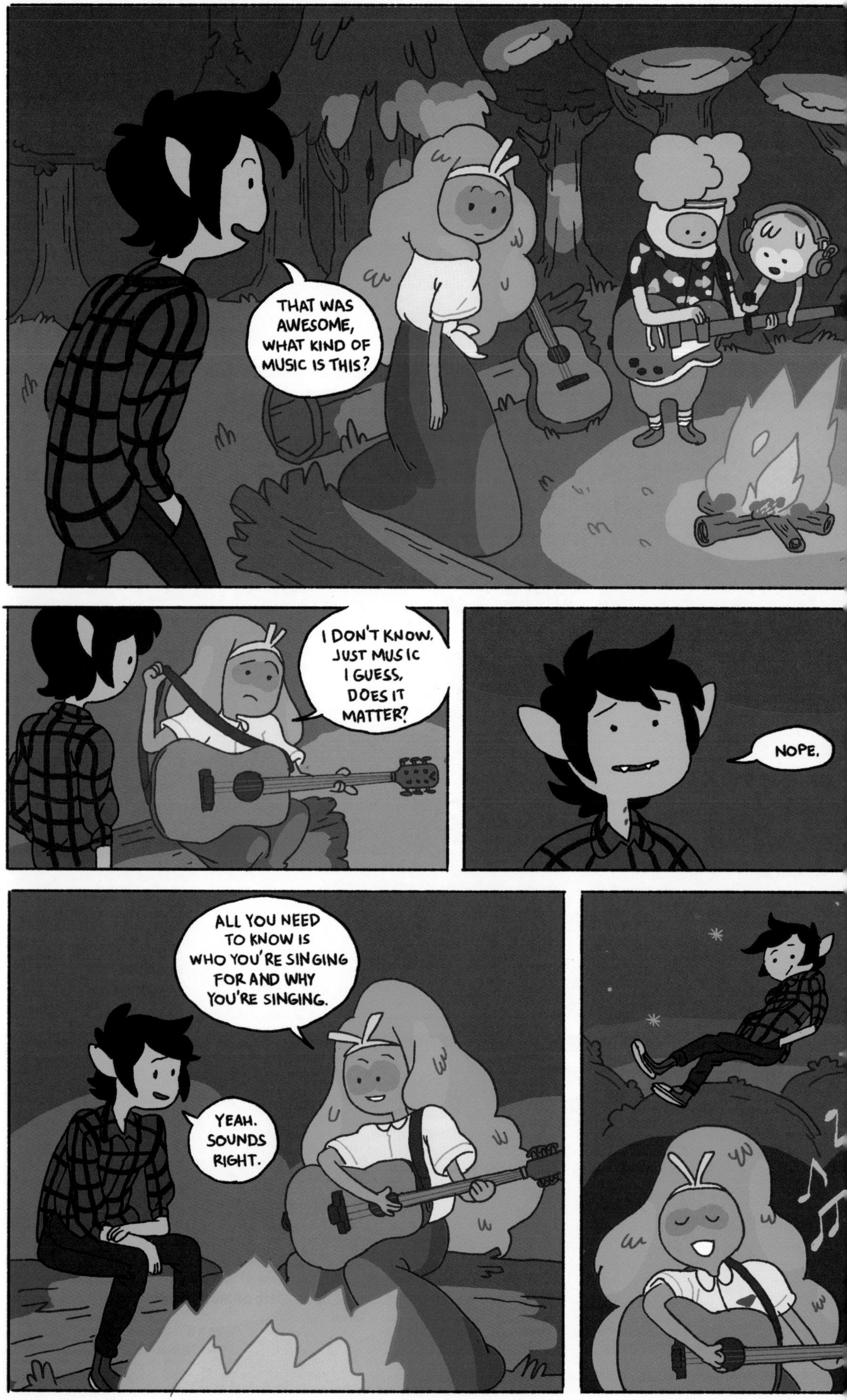
THAT WAS AWESOME, WHAT KIND OF MUSIC IS THIS?
I DON'T KNOW. JUST MUSIC I GUESS. DOES IT MATTER?
NOPE.
ALL YOU NEED TO KNOW IS WHO YOU'RE SINGING FOR AND WHY YOU'RE SINGING.
YEAH. SOUNDS RIGHT.

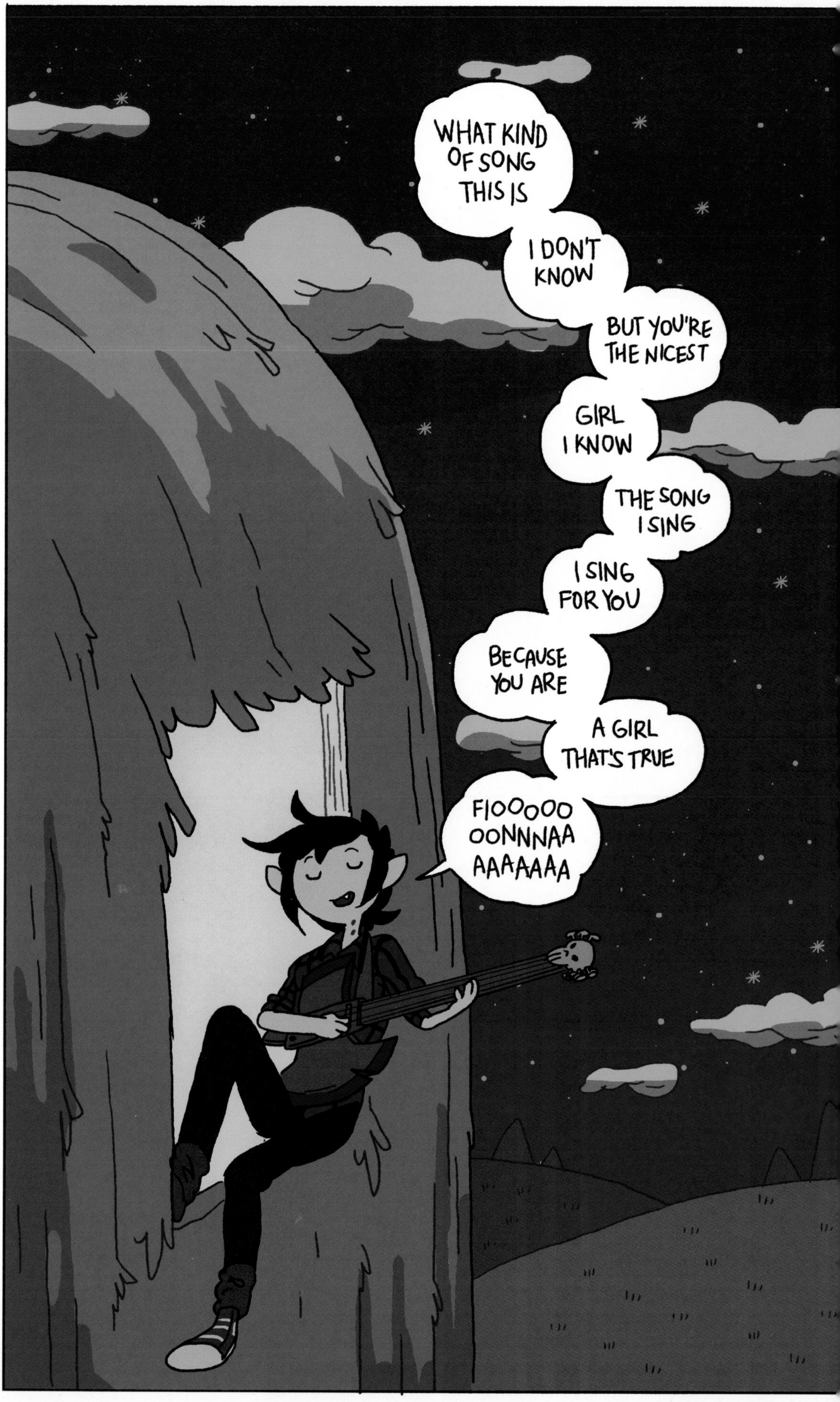
WHAT KIND OF SONG THIS IS
I DON'T KNOW
BUT YOU'RE THE NICEST
GIRL I KNOW
THE SONG I SING
I SING FOR YOU
BECAUSE YOU ARE
A GIRL THAT'S TRUE
FIOOOOO OONNNAA AAAAAAA

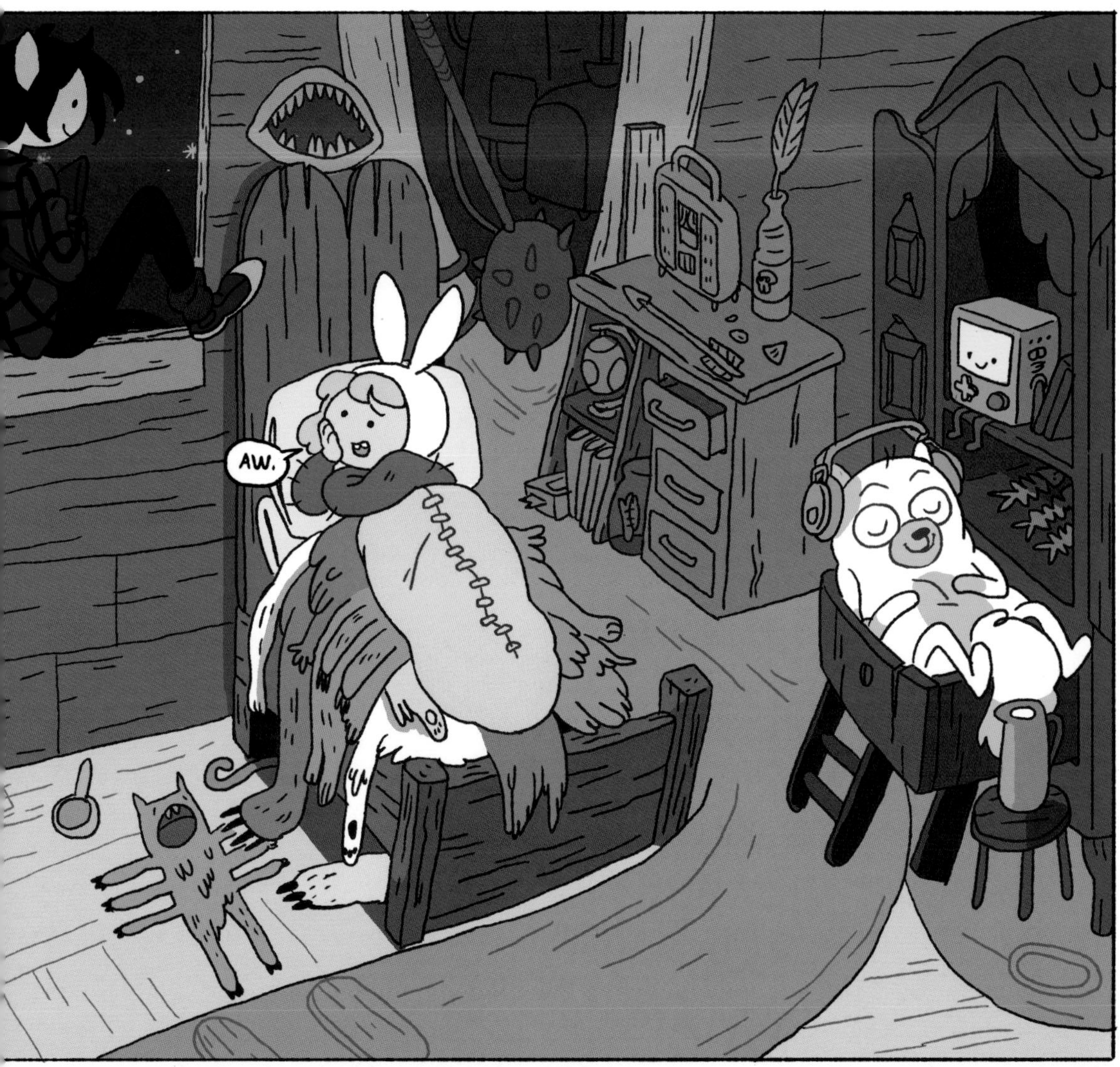
AW.

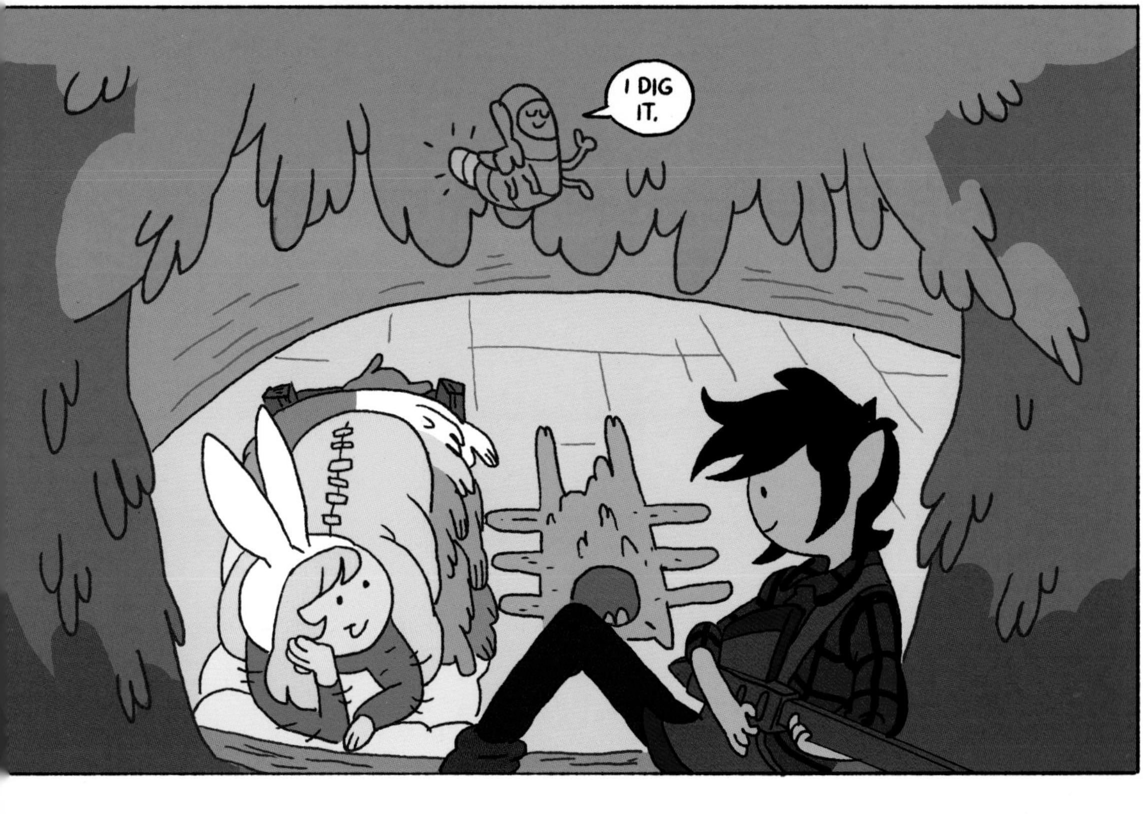
I DIG IT.

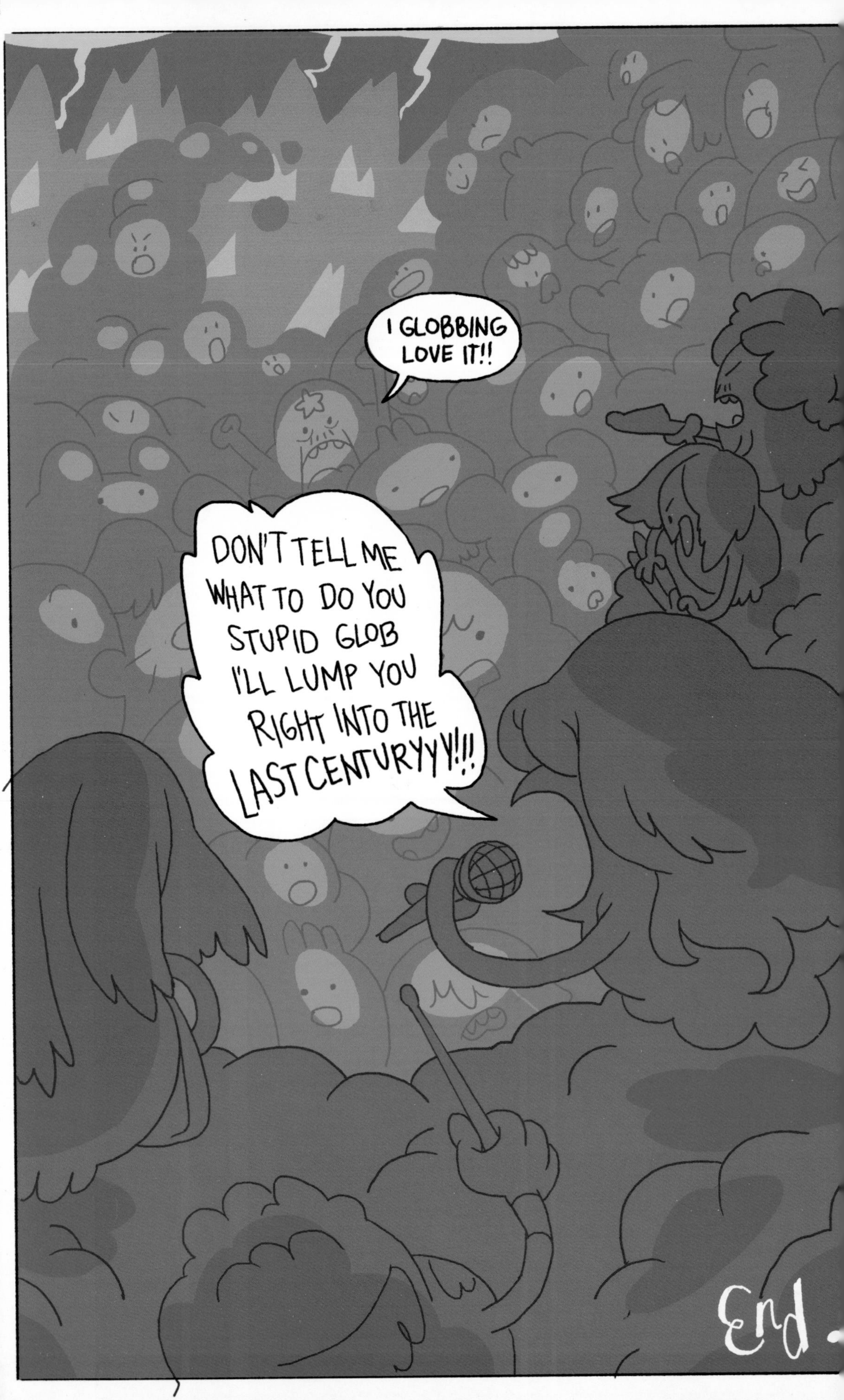
I GLOBBING LOVE IT!!
DON'T TELL ME WHAT TO DO YOU STUPID GLOB I'LL LUMP YOU RIGHT INTO THE LAST CENTURYYY!!!
End.

COVER GALLERY

Issue #5 Main Cover

RENÉE PARK

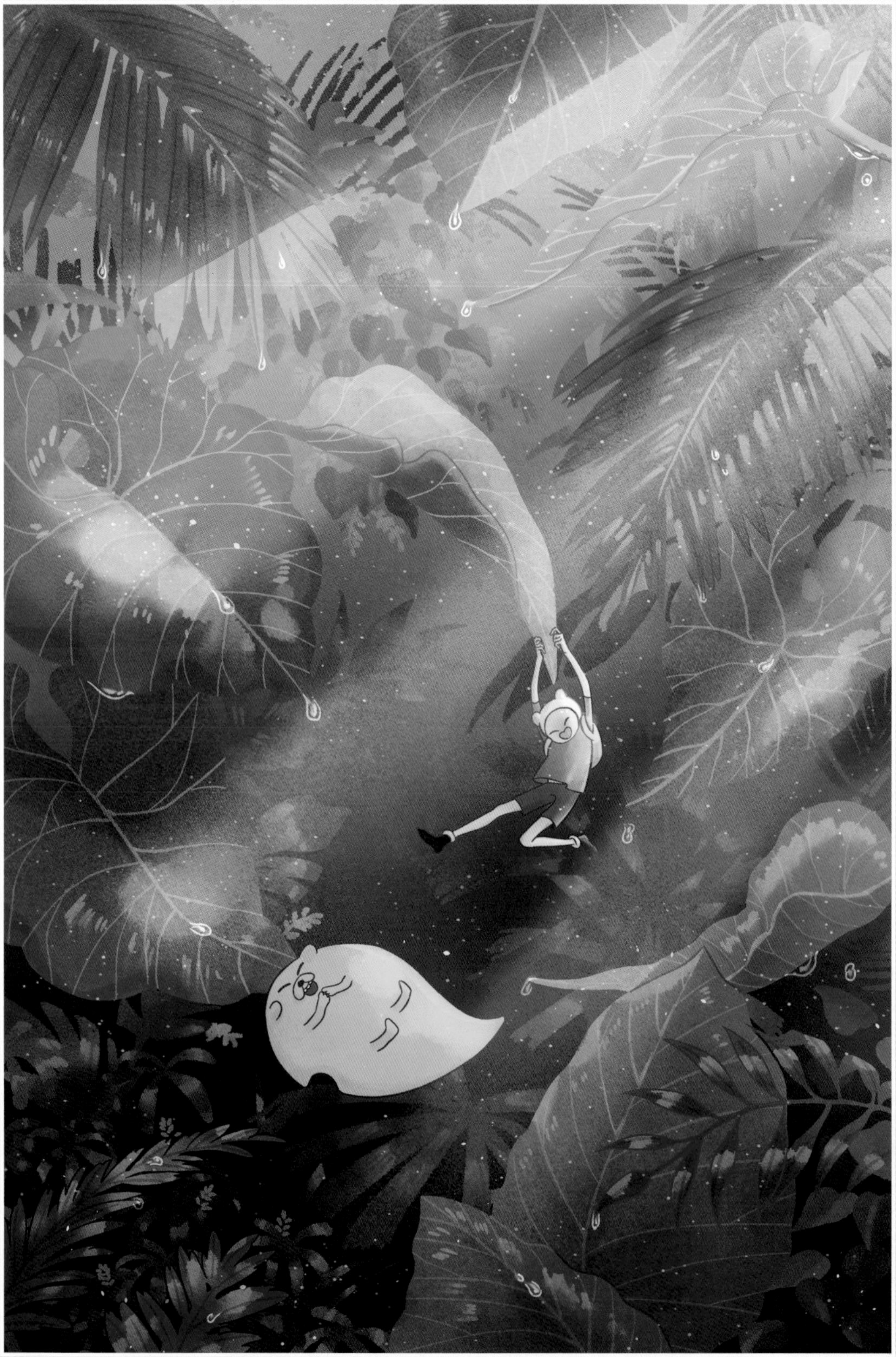

Issue #5 Subscription Cover

SHAUNA J. GRANT

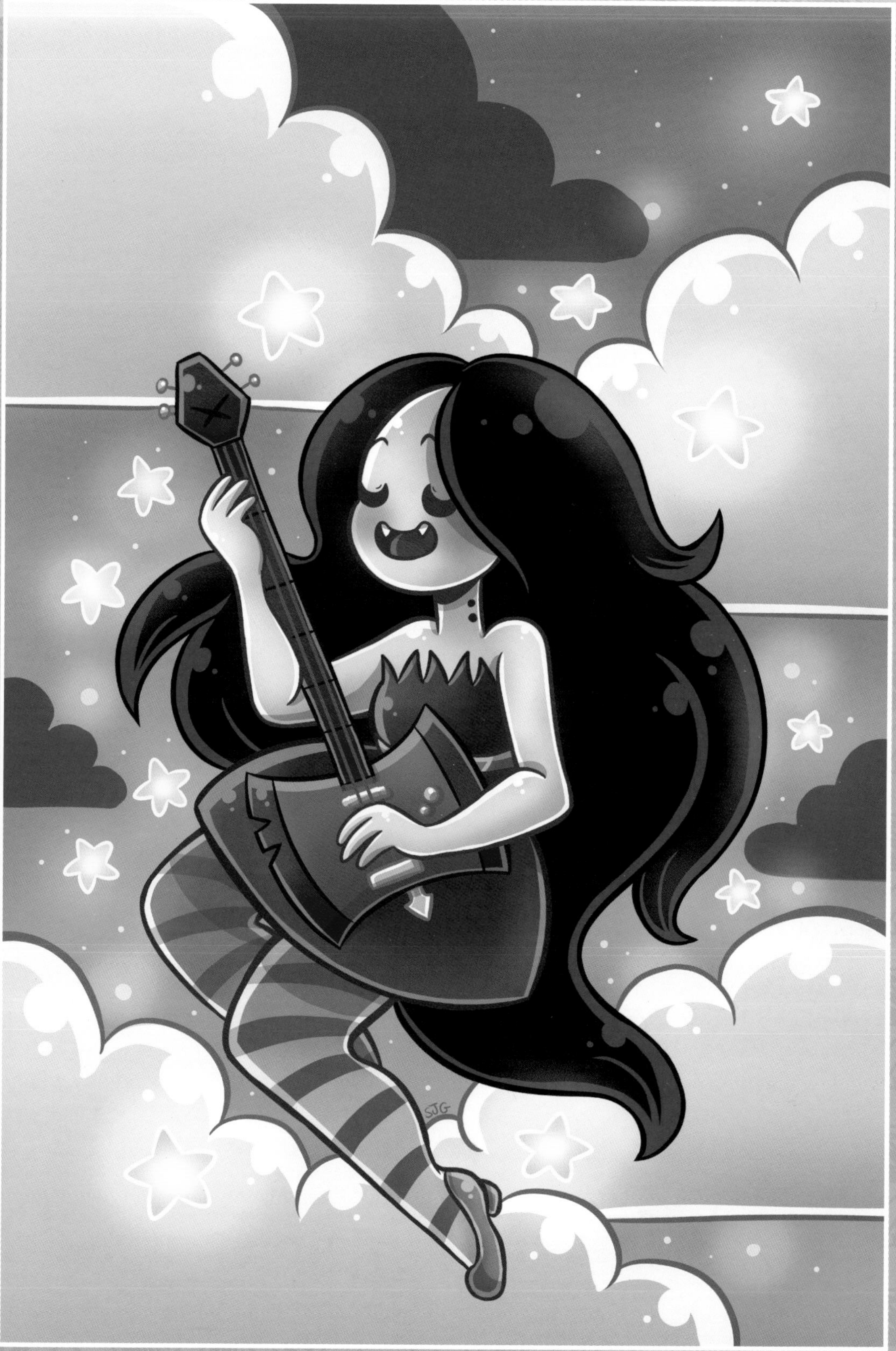
SJG

Issue #5 Variant Cover
SIMON LeCLERC

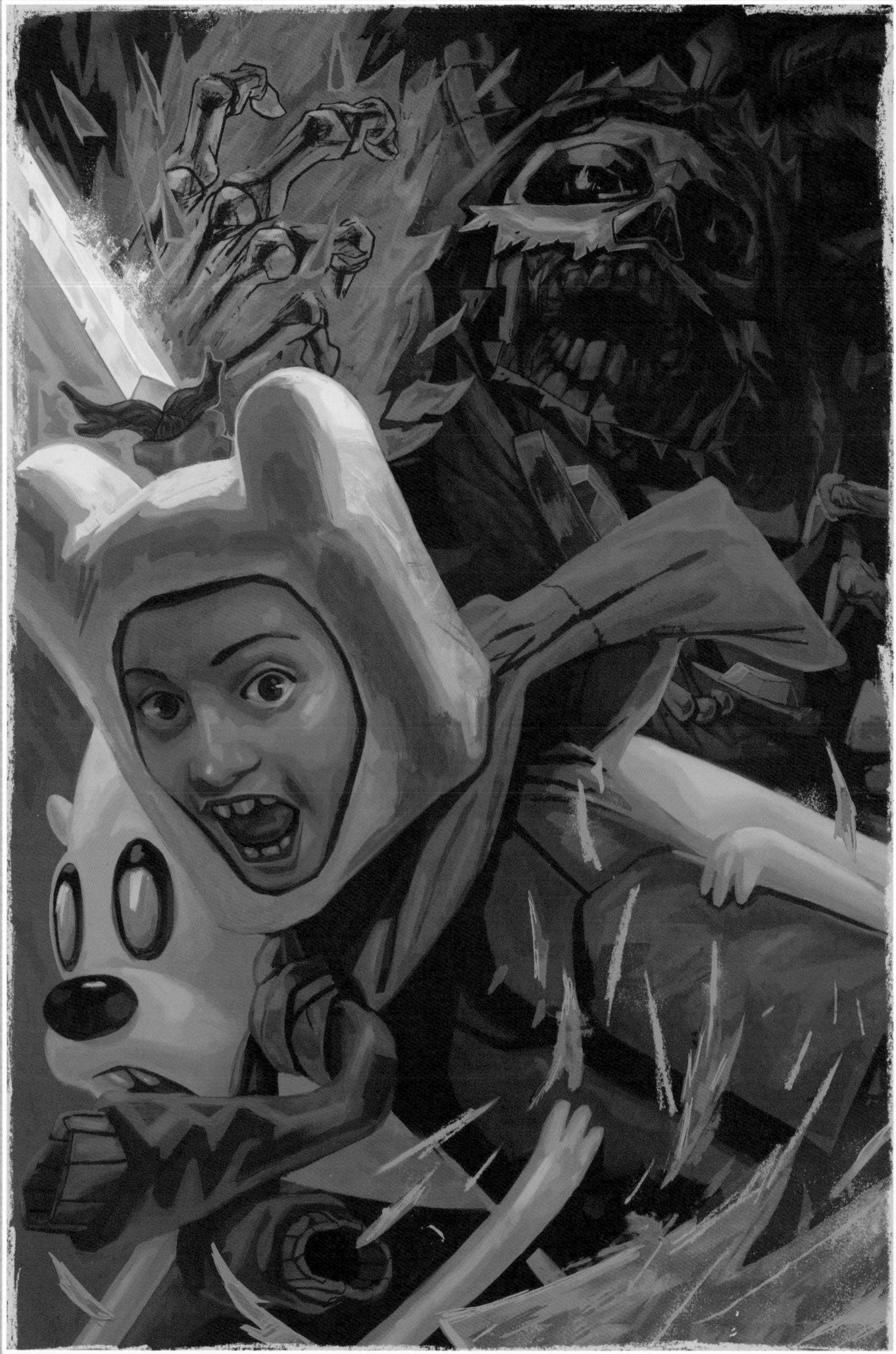

ssue #6 Main Cover

JORGE CORONA

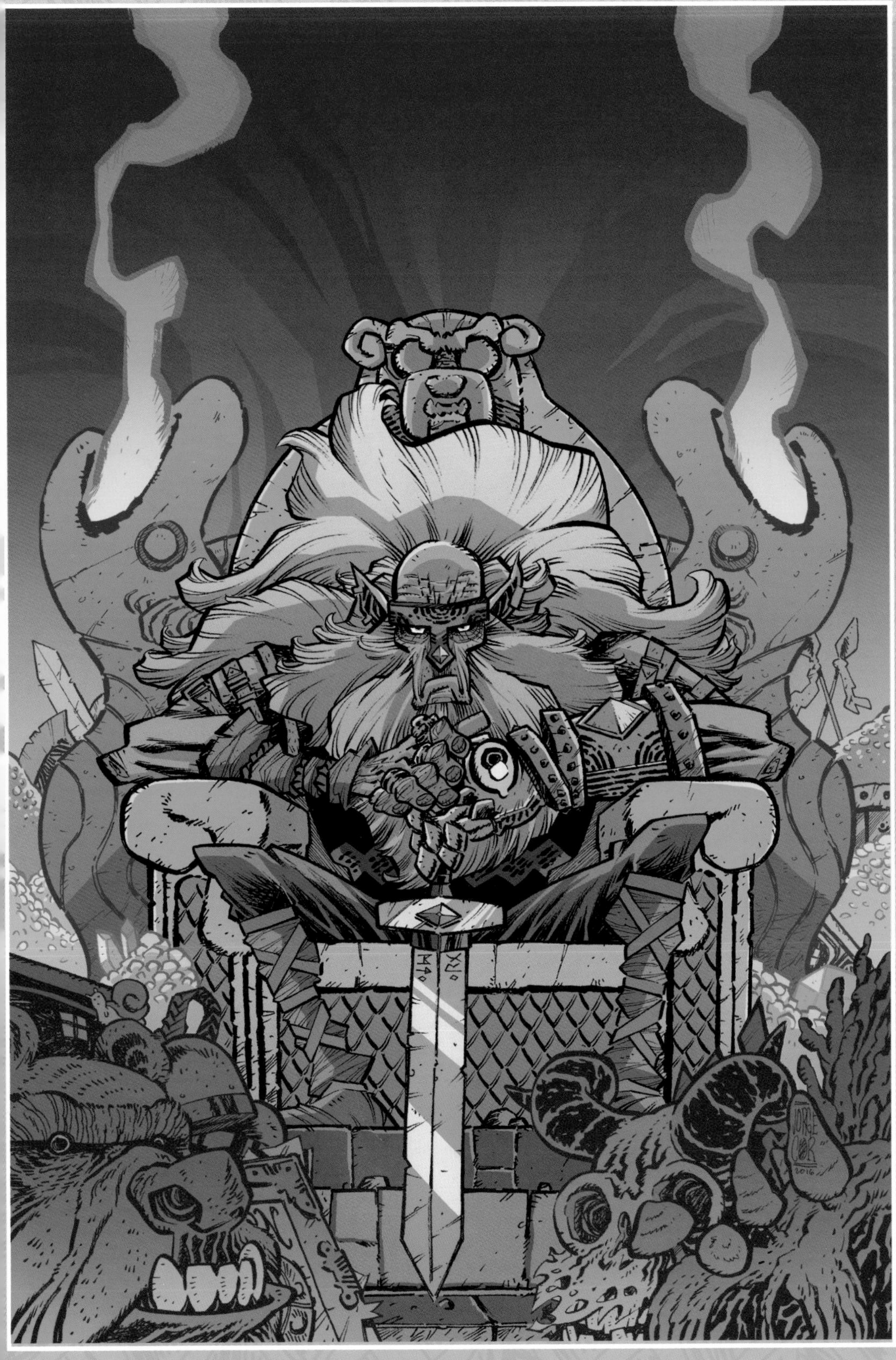

Issue #6 Subscription Cover
DIIGII DAGUNA

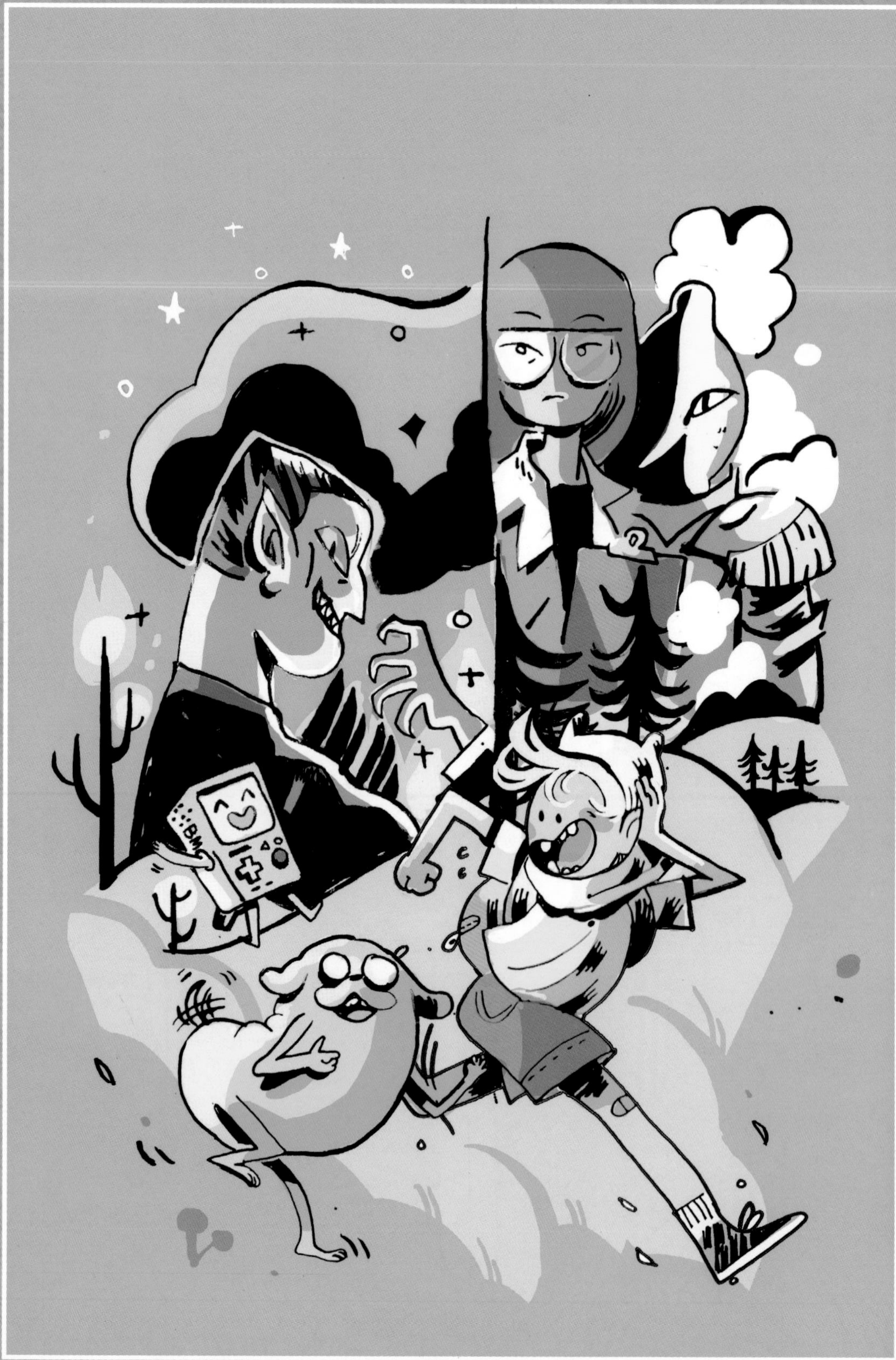

Issue #6 Variant Cover

COLLEEN COOVER

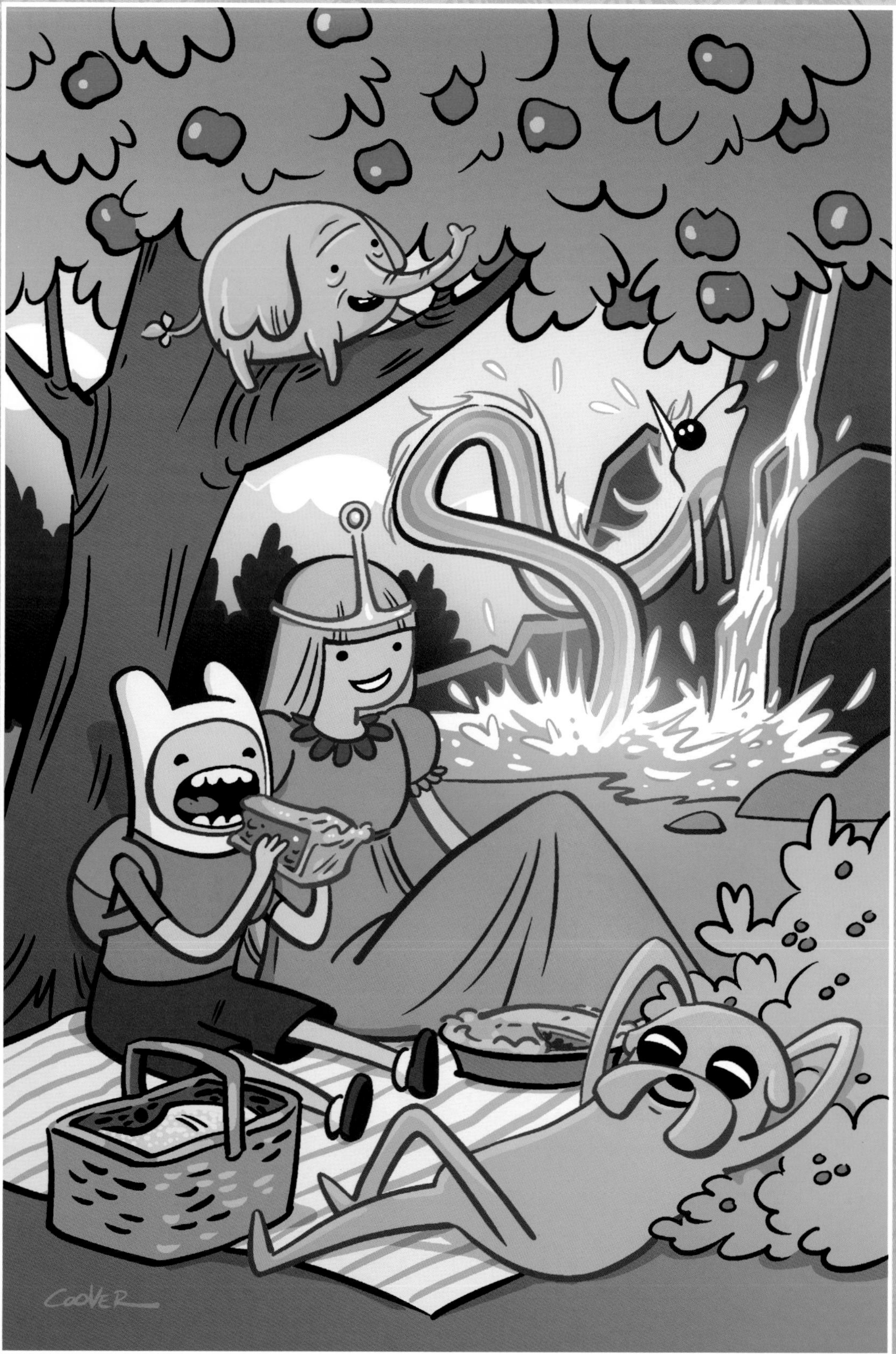

COOVER

Issue #7 Main Cover

EVA CABRERA

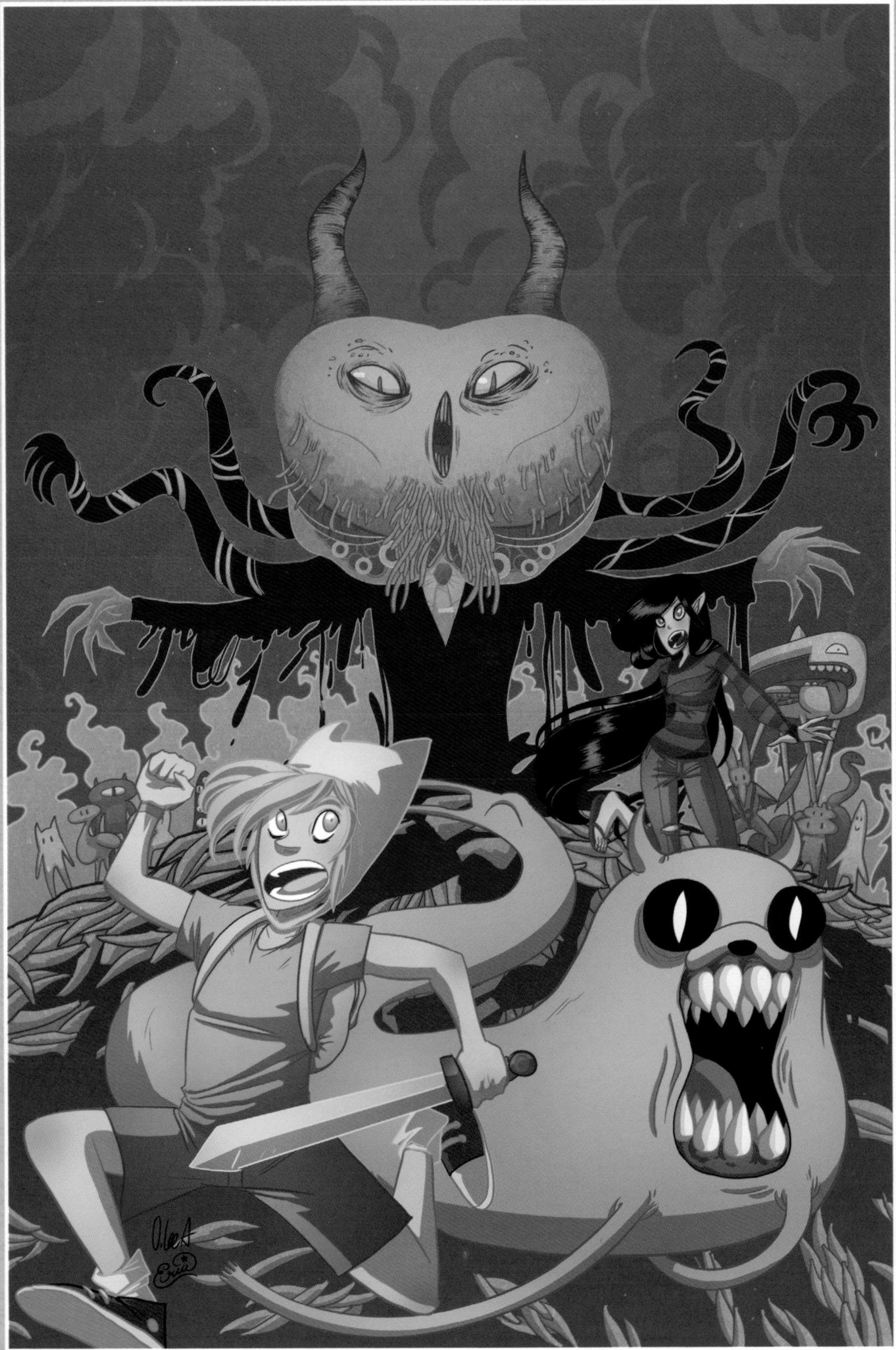

Issue #7 Subscription Cover

MEG DAUNTING

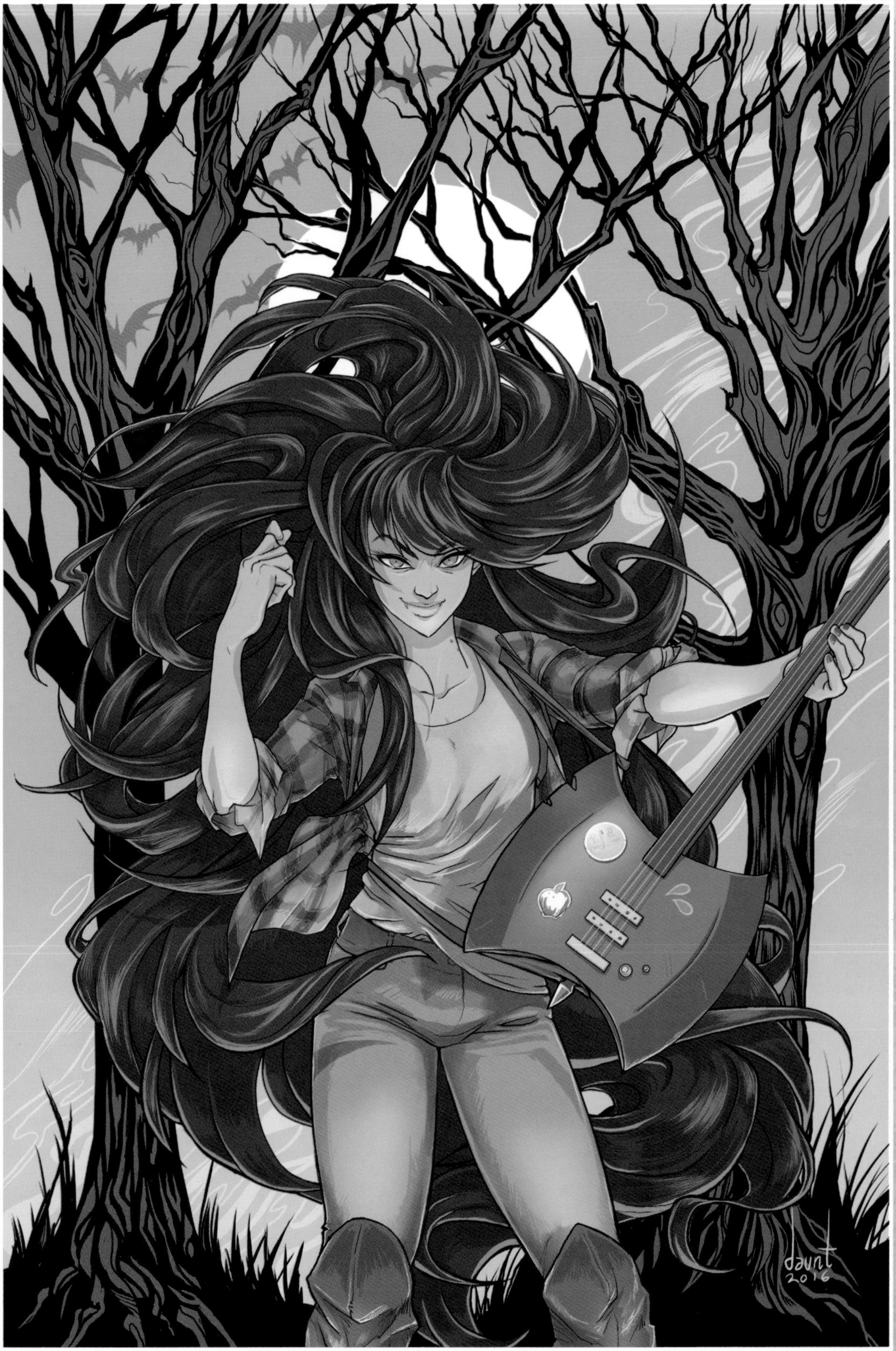
daunt
2016

Issue #7 Variant Cover

ANGELA RIZZA

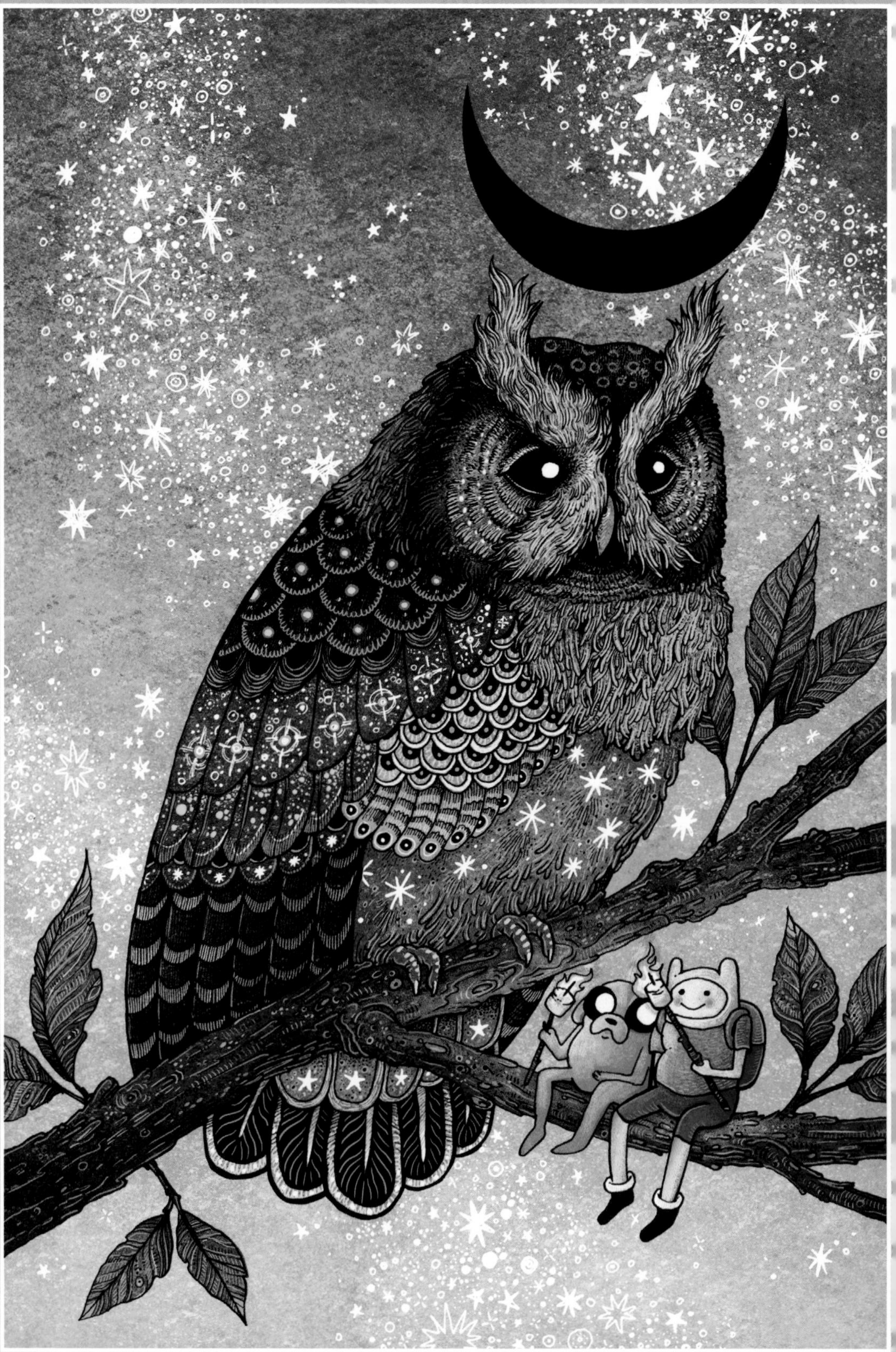

Issue #8 Main Cover

MEG OMAC

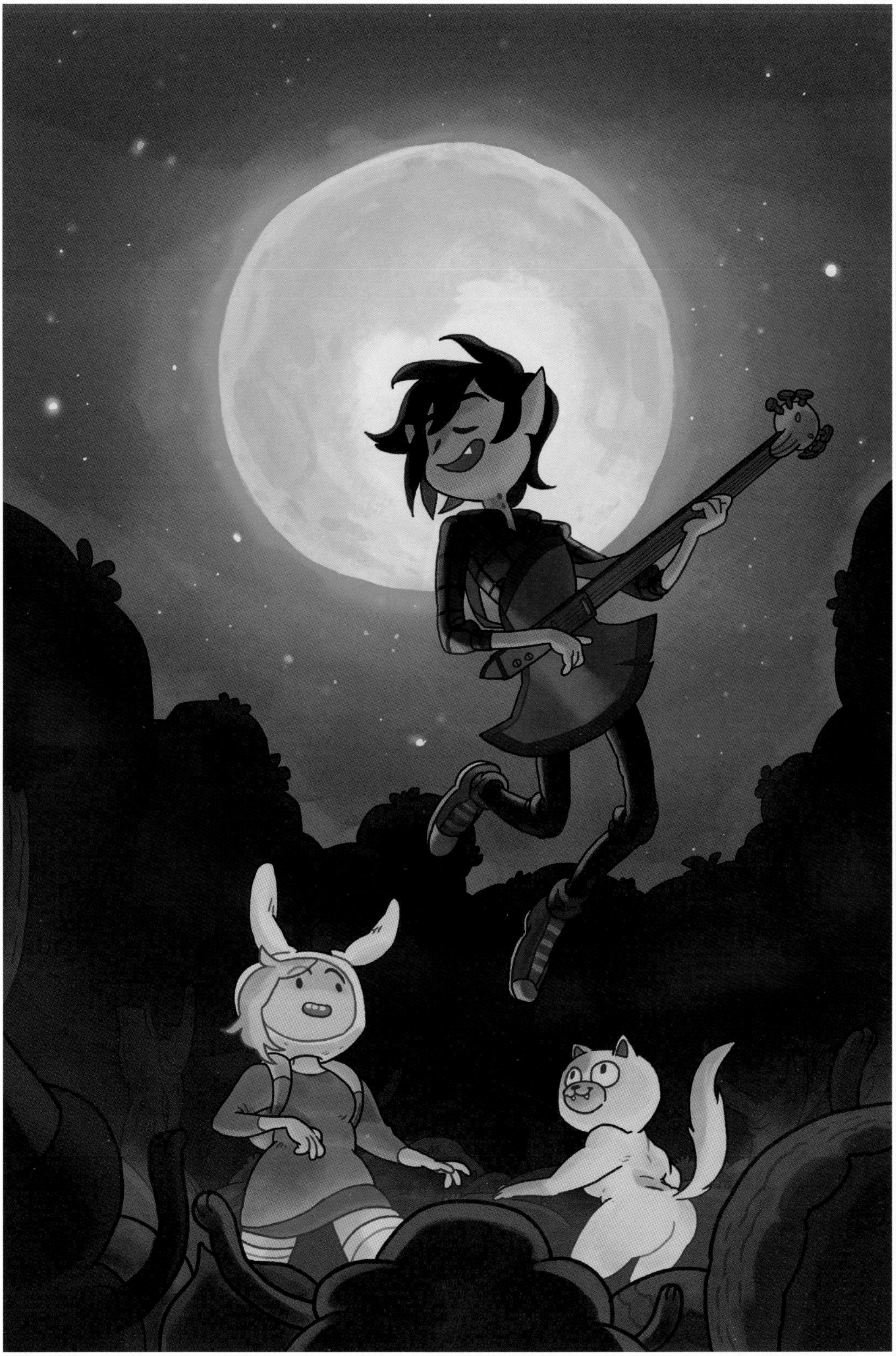

Issue #8 Subscription Cover

DEREK KIRK KIM

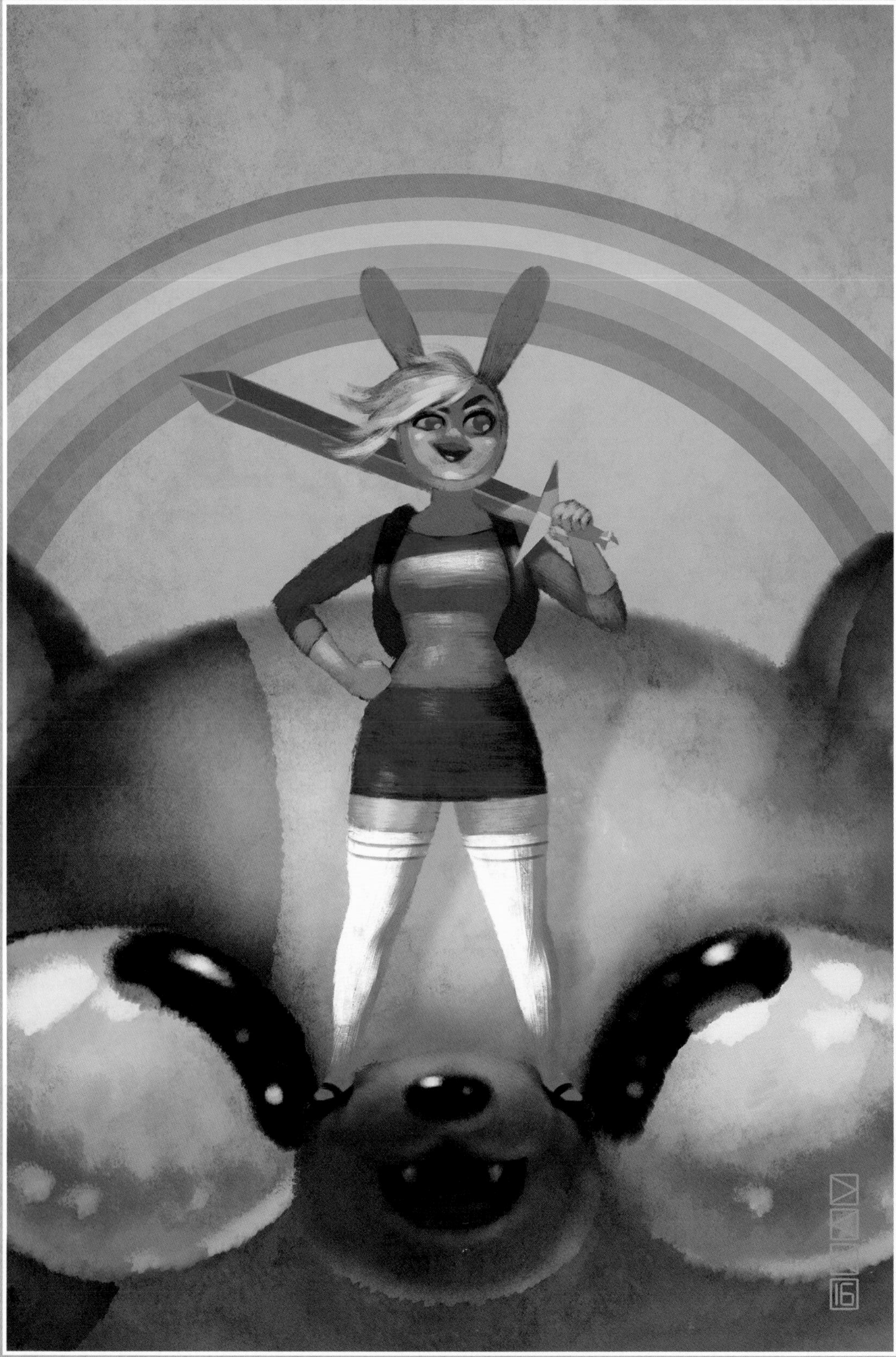

ssue #8 Variant Cover

BEN CONSTANTINE

WITH COLORS BY WALTER BAIAMONTE

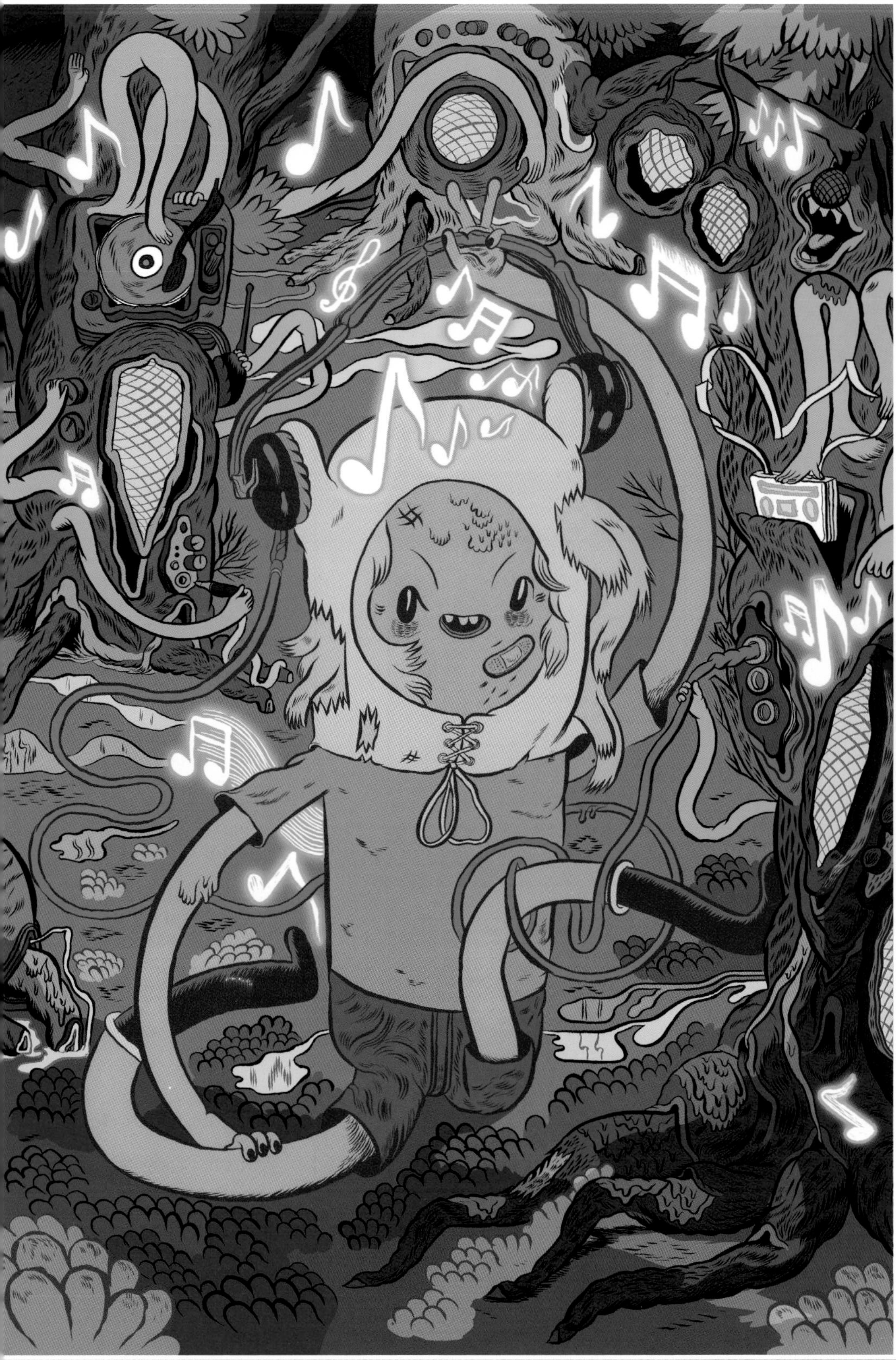

DISCOVER
EXPLOSIVE NEW WORLDS

Adventure Time

The Amazing World of
Gumball

Steven Universe
Volume One

Over the Garden Wall
"A unique, delightful read."
—Comic Book Resources

Garfield
By Jim Davis

Charles M. Schulz
PEANUTS

kaboom!™

AVAILABLE AT YOUR LOCAL COMICS SHOP AND BOOKSTORE

To find a comics shop in your area, call 1-888-266-4226

WWW.**BOOM-STUDIOS**.COM

Adventure Time
Pendleton Ward and Others
Volume 1
ISBN: 978-1-60886-280-1 | $9.99
Volume 2
ISBN: 978-1-60886-323-5 | $14.99 US
Adventure Time: Islands
ISBN: 978-1-60886-972-5 | $9.99

Regular Show
J.G. Quintel and Others
Volume 1
ISBN: 978-1-60886-362-4 | $14.99
Volume 2
ISBN: 978-1-60886-426-3 | $14.99

Regular Show: Hydration
ISBN: 978-1-60886-339-6 | $12.99

The Amazing World of Gumb
Ben Bocquelet and Others
Volume 1
ISBN: 978-1-60886-488-1 | $14.99
Volume 2
ISBN: 978-1-60886-793-6 | $14.99

Over the Garden Wall
Patrick McHale, Jim Campbell and Oth
Volume 1
ISBN: 978-1-60886-940-4 | $14.99
Volume 2
ISBN: 978-1-68415-006-9 | $14.99

Steven Universe
Rebecca Sugar and Others
Volume 1
ISBN: 978-1-60886-706-6 | $14.99
Volume 2
ISBN: 978-1-60886-796-7 | $14.99

Steven Universe & The Crystal Gems
ISBN: 978-1-60886-921-3 | $14.99

Steven Universe: Too Cool for School
ISBN: 978-1-60886-771-4 | $14.99

Peanuts
Charles Schultz and Others
Volume 1
ISBN: 978-1-60886-260-3 | $13.99

Garfield
Jim Davis and Others
Volume 1
ISBN: 978-1-60886-287-0 | $13.99

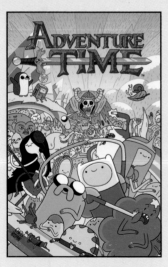

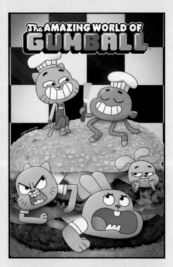

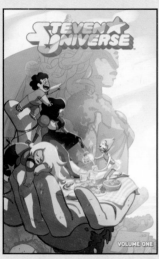

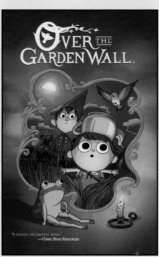

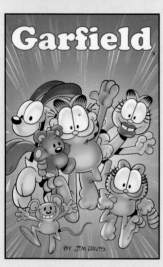

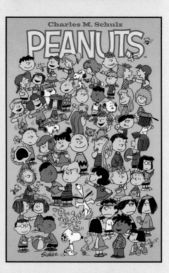

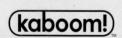